The branches were like spiders

From childhood, Thornton had played in these woods, and he usually could slip through them like a shadow.

He snatched up his bicycle, wheeled it to the dirt road, then mounted it. The dark woods towered on each side of the road. With despair, he looked at the giant trees, their heavy branches casting lengthening shadows.

His mother was mad at him. He had done the bad thing, said the bad thing.

That long-ago unreal night with the dead person had become real again. He had told. Now the dead person would come back for him.

He pedaled hard, pumping to make it up the steep hill. Sweat dampened his hair and dripped, burning his eyes. He pumped his bike harder.

He had magic. He kept telling himself that it would protect him from the dead person. He believed that.... He had to.

D0191556

Dear Reader,

You asked for it, and we're delighted to bring it to you—two more Harlequin Intrigue novels each month!

Now you can get a double dose of derring-do as all your favorite Intrigue authors bring you even more heart-stopping suspense and heart-stirring romance.

Our exciting new cover promises the best in romantic suspense—and that's just what you'll find in the four Harlequin Intrigue novels each and every month.

Here's to many more hours of happy reading!

Sincerely,

Debra Matteucci
Senior Editor & Editorial Coordinator
Harlequin Books
300 East 42nd St., 6th floor
New York, NY 10017

Child's Play

Bethany Campbell

Harlequin Books

TORONTO • NEW YORK • LONDON
AMSTERDAM • PARIS • SYDNEY • HAMBURG
STOCKHOLM • ATHENS • TOKYO • MILAN
MADRID • WARSAW • BUDAPEST • AUCKLAND

To Betty Allsup and the rest of the troop

Harlequin Intrigue edition published September 1992

ISBN 0-373-22196-7

CHILD'S PLAY

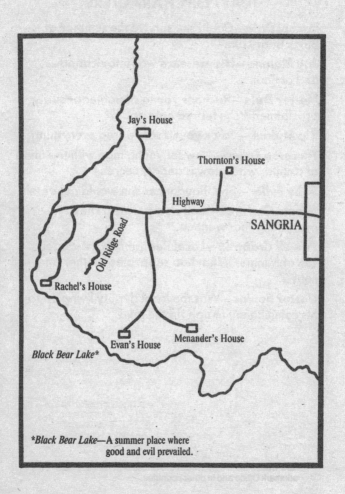

Jay's House

Thornton's House

Highway

SANGRIA

Old Ridge Road

Rachel's House

Evan's House

Menander's House

Black Bear Lake*

*Black Bear Lake—A summer place where
good and evil prevailed.

CAST OF CHARACTERS

Rachel Dale—Could she survive the summer at Black Bear Lake?

Jay Malone—His presence was intoxicating . . . and ominous.

Mercer Dale—Rachel's young daughter proudly proclaimed "she feared nothing."

Kip Malone—Jay's young son feared everything.

Thornton Fuller—A sweet young man with the mind of a child, who knew a deadly secret.

Ruby Fuller—She thought her son would *never* tell.

Minnie Crabtree—Ruby's sister who knew everything that went on.

Powell Crabtree—Local Realtor and estranged son of Minnie. What had separated mother and son?

Castor Bevins—Was the local deputy living up to his commitment to uphold the law?

Found a peanut,
Found a peanut,
Found a peanut,
Just now.
Just now I
Found a peanut,
Found a peanut,
Just now.

Cracked it open,
Cracked it open,
Cracked it open,
Just now.
Just now I
Cracked it open,
Cracked it open,
Just now.

It was rotten,
It was rotten,
It was rotten,
Just now.
Just now
It was rotten,
It was rotten,
Just now.

Ate it anyway,
Ate it anyway,
Ate it anyway,
Just now.
Just now I
Ate it anyway,
Ate it anyway,
Just now...

—Children's Song

Prologue

They were big people. Sometimes they used big words. Even so, he could not forget.

For once in his life, nothing hid in the fuzzy places in his head. He remembered everything. He remembered how angry they had been at him. Mean angry.

"You know what the name of this town means? *Blood.* Think about it.

"Don't *ever* tell what you saw or heard tonight—or blood'll flow. Yours. It'll flow until you're as dead as that one there."

A finger pointed. It pointed toward the body with its white, still face. The face had a scary hole in its forehead.

"*Some* dead people don't like to be talked about. Understand?"

The finger kept pointing at the scary hole.

"Dead people like this hear everything you say. They do. They *know.*

"Dead people like this, if you talk about them, they come back. They come back and make you dead, too. They take you. They take you down a river of blood.

"Know where they take you? To hell. Forever. They drown you in blood. They burn you in fire. Forever.

"Understand? *Never talk about this.* This is a bad thing. It could kill you. Pretend this never happened. Or you die. Understand? Understand?"

Sometimes he understood. Sometimes he didn't. Sometimes he worked so hard to pretend there hadn't ever been a dead person that the pretend became true—nothing had happened. He was safe. Safe.

Other times, he thought it had happened in a bad dream. He thought this because he'd had such bad dreams since. Maybe the first time was a dream, too. Maybe he just kept dreaming about a dream.

Yet, at other times, he *knew* it was real. He could still see the dead face. It was wet from the blood being washed off. But blood was still in the hair. Blood was in the hole in the forehead. The mouth hung open like it was going to talk. But it didn't. The eyes were blue. They stared and never blinked.

And its ears, he thought sickly. He remembered its ears under its bloody hair, its funny-colored bloody hair. Its ears might have been listening that night. They might be listening still.

The thought made him dizzy. Thinking and remembering about the dead person hurt his head. He would have to go to his dresser drawer. He would have to open his secret box. He wore the key to the box around his neck. He would open the box. Then he could stare at the magic.

He had taken the magic. He'd taken it that night because they scared him so bad.

They'd *said* it was magic. They said so. They said that the dead person "had held a handful of magic." But not anymore. They had the magic back. They were safe. That's what they said.

He'd seen the magic shining out of the open suitcase. There was a lot. From the way it gave off light, he could tell it was strong.

The dead person must have lost it and got dead, he'd thought. Got apart from the magic, then apart from life.

Magic took care of you. He knew that. Maybe it kept the life in you.

And there was so much shining there that night, nobody would know if he took a little. If he took just a little bit, the things they said might not come true. He'd be safe.

He'd waited until their backs were turned. He'd waited until they were moving the body. He put his hand in the suitcase. He'd taken as much magic as he could hold and hide.

When he got home, he hid it safe in his secret box. His hands shook. *It's mine,* he'd thought. He felt relief, but fear, too. The feeling was sick and wild in him.

So, when the dead person seemed too real and he got scared, he opened the box. He looked at his bit of the magic. It glowed. It made bad thoughts go away.

Then at last, after a long, long time, he'd stopped being so scared. Instead, he felt what people often said he was. Special.

For a while what had happened hardly scared him at all. Oh, it scared him *some.* But it did something else, too. It made him feel important.

For a while, the dead person didn't seem so real anymore. He began to feel safe. Most of the time.

But then everything changed. It got real again. It got scary again.

It changed when the summer people came back.

It happened because of the children.

Because of them, something terrible got loose.

The dead got loose. The dead were coming back. They would kill people. They would take them in a river of blood.

They come back, you know.

Chapter One

She was going to have to talk to the man. She didn't want to, but she had to. Things had gone too far.

He was the sort who gave off an unfriendly aura that crackled, *Leave me alone.* The dark glower of his brow said it. The hostile blue flash of his eyes said it. He never smiled, not even at his own son.

She knew he was well-to-do and that his wife had died. She had heard he was well-known in his field, which was some kind of sport.

He was also just handsome enough, in a rough-hewn sort of way, to be conceited. When she finally went to speak to him, he would undoubtedly think she was another of the summer's young divorcées trying to meet him, intrigued by his Heathcliff-on-the-moors act.

But that wasn't it. She wasn't impressed—quite the opposite. Other women might find his moodiness and mysteriousness attractive. She did not. No. She had to talk to him about their children.

Rachel Dale had journeyed to this summer house on Black Bear Lake in Sangria, Missouri, to put her career on track, her mind in order, and to solve the burgeoning problems with Mercer, her six-year-old daughter.

So far, perversely, nothing had gone according to plan. Her dissertation was going slowly, as if each paragraph were a huge stone she had to hew from a quarry, drag uphill single-handedly, then set ponderously into place.

Besides, the subject was starting to give her nightmares. She was writing about the psychology of the serial killer, and it was affecting her nerves. In dreams she kept meeting the Hillside Strangler, the Yorkshire Ripper, the Vampire of Sacramento. They came knocking at her door, a vivid mad gleam in their eyes that said, "You know too much. You have to die."

A woman who had dreams like that, she told herself darkly, wasn't getting her mind in order. Especially a woman who aspired to be a doctor of psychology. She still bore mental scars from her divorce five years ago. Somehow, she had found herself married to Damon, who was explosive and melodramatic. Memories of him continued to haunt her. It still amazed and confounded her that she had married such a man.

"Your own father was subtly...abusive," Henry had said. "You were looking for a father figure. Nothing wrong with that." He'd smiled in self-satisfaction. "Next time just pick one who'll be adequate."

Dr. Henry Bissell of the University of Nebraska had first been her professor, then her mentor, then her friend. Now he hinted that when she had finished her dissertation, it would be satisfactory to him to become her husband. He was sixty, exactly thirty-two years older than she was.

She supposed she would marry him. What was romantic love but a temporary psychosis, anyway? Romantic love had gotten her into the mess with Damon. Down with desire, away with passion, long live companionship, she thought with hardened practicality.

Henry was cool, intelligent and wry, a tall man with silver hair and an air of certainty. He had loaned her his condo for the summer, rent free, to finish her dissertation. It was an incredibly generous gift that she shouldn't have accepted if she didn't intend to marry him.

Besides, she kept telling herself, Mercer seemed to like him well enough. Her daughter's antics never bothered him. "She's creative," Henry said indulgently. "She's expressing herself, that's all."

Mercer expressed herself, all right. Like many of the children who spent the summer in the isolated houses scattered about the lake, Mercer attended a supervised play group in town. Yesterday she had expressed herself by getting a headlock on an eight-year-old boy and squirting half a bottle of suntan oil down the back of his jeans.

Mercer had said she'd done it because the boy, Wesley, had picked on her special friend, Kip, a little boy of five. Mercer was frequently all too zealous in the cause of justice.

Wesley's mother hadn't seen the act as justice. Enraged, she had telephoned Rachel. "What kind of *hellion* are you raising?"

Rachel had glanced uneasily at Mercer, who was happily playing a video game in which she blasted enemy planes out of an aqua blue television sky.

I should have known something was wrong, Rachel had thought bleakly. Mercer had skipped up to meet her, for once all too eager to leave the play group, chattering and waving goodbye to Kip, who sat looking forlorn as usual while he waited for his father.

"I...didn't know anything happened," Rachel said lamely. "Mrs. Crabtree didn't say anything."

"No," Wesley's mother snapped. "Mrs. Crabtree had poor Wesley in the bathroom trying to clean out the mess in his jeans. He was *humiliated.* He was *crying.* Those were his brand-new jeans, and he was wearing a brand-new Mutant Ninja Turtle T-shirt. That amount of oil will not come out, or out of his underwear, and of that, the less said the better. I expect you to pay the bills for all this."

"I'll be glad to," Rachel said as calmly as she could. "And I'll speak to Mercer."

"You should do more than *speak,*" Wesley's mother sneered. "That child needs an old-fashioned spanking. I hear you're a psychologist, so you probably don't believe in good old-fashioned discipline. Well, your child is turning into a rotten apple and spoiling the whole group."

Rachel winced, forcing herself to stay cool. There were certain children whose misbehavior always got pilloried worse than others: teachers' kids, preachers' kids, army brats and psychologists' kids. She knew. Her father had been a chaplain in the army; her mother had been a teacher.

"I told Mrs. Crabtree how unhappy I am," Wesley's mother continued, malice oozing from her voice. "I know this isn't the first complaint about your daughter. I'd hate to ask her to be barred from the play group. But I will—if you can't control her any better."

Rachel took a deep breath and counted to ten. "I'll talk to Mercer and Mrs. Crabtree," she said with a serenity she didn't feel.

"Another thing," Wesley's mother added, the air almost hissing between her teeth. "She's provoking that poor, pitiful creature—Thornton Fuller. His mother brings him to the Crabtree house all the time. Mercer and that snively Malone child are insufferable to him. You'd better teach that little lady some manners."

Rachel stiffened. Thornton Fuller was twenty or so, yet his IQ was probably not as high as Mercer's. All the summer people had been told about him: he was sweet natured, more childlike than many of the children, and he yearned to be accepted by them.

Although the vacation houses were scattered through the forest and along the edge of Black Bear Lake, Thornton was sure to come sooner or later, riding his battered bicycle, calling on summer visitors if they had children or even a dog. Thornton loved dogs inordinately, too. He always used the same words to introduce himself: "My name is Thornton. I got a whole shelf *full* of toys."

"Mercer *likes* Thornton," Rachel objected. "She's always treated him well. I wouldn't allow anything else."

"Ha," said Wesley's mother snidely. "That's easy to say. It's one thing for Mercer to pick on ordinary children, but when she starts tormenting *afflicted* ones ... Well, I've said what I had to say. *Watch* that child of yours—I mean it."

She hung up the phone with a crash that made Rachel's ear ring painfully.

She stood for a moment, her head spinning with emotions.

"Mercer," she'd called in her most relentless voice. *Maybe Wesley's mother was right,* was the small niggling doubt in the back of her mind. *Maybe I'm such a lousy psychologist I can't even raise my own child without one crisis after another. Or maybe I'm a lousy mother. Or both.*

Mercer appeared in the doorway.

"That was Wesley's mother," Rachel announced stonily. "She said you threw Wesley down and squirted suntan lotion down his pants. Well?"

"Well," Mercer said with a righteous shrug, "he asked for it."

Rachel gazed at her daughter, half in anger, half with a growing feeling of helplessness. Mercer was eerily like a smaller version of herself: the same shoulder-length dark hair, the same straight nose and high cheekbones, the same stubborn mouth. But under Rachel's curved brown brows were troubled blue-gray eyes, and under Mercer's were alert dark ones, her only outward legacy from her father.

Rachel put her hands on her blue-jeaned hips. "Why? Why did you squirt oil down Wesley's pants?"

"Because he sat on Kip's head and was going to make him eat a worm," Mercer said, folding her arms and staring up at her mother. "It was a big black worm. With fur."

Rachel sighed. "Mercer," she said, "you can't fight Kip's battles for him. This has got to stop."

"You want him to eat a worm with fur?" Mercer asked indignantly.

Rachel knelt before her daughter, taking her firmly by the shoulders. "No. But it's not your place to stop it. Let Mrs. Crabtree do it."

Mercer rolled her eyes expressively. "Mrs. Crabtree," she said, putting a twist on the name, "never sees anything. Besides, she doesn't like me—or my friends."

Rachel sucked in her breath in frustration. Minnie Crab-tree was a teacher during the school year. The widow of a minister, she apparently ran the play group for extra money. Rachel had to admit the woman did not seem fond of Mercer. Still, in supervising the group, Minnie Crabtree had responsibilities, and she had to meet them.

"You *tell* Mrs. Crabtree when there's a problem," Rachel said, squeezing her daughter's shoulders for emphasis. "And what's this about you and Kip being mean to Thornton?"

Mercer's nose wrinkled in disdain. "We're *not* mean. It's just he always wants me to pay attention to him. All the time. It *bugs* me. And he scares Kip and Evan. They don't like him."

Rachel sighed. Evan was a stolid-looking little boy, whose mother seemed nervous and unhappy. The sort who might see something to fear in Thornton and convey that fear to her son.

But Kip Malone was another matter. He was the son of the brooding Jay Malone, the man to whom Rachel was going to have to speak. The man to whom she did not *want* to speak.

Although Kip was a sturdy, if skinny, five-year-old, he had a mysterious air of fragility about him, as if he were really a little old man disguised as a child. He always looked in pain, as if some secret disease gnawed him from within.

He had joined the play group only two weeks ago, and had immediately attached himself to Mercer. He was as devoted to her as an adoring slave. Mercer, in turn, became his jealous protector. It was a clear instance of opposites attracting, and the combination brought out Mercer's combativeness full force.

Kip, because of his timidity, was always being teased. Mercer was the sort who raged against any injustice, and she was delighted not only to avenge anything done to Kip, but to avenge it in style.

Mercer's growing attachment to Kip disturbed Rachel. At first she was glad Mercer had a special friend. But Kip, it turned out, was not allowed to come to Mercer's house. The reason infuriated Mercer and Rachel both. His father said Kip could not visit a *girl* to play. Rachel had loathed the man from that moment on, although she felt sorry for his son.

Whenever Jay Malone saw Rachel delivering Mercer or picking her up from the play group, he shot the pair of them a glance that was almost openly antagonistic. He never said so much as hello. He hardly spoke even to his son, and Kip didn't speak to him. Father and son only nodded when they met, and Kip always seemed sad to be going home with this stony man.

"Why is Kip frightened of Thornton?" Rachel asked carefully. "Didn't you tell him Thornton wouldn't hurt anyone?"

"Yes," Mercer objected, trying to wriggle from her mother's grasp. "He doesn't believe it."

"Why?"

"I don't know," Mercer said impatiently. "It's something his father told him. To stay away from him. It's not Kip's fault. But Thornton *won't* understand, and he *won't* leave us alone. I'm *tired* of him."

Rachel released her daughter and stood staring down at her sternly. "I won't have you being mean to Thornton. And you've got to stop fighting Kip's battles. He has to learn to fight for himself."

"Yeah, sure," Mercer said sarcastically.

An unpleasant wave of understanding passed between mother and daughter, almost as jolting as electricity. Kip was a problem. He brought out Mercer's worst, but she would never willingly give him up. Rachel put her hands on her hips again.

"I'm going to talk to Mr. Malone about this," she said. "All of it—about Thornton, too. Understand?"

She said it crisply, all business and confidence, but she felt uncertain about facing Malone. He seemed sullen, arrogant and cold. He was chauvinistic and obviously prejudiced against special people like Thornton. How did one talk to such a man?

She sighed, crossing her arms. She would speak to him, anyway, after play group tomorrow. Kip usually arrived early, before Rachel came with Mercer. But Rachel often saw the Malone man coming to pick up his son. She would speak to him then, and she hoped he would listen.

What had been his sport? Baseball? Football? She didn't remember and didn't care. She had never been attracted to athletes. Jocks, she'd thought in contempt. Nothing but muscles, even between their ears. Poor little Kip Malone. Exactly the wrong child for such a man to have.

"Be nice to Kip," Rachel said, her tone gentler. She touched her daughter's hair. "But be nice to Thornton, too. You can have more than one kind of friend, you know."

Mercer gave her a rebellious look and set her mouth more firmly. She moved away, sat down before the video game and once more began to blow enemy planes out of the sky.

She was excellent at it. And she loved war games best of all, which Rachel thought appalling, but Henry told her not to worry. "She's just releasing hostility. It's normal. Don't worry about it."

But Rachel worried.

HE'S HARMLESS, everyone said. He loves children, they said, and he's like a child himself; he's really quite harmless. Be kind to him, people said.

But Mercer, splashing in the pool at Mrs. Crabtree's house with the other children the next day, was sick to death of being kind.

Thornton was making her crazy. "Thornton," she said, firmly. "*No.* Go away. Kipper and I are going to be Godzillas, and Evan's going to be Tokyo, and we're going to squash him. Go *away.*"

Thornton squatted beside the pool. He was a rather handsome young man. He was overweight, but his face was sweet and boyish with long-lashed blue eyes. He wore a red baseball cap, and beneath its shade, his beautiful eyes were clouded with disappointment.

"Mer-cer," he whined. Although he was strong enough to ride his bike up and down the hills for hours, he had a high voice, almost like a girl's. Mercer hated it when Thornton whined. She knew he was "special," but she got sick of his demanding special treatment from *her*.

Kip and Evan were both a year younger than she, and both had joined the group only two weeks before. Mercer had been delighted to discover she could boss them completely, making them play whatever she wished. She planned every play period like an army sergeant.

Before they had come, Mercer had seemed fascinated by Thornton and talked to him often. But now she hardly noticed him. Now Mercer ignored him in favor of the younger boys, and Thornton was jealous. She, in turn, was fiercely tired of Thornton interfering with her plans.

"Mer-cer," Thornton begged. He glanced over his shoulder, where his mother sat in a lawn chair, talking to his Aunt Minnie, who ran the play group.

Neither Minnie nor his mother paid any attention to him and Mercer's small group; they watched the other children playing in the deep end of the pool. That was good, because for some reason the adults didn't like him to talk to Mercer, Evan and Kip.

"Don't play with *them* all the time," Thornton supplicated. "Come on."

"Stop bothering me," Mercer said with an impatient fling of her wet hair. "I got constitutional rights. You're invading my privacy."

She held her nose and slipped under the water until only her feet stuck out. She wriggled them in disdain at Thornton.

Thornton sighed unhappily. She was always saying things too grown-up, like, "You're invading my privacy."

The other day she had said, "Thornton, I got priorities, and you're not one of them." He'd had to ask his mother what "priorities" meant. When he found out, it had hurt his feelings.

Still, he really liked Mercer. She was so smart. He wanted so much to be her friend. Maybe her smartness would rub off on him. People would be impressed that he had such a smart friend.

She had other gifts, too. She did things Thornton envied with all his heart. She could cannonball fearlessly off the high board of Minnie's pool, yelling louder than any boy.

Mercer could ride a bicycle with no hands, she could hold her breath and stay underwater for a full minute and a half, she could snort and squeal *exactly* like a pig, and she wasn't afraid of snakes. She had found one in Minnie's azaleas. It was as long as her arm, but she'd picked it right up. All the other children screamed, and Minnie had, too.

Thornton couldn't believe how brave she was. Everything Mercer did seemed wonderful, and he wanted to be her best friend. For a while, he had been.

But now she preferred the littler boys who had joined the group, the plump, silent Evan and skinny little Kip, who was a fraidy-cat.

Blub-blub-blubbety-blub. Mercer made giant bubbles roil up out of the water. Then she righted herself, wiping the dark hair out of her eyes, and stared with indignation at Thornton. "Go away," she ordered. "I'll tell your aunt—and your mother. Go away and let us play. Evan, you float facedown. You're an island. Tokyo's an island."

"No," Thornton insisted in his high, labored voice. It was always hard for him to drag the right words out in the right order. "I want you to sing for me. Sing, or I *won't* let you alone." His voice was petulant with warning.

Kip edged back imperceptibly into the deeper water. None of the children had ever seen Thornton even vaguely threatening before. Kip's eyes opened wider in apprehension.

"Sing what?" Mercer demanded, putting her hands on her boyish hips.

"Sing 'Found a Peanut,'" Thornton said, trying not to seem intimidated. "You know. The 'Found a Peanut' song."

Mercer's patience shattered. "No," she said flatly. "There's ten million verses. I don't have time. We're going to be Godzillas."

She raised up her arms like a monster. She let a mad gleam shine from her eyes. "Go away," she ordered, "or I'll Godzilla you. *Rrroorroawwwrr!*"

For a small girl she made a frightening roar and stalked toward him, splashing through the water with the heavy, threatening gait of a giant lizard.

Thornton was impressed and almost backed away. Mercer crossed her eyes and stretched her mouth into a lizard's leering snarl. She was funny, but scary.

Still, Thornton sensed she would not respect him if he let her scare him off. Stubbornly he stayed put and stuck out his tongue, which made her even more furious.

"Thornton!" she cried. "I'll splash water all over you. I will!"

"I don't care," he said obstinately. "*You'll* just get in trouble. Minnie'll make you get out of the pool. Then you can't play at *all*. So there."

Mercer stopped, surprised at his craftiness. She and Thornton eyed each other, while Mercer's mind spun, trying to think of a way to get rid of him.

She crossed her arms, looking as stern as possible. "If you don't go away, I won't like you anymore," she said, her voice cold. He had incensed her so much she had forgotten all the promises she'd so recently made her mother.

Thornton flushed with hurt. Mercer ought to like him as much as he liked her. It was only fair. They were alike. She had freckles and so did he. She had broken her arm once falling off her bike and so had he. She had no father and neither did he. They could be almost like sister and brother if she would let him. If only.

Thornton was desperate. He looked as if he might cry. "Please, Mercer. Just once. Sing 'Found a Peanut.'"

Mercer set her jaw and shook her head. She wished she had never showed off by singing the song for him in the first place. It was such a long, complicated song, about finding a peanut and all the consequences that followed, including dying and going first to heaven, then to hell.

Why it so fascinated Thornton she didn't know. Ever since she'd sung it, he'd pestered her to sing it again and again. She'd sung it last week until she was blue in the face, and he still wasn't satisfied.

Now he was pleading, but this did nothing to melt her resistance. She decided ignoring him was her only course.

"Thornton," she said with all the disdain of royalty, "I am going to ignore you." She turned her back on him. "Float," she commanded Evan. "Kip'll try to sink you, then I will."

Thornton was desperate. He didn't know what to do. He wanted Mercer to talk to him.

"I know a secret," he said recklessly, frantic for her attention. "I know a bad secret. It's about your house."

Mercer kept her back to him, but nervous little Kip watched him with real alarm in his eyes.

"It's about Kip's house, too," Thornton pressed on, watching Kip's face grow more fearful. Evan looked up at Thornton with curiosity instead of his usual disdain.

Mercer turned to face him again, her expression defiant. "*What* secret? You don't know any secrets."

But in truth he had struck a nerve. She and Kip and Evan were, like most of the children in the group, "summer people." They lived in houses strange to them, houses isolated in the woods that bordered the lake.

Drunk with having her attention, Thornton rushed on, "Somebody got killed at his house—last year," he said sinisterly, pointing at Kip, who blinked and paled.

Thornton narrowed his eyes and looked at Mercer, who stood in her same rebellious stance. "And they took them to *your* house," he told her. "They took a *dead* person to your house."

For a moment Mercer said nothing. She looked at the little boys, who seemed frightened, then back at Thornton. "You're a big liar," she said, cool as ever. "I'm going to tell my mother on you. My mother knows all about murder. So *there*."

Thornton's confidence ebbed. He suddenly realized he had said what he'd been told never to say.

Fright swept over him. Then, in growing panic, he remembered the warning that had kept him quiet for so long. It would make them keep quiet, too.

"You *can't* tell. If you tell," he said, watching their faces, "the dead person'll come back and *get* you."

In spite of the hot June sunshine, a shiver rippled down Mercer's back. "Ha," she shot back. "The dead person'll get you first. *You* already told."

Her logic frightened him and once again drove him to say more than he should. "Ha, yourself," he answered with more bravery than he felt. "I got magic stuff. Ch-ch-charms, like. Gold ch-charms." It was hard for him to get the word out. "Nothing can hurt me."

"Charms?" Mercer demanded suspiciously. "What kind?"

"Things—something I stole," Thornton said. At last he had her full attention, but he was terrified at the price he'd paid for it.

"You're not brave enough to steal," Mercer retorted, but she wasn't sure. "And you don't know anything about a body. How would *you* know?"

"I saw it," Thornton answered stubbornly.

"Yeah?" Mercer challenged. "What'd it look like?"

Thornton's face got red and his lower lip stuck out petulantly. He actually looked as if he was trying to remember, which took Mercer aback.

Then he mumbled, "It looked dead." His brow furrowed. "And its hair was kind of green."

Mercer laughed. "Oh, you big liar," she said in triumph.

Thornton's face got so red and his chin so trembly that he looked as if he might cry.

"Green hair," Mercer mocked. Then she noticed fat little Sean Alan Menander had crept up on them, the way he always did. She splashed water at him. "Go away, Sean

Alan! This is a private conversation." Her aim was true. Sean Alan thrashed off, rubbing his eyes.

She turned her attention back to Thornton. "You never saw any body and you never had any charms—so there."

Thornton glanced nervously at his aunt and mother, still talking by the pool. "Shh, be quiet. I wasn't supposed to tell," he said, fear rising in his voice. "But if you say anything, the dead person'll come get you."

Mercer stared at him without blinking. She knew she and Thornton were having a contest of wills. But she would not be dominated, no matter what scary thing he made up.

Then, behind her, she heard a gulping noise. She turned and saw that Kip was crying. His rib cage shook with suppressed sobs, and Evan's plump face had an expression of fright mixed with queasiness.

Mentally, Mercer said the worst word she knew. She knew how Kip hated to cry. He hated it because his father scolded him for it and said boys should never cry. Kip missed his mother all the time, and he was ashamed when he made his father feel embarrassed.

Mercer moved to Kip and wound her arm around his shoulders. "*Now* look what you did, Thornton," she accused, making her voice loud enough so that the adults would hear. "You leave us alone!"

Thornton's aunt did hear. "Thornton, are you making mischief? That's not like you. Get over here, you hear me? And Mercer, did you splash Sean Alan? You let him play. Thornton, get *over here,* I said."

Thornton, looking humiliated and frightened, rose from his crouching position. He kept watching Mercer's stubborn little face. Whatever emotion shone in her dark eyes was not respect. He didn't know what it was. He had done a terrible thing. He knew, although he couldn't put it into words, that he had betrayed himself for her. Didn't she even care?

"Thornton!" Minnie Crabtree's voice was sharp. "Get over here right now."

Thornton shrugged guiltily and shuffled, head down, toward his mother and Minnie.

"Don't listen to him," Mercer told Kip fiercely. "He's just making stuff up."

But Kip was so frightened he was actually shaking, so Mercer pulled him closer to her and let him cry against her shoulder. "Hey," she said more gently, "it's okay. Don't be scared."

But Kip cried harder and Mercer knew why. He wanted his mother, and he couldn't have her ever again. She was dead, just like the person Thornton had talked about.

Evan still had his sickly look, but he stared contemptuously at Kip. "Oh, don't be such a crybaby," he said.

"You shut up," Mercer snapped, "or I won't let you be Tokyo."

But they all knew that none of them would be Godzillas or Tokyos that day. Somehow it was ruined.

Then they saw the gate swing open, and Kip's father walked into the yard, the sun shining on his black hair and his white shirt.

"Stop," Mercer commanded, shaking Kip lightly. "Your dad's here."

Kip stepped away from Mercer guiltily and did his best to scrub his eyes dry.

His father came to the pool's edge. He was a tall, dark man who looked nothing like Kip. His face was always so serious it looked bleak, even cruel, and his tone was always harsh.

The man looked down at Kip without smiling. Kip was still rubbing his eyes.

"What's wrong?" his father asked. He had a low voice, deep, raspy and without sympathy.

"Nothing," Mercer lied for Kip blithely. "He got chlorine in his eyes. Want to see me spit water through my teeth? Look—I'm a fountain."

She took in a great mouthful of water and squirted it in an arc, attempting to distract the man by showing off. He ignored her.

"Get your things," he said shortly to Kip, then turned and walked away to stare out over Minnie's azalea garden. Kip, still wiping at his eyes, scrambled from the pool and ran across the tiles to fetch his towel and beach bag.

Mercer watched, hoping he was all right. She allowed herself one last withering glance over her shoulder at Thornton, who now sat hunched by his mother's side, his head down. He looked half-sick with dread and regret.

Good, thought Mercer with satisfaction.

At that moment, though, her mother came through the gate, tossing a cursory smile to Minnie and Thornton and Thornton's mother.

But Rachel only nodded at Mercer and walked past the pool to the edge of the azalea garden.

Oh, no, Mercer thought, her heart shriveling unhappily. She'd hoped her mother would forget, but she hadn't. She was going to talk to Mr. Malone.

Rats! Mercer dived underwater. She lay on the bottom, pretending to be a killer squid, lurking.

RACHEL RECOGNIZED the Malone man's broad back, his dark hair. He wore blue jeans and a white polo shirt. Hesitantly, she reached out and tapped his shoulder. It was a hard shoulder, hot with the sun. "Mr. Malone," she said.

He moved as if he'd been stung, quickly wheeling to face her. She felt as if her touching him had violated some strong and private taboo.

He studied her face unamicably. He had eyes of extraordinary pale blue, made all the more startling because of the blackness of his hair, brows and lashes. Now the black brows drew together in a questioning frown.

"Mr. Malone, I'm Rachel Dale, Mercer's mother. We need to talk about our children. There's also the matter of your son's attitude toward Thornton. You know who I mean by Thornton," she said, nodding back in Thornton's direction.

Malone said nothing at all for a long moment. The children in the pool shrieked and splashed. A blue jay jabbered in a sugar maple. The azalea leaves nodded in the wind. He stood, looking at her with those disconcerting ice blue eyes.

"You're the psychologist?" he asked at last, no emotion in his voice.

Rachel nodded, supposing he had this news from Kip or some other child's parent. She tried to give him a friendly smile, but it failed, feeling weak and false on her lips.

He said nothing. His expression changed not one whit. Then he looked past her, dismissing her, and strode away, leaving her standing there.

"Come on," she heard him say to his boy in a clipped, cold voice. Rachel turned, her heart beating hard, and watched as Kip, holding his towel and beach bag, cast a hopeful glance toward the pool, looking for Mercer.

Mercer rose up at that moment in an explosion of water, waving her arms and legs frantically. "I'm a killer squid!" she shouted to Kip with delight. "I'll protect you from everything! Everything!"

Rachel saw the boy smile shyly, sadly, at the splashing little girl. At that moment, her own heart went out to him, shot straight to him like an arrow.

Damn his father! she thought angrily.

She would help this child if she could, in spite of the father's loutishness. And she would help her own child, too, she swore. And even poor Thornton. She would help them all if she could.

She walked to the pool's edge and reached out her hand. Mercer swam to her and took it, letting her mother pull her up. "I'm a squid. You caught me," she said. "But I'll break free. You'll see."

"I'm sure you'll live to squid another day," Rachel said. She was upset and insulted by Jay Malone's rudeness. But she would do what she could today.

"Let's talk to Thornton," she told Mercer. "I want to make sure that things are back to normal with you two."

"Ahh, Mom," Mercer complained. Her mother would never believe that Thornton wasn't becoming a bigger pest with every passing day. Never.

They stood, hand in hand, blinking against the bright afternoon sunlight. Mercer was relieved and Rachel was puzzled. Minnie Crabtree and her sister were helping a little girl who had cut her foot on a pebble.

But Thornton was nowhere to be seen. He had disappeared.

Even his own mother didn't know that he was riding his bicycle as quickly as he could toward the ridge overlooking the lake, his head low over the handlebars. The ridge was where he always went when he was troubled. Tears stung his eyes, streaked down his face, leaving tracks.

He realized now what he'd done and how terrible it was. And how scary. He sobbed and pedaled harder.

Now he had done it. Now he had told and the dead person would come back.

The dead person would come back to kill them all.

CONFESSION

They say Rachel Dale was tired of death. Hey! I can relate. *It reminds me of that dear old mother of mine: the Queen of the Dead.*

I always knew Thornton would talk.

I knew as long as he was alive I was living on the edge. But I grew up on the edge. Like razor blades, the sharper, the better.

The murder was perfect. *Or would have been perfect, if Thornton hadn't blundered along. I'm no fool. I knew he couldn't keep his mouth shut forever.*

When he talked, the dying would start again. Do you think I minded *that? I just didn't know that the Dale woman would be drawn into it so deeply. Along with Malone.*

And their children, of course. Their beautiful, precious children.

Chapter Two

Mercer was quiet all afternoon, which Rachel did not understand, but appreciated. From her desk, she stared out the front-room window of the condo, watching the child.

Mercer waded outside at the lake's edge, trying to catch minnows in a jar. Every afternoon she caught them laboriously, one at a time, putting them in an old bucket.

Then, when the sun fell, after lecturing them sternly, she set them loose again. She thought she was warning them, teaching them to be careful.

Rachel smiled and shook her head. Her smile faded slightly when she remembered the Malone man, staring at her with those eyes of pale arctic blue.

For a moment, she had been riven through by his gaze, as unsettled and agitated as if she had grasped a live wire and its power had coursed through her body, shaking and burning. A perverse thrill had pulsed in the sensation, almost sexual.

Rachel almost laughed at the thought: sexual titillation. From someone like *him*. Henry was right; she'd been alone too long. It really was time she remarried. Only this time, as Henry said, sensibly.

Her smile faded completely when she turned back to her research notes. Murder. Always murder.

Until her dissertation was done, she was forced incessantly to think of murder. It hung over her like a cloud that every day grew larger, darker and more poisonous.

"You can break ground with this study," Henry had told her. "Make a name for yourself," he'd said. "Most important, you can publish."

Publish, she thought, shaking her head over her notes. In the academic world it was always publish, publish, publish. Publishing was the life's blood of a university career. It had dominated Henry's world for thirty years. Soon it would dominate hers, as well.

She frowned and marked a margin in her notes. If it wasn't for Henry, she might be going into private practice, devoting herself to patients, eliminating the teaching and research and writing.

But it had become an unspoken agreement between them that she would follow in his prestigious footsteps. Her work was an extension of his own research. If they married, he would share with her his considerable reputation and expertise on psychotic murder—no small gift. She, in turn, would carry on his work.

She stirred uneasily. *If* they married.

For no reason at all she remembered reaching out to touch Jay Malone's wide shoulder. His white shirt had gleamed so brightly in the sunshine that it dazzled, and it was surprisingly hot beneath her touch. She had been thrown off guard, as if she had touched a man who burned with white-hot fire from within.

Perhaps that was why when he'd turned his eyes, they had shot through her with a bolt of pure coldness.

Oh, heavens, she thought, angrily erasing an erroneous mark. Why think of him? It seemed more and more inevitable that she and Henry would marry—eventually. It would be sensible, it would be practical.

Was she having qualms about what it *wouldn't* be? It wouldn't be passionate. It wouldn't be physical. Henry was not passionate or physical. Theirs would be a marriage of minds, careers.

She didn't want passion anymore. She hadn't wanted it since she'd escaped from Damon. Passion was dangerous, it was a disease, and she'd frozen it out of her system forever.

She cradled her forehead in her hand and studied a sheet of statistics about victims. Passion could make a person a victim. She would never be a victim again. All she wanted for herself and Mercer was safety—safety and security.

The doors from the deck slid open and Mercer erupted into the room. "Why're you sitting in the dark?" she demanded.

Rachel looked up. Across the lake, the sun was sinking, and the room had grown shadowy. She'd been so lost in her mingled thoughts of marriage and murder that she hadn't noticed.

Mercer switched on the light. The child was covered with mud, like some lake sprite who lived among the wild flags along the shore. She carried her bucket, empty once more of minnows.

Rachel smiled. "You like it here, don't you?"

Mercer shrugged one sunburned shoulder. "Sure. I just wish there were more kids around. I wish Kip or Evan lived next door."

Rachel diplomatically ignored the remark. The other half of the condo was empty and for sale. She supposed Evan McInery's family was all right; she knew little of them, except that the mother always looked unhappy. But the thought of living next to the Malones, father and son, was too disquieting to entertain.

"I mean," Rachel went on, "it was nice of Henry to let us use this place, don't you think?"

Mercer shrugged again. "*He's* not using it."

"But you'd like to come back? Would you like to come every summer?" Rachel was trying to lead up delicately to the subject of Henry's being with them. She had never said anything to Mercer about actual marriage, and she suddenly felt the discussion was long overdue.

"Come back?" Mercer asked, picking at a scab on her elbow. "Well, yeah. If Henry doesn't want to."

"I'm talking," Rachel said carefully, "about Henry coming with us."

Mercer's brown eyes snapped up with sudden alertness. She stared at her mother a long time. "Yuck," she said.

"Yuck?" Rachel repeated, wounded. "What's the matter with Henry? I thought you liked him."

"Are you talking about him being my *father?*" Mercer asked with a mixture of surprise and disgust.

"Well...yes," Rachel admitted, surprised at the child's reaction. "We talked about it a bit. He's a...smart man and he likes you. He'd make a good father."

Mercer frowned and again picked at her scab. "He'd make a better grandfather. He's old. He's *real* old. You better not. He'd just up and die on us."

Rachel stared at her, shocked.

Mercer took a long piece of water vine from her bucket and wound it around her head like a ragged crown.

"If you got to marry somebody, why don't you marry Mr. Malone?" Mercer asked, her face lighting with happy inspiration. "Then I'd have a brother. That'd be better."

Rachel was struck speechless.

"*Ga-rump.* I'm a frog princess. *Ga-rump,*" Mercer said, hopping across the room, swinging her bucket. "Kiss me and make me human."

She hopped to Rachel's side, and Rachel bent and kissed the warm, mud-streaked cheek. She had a sudden vision of sleeping beside Jay Malone—and forced it out of her mind. She would talk again to Mercer later.

"Come on, princess, into the royal tub," she said.

Mercer ran down the hallway toward the bathroom. She stopped suddenly and looked over her shoulder. "Mom, dead people can't come back and get you, can they?"

Again Rachel felt a frisson of shock. Where had Mercer come up with *that* one?

"Dead people? Get you?" Rachel said with distaste. "Of course not. Don't even think such a thing."

"Just making sure," Mercer said and darted into the bathroom. But for the rest of the evening she was unusually quiet and seemed lost in her own thoughts.

Outside, from behind tall cedar trees that edged the lot, Thornton stood, watching Mercer's house. His bicycle was hidden up the hill, deeper in the woods. He shifted uneasily from foot to foot, weary of standing.

He had watched Mercer play from after supper onward, and now he stood restless guard at her house, trying to protect her from the terrible thing he had done.

He knew what he had told her was true, and it scared him so sick that his stomach wrenched and his hands wouldn't stop sweating.

If you told killed people's secrets, they could come back and hurt you until you died, all covered with your own blood. And he had told.

And Mercer might tell, too. She might tell because she was Mercer and wasn't afraid of anything. Then the dead person would come after her to kill her. What could she do? She was brave, but she was only a little girl.

He had his magic. But Mercer had nothing. Who would protect her? There was nobody, only him.

His charms gave him powers, and he believed in them, but he was confused. He didn't know how much power. He prayed it was enough. His mother had taught him to pray long ago. He kept praying and praying, even though his stomach felt sicker and sicker.

He watched Mercer's house until all the lights went out. Then, unsure what to do, he made his way through the woods and rode his bicycle all the way to Kip's house. There, too, he stayed hidden, watching, guarding, until all the lights went out.

What have I done? Thornton kept thinking in terror. *What have I done?*

THE HOUSE JAY MALONE had rented for the summer stood by itself at the end of a long dirt road that led to the lake. He had come back to Missouri for the summer because once, years ago, Missouri had been home, and somehow he had to find a way to make a home for the kid and himself.

But coming here was a mistake. Who had said you can't go home again? He'd been right, damn him.

And this place—this overpriced vacation mansion in the middle of nowhere—was no place for a kid like Kipper. Jay saw that, too, now that it was too late.

That was always how he saw things with Kipper—too late.

He watched the boy sitting, thin shoulders hunched, in front of the television set. Kip was watching the same movie on the VCR he had watched for the past three nights. The fool thing seemed somehow to comfort the kid.

Jay sat at the dining-room table trying to adjust the drag on his son's fishing reel. He didn't know why. Kip hated to fish. The first time this summer he'd seen a fish thrashing, the hook skewed through its jaw, he looked sick.

Jay had realized then, with a familiar sinking feeling, that the kid couldn't bear to see the fish suffer. He'd realized it, of course, too late.

He ran his hand through his hair and swore inwardly. He kept toying with the reel just to have something to do. It was the anniversary today. Death's anniversary. A year ago today Cindy had died.

Correction. A year ago today, Cindy had been killed.

He ground his teeth, wishing for the ten thousandth time that day that he had a drink. So he could forget, even for a few drunken hours. So he'd stop replaying it in his head all night the way he had all day today.

He wanted his wife. He wanted a drink. He was never going to be able to have either again. He was a widower with a son who didn't need a drunk for a father.

And Jay had been that, quite simply drunk, for the first three months after Cindy's death. He drank from the time he got up until he passed out at night, trying to forget.

But every time he looked at Kip, he remembered. God, but the boy was like her. He was like her in every way: the fair hair, the fair skin, the serious hazel eyes, the slight build. Like her he was sensitive, with a heart too easily touched. Like her he was shy.

And the two of them, Cindy and Kip, had a natural rapport, a rapport that Jay had never achieved with the boy. He'd never thought much about it back then. He was away so much, and Cindy needed something. He was glad she had the kid.

Now she was gone. A year ago today, she was gone.

Kip's video ended and he looked up at Jay with eyes shadowed with worry. "Dad?" he asked in a small voice. "Could I watch it again?"

Jay studied him unhappily. Why did Kip always seem *afraid* to ask him for anything? Was it Jay's fault, for trying too hard to teach the boy *not* to be afraid? And why did Kip keep watching that crazy film about little blue fairies or something? Couldn't he watch cowboys or detectives or spacemen or dinosaurs like a normal boy?

But something in Kip's face tonight brought out a weary gentleness in Jay. If the cartoon comforted the kid, let him have it. "Sure," he said gruffly. "Rewind it. Watch it again. It's fine, man."

If Kip was pleased, he didn't smile. Solemnly he hit the rewind button. Then, as if his mind were a million miles away, he put his thumb in his mouth and rubbed the satin inner ear of a stuffed rabbit, a creature so ragged it should have been thrown away long ago.

For once Jay didn't tell him to take his thumb out of his mouth. Neither did he tell him to stop rubbing the rabbit's ear. The boy was too troubled.

He'd been troubled ever since Jay had picked him up from the play group. Did Kip somehow realize that it was the anniversary of his mother's death? Or had he just picked up Jay's vibes? Kids could do that, couldn't they? Kids and animals?

"He's insecure," the psychologist had told Jay about Kip. "The suddenness of his mother's death—and he's by nature an exceptionally sensitive child...."

Then the psychologist had tried to start in on Jay him-self, asking all those snide little questions, like was Jay feel-ing guilty maybe? For being out drinking with his friends the afternoon Cindy died? For not having been as good a hus-band as he might have? For perhaps secretly *resenting* Kip? What had Jay felt for his own father? Jealousy?

To hell with it, Jay had said in disgust. He'd had a belly-ful of psychologists and psychiatrists. They were the ones who'd gotten Cindy's killer off with a couple of years in a hospital instead of a lifetime in prison like the animal de-served. "Diminished capacity," the headshrinkers had said.

Some kid with too many problems and too many pills had taken his father's car and gun and started driving around L.A. It was broad daylight, but he began shooting out of the car window while he passed a little shopping center, trying to shoot out signs, he said.

He shot out signs, all right. And he shot Cindy. He said he didn't know why he did it. He said he didn't actually *re-member* doing it.

But he had. He shot her in the back, and she died on the sidewalk before the ambulance even got there. Beside her was a paper bag with two new pairs of kids' pajamas spill-ing out. She had gone shopping to buy Kip pajamas. They had ended up drenched in her blood.

A year ago today.

He heard Kip restart the movie, the all-too-familiar jin-gle-jangle of its theme music.

He put his elbow on the table and passed his hand over his eyes. By all that was holy and unholy he wanted a drink.

He'd felt like a maniac all day. While Kip was at the play group, Prosky, the assistant manager of the team, had called him again from L.A. Today of all days.

"Look," Prosky had said, "don't walk away like this. You got some good years left. You realize the money you're giving up? The team needs you. Look, you can come back. What you need to do is talk to somebody. See somebody. Work this out. I've got the name of a doctor in St. Lou-is—"

Jay had wanted to scream, actually scream like a crazy man, "She died a year ago today, you idiot! You want me to talk *hockey?*"

Instead, he'd snarled something obscene and hung up. He was retired now and he intended to stay that way and he never wanted to see L.A. or another shrink as long as he lived.

He sighed harshly and passed his hand over his eyes again. He felt like a maniac, all right. Which hadn't given him the right to be rude to the woman at the play group—the girl's mother, the Dale woman.

She was beautiful in her way, quiet and with a certain classiness in her bearing. The first time he'd seen her, he'd felt an empty sensation in his chest and a quickening in his groin. It was the first time he'd felt such a sensation since Cindy's death, and the surprise at it was flooded out by a tide of guilt, dark and gritty, like silt.

But then he'd found out who she was and what she was, and he didn't even want to look at her again.

Besides that, she had that diabolic roughneck daughter who tried to run Kip's life at the group, and worse, Kip adored the little hellcat and considered her his best friend.

A girl—his son's *best friend.* Practically his only friend. It had come to that. Jay felt half-sick. How was he supposed to raise his son to be a man? He couldn't understand the kid at all.

He shook his head and set the reel aside. What was the point of fixing it? Kip would never learn to fish. Or hunt. Or maybe even play ball—he wasn't the most coordinated of kids. Jay repeatedly tried to teach him to catch, but Kip fumbled half the time and seemed to hate his own failure.

Jay turned and stared at his son again, sitting very quietly, watching the blue elves rush around. He still stroked the rabbit's ear and he still sucked his thumb, as he always did when disturbed.

With shock, Jay realized that tears were silently gliding down the child's face. Kip was crying, soundlessly and steadily. The boy gave an almost silent hiccup, hugged his rabbit tighter and kept right on crying.

Alarmed, Jay sprang to his feet and went to the boy, standing over him. "Kip?" he asked. "Kip? What's wrong?"

Kip didn't answer. He looked up briefly, tears welling steadily in his eyes. He stared at Jay almost as if he feared him. Guiltily, he took his thumb out of his mouth and turned his face back to the television, biting his lower lip.

Agony went through Jay like a spear. He bent over and picked the boy up in his arms. "Kipper," he whispered in the boy's ear. "Kip—hey, come on, man, what is it? What's wrong, buddy?"

Kip shook his head and refused to speak. Jay looked down and saw the struggle in the child's face. How many times had Jay told him that boys didn't cry? But the kid was full to overflowing with misery, and now he was afraid to show it.

Oh, God, Jay thought, maybe it was all right for boys to cry sometimes. He hugged the child tighter. "It's okay, Kip," he said, trying to sound gentle. He didn't know if he succeeded. "It's okay, man."

Kip looked at him with a mixture of hope and disbelief. Jay nodded, feeling his innards knot with pity for the child. He nodded again. "It's okay," he repeated. "Maybe this is the one night in the year it's okay."

Kip's face crumpled and he buried his face against his father's shoulder, sobbing. Stricken, Jay tried to soothe him, but the boy would not be comforted. He clutched his father's shirt convulsively and cried hot tears into it.

Jay's face twisted with pain for his son, and he paced back and forth, as Cindy had done when the boy was a baby. In the background, the cartoon characters cavorted, singing a silly song.

"Tell me," Jay said, almost fiercely. "Tell me what it is."

But Kip only cried harder. The more Jay asked, the more wildly Kip refused to talk. In confusion, Jay realized it wasn't grief tearing the boy apart, it was fear, pure and terrible. But fear of what?

He stopped asking questions because they only upset Kip more. At last he simply put the boy into his bed with his rabbit, then sat beside him, one hand protectively on the child's sobbing back. "Hey, I'm here, man. I'm here. I wouldn't let anything get you."

He might as well have said nothing. The boy didn't seem to hear.

Exhausted, Kip finally cried himself to sleep. Just as he dozed off, he slipped his thumb into his mouth again. Jay automatically reached to pull it out, then checked himself. He let the thumb stay.

He sat beside the boy for three hours to make sure he didn't wake up again. Sometimes Kip turned, whimpering in his sleep, but he did not awaken.

At last Jay rose tiredly and turned out the light. He left a night-light burning and the boy's door open. He glanced at the clock in the dining room. It was one minute after midnight.

He felt exhausted himself, as if he'd just played a tie game in hell. He went through the house switching off lights, grateful it was after midnight.

That meant the anniversary of death was over.

He fell asleep with all his clothes on, without even turning down the covers of his bed.

FROM HIS HIDING PLACE among the scrub cedars and locust trees, Thornton watched the last light in the Malone house blink off.

Now he was frightened for another reason; his mind spun giddily, dizzied by his growing multitude of fears. He was out late, far too late. His mother would be angry. What could he tell her? He did not dare tell her the truth.

His heart hammering, Thornton went for his bicycle and rode home along the dark roads as swiftly as he could. His head was so full of worry that it banged with pain, and his stomach squirmed. What was he going to do? He had opened up the pit of hell. He had told the truth about the dead person.

And now it could never be untold.

MERCER AWOKE AT DAWN, yelling and fighting with sheets. She had dreamed she was in the basement of the condo.

The basement was a spooky place. It had damp concrete walls, but its floor was nothing but a rubble of disturbed earth. Her mother said the condo was built like that because it was on a steep, where it would cost too much to pour a concrete floor.

Mercer didn't understand anything about concrete, but she knew a spooky place when she saw one. Until now, it had been pleasantly eerie to her, an excellent place to stalk toads and spiders.

But in this morning's dream, nothing as lovely as a hunt awaited Mercer in the basement. An undead dead man did, and she could hear him clawing his way up through the dirt to get her. Scrabble, scrabble went his hands beneath the earth.

The dream-Mercer stood, watching an uneasy patch of earth heave and shift, listening to the scratching of the dead man's fingers. As sometimes happened in dreams, she found it impossible to move. Her limbs were leaden, useless.

Suddenly a greenish hand with rotting flesh shot up through the clods of earth like some evil, slimy flower. With the finality of a death sentence, it clamped around her ankle, cold and stinking.

Then a second terrible hand clawed its way through the earth, joining the first, chaining her ankle in an unbreakable grip. At the same moment, a man's head, decayed and grinning, rose and stared at her triumphantly with lidless eyes.

"No, you don't!" Mercer cried. She kicked at him with all her might, struggling to break free, but he only laughed. "I'll bust you to pieces!" she shouted. "No, no, no!"

Rachel was there when she woke up, shaking her. "Mercer, wake up. You're having a nightmare."

Mercer's eyes opened in confusion. She saw her mother's concerned face and relaxed.

"You're all right, honey," Rachel said, bending to kiss her forehead. "It was just a dream."

"Some dream," Mercer grumbled, pulling the sheet up around her neck.

Rachel smoothed the girl's hair away from her brow. "Do you want me to stay with you awhile? Do you want a drink?"

Mercer yawned groggily. "I dreamed I had to beat up a guy. He was trying to *get* me."

"Oh." Rachel smoothed the child's hair again. "Well, you're very brave and strong. I'm sure you won."

Mercer's eyes fluttered tiredly. How irritating, she thought, to wake up before she could overcome her enemy. How irritating to be frightened, too; she wasn't used to it. Dimly she realized she'd been frightened because of something Thornton, of all people, had said.

"Going back to sleep?" Rachel asked, adjusting the bed's light cover.

"Umm," Mercer mumbled and slipped back into sleep. The child tossed uneasily for a few moments, but then seemed to lapse into peacefulness. Rachel sat by her until she was quiet again.

How unlike Mercer, Rachel thought, going back to her own room. Maybe the child was picking up some of Rachel's own uneasiness, having to think about murderers and victims all the time. How could Mercer not, as oppressed as Rachel was by violence and bloodletting?

We're going to have to lighten up around here, she thought as she slipped back between the sheets. Perhaps they should have a weekend devoted to wholesome silliness, rent two dozen Warner Brothers cartoons and make themselves laugh a lot.

Drowsy, she had a sudden image of Kip Malone, who hardly ever laughed, and his ice-eyed father, the man who never so much as smiled. In her mind's eye, she saw Jay

Malone's dark face, staring at her with those astounding light blue eyes.

An odd knot formed and tingled in the pit of her stomach, sending frissons down her thighs. She knew that feeling, had once known it all too well. *No!* she commanded. She had disciplined herself rigorously against such feelings. She had overcome them.

The birds had already begun to twitter sleepily in the trees. She ignored them and fell into a restless sleep.

AT BREAKFAST Mercer was quiet again, thoughtful. Rachel poured her a glass of juice, then turned to make coffee.

"Mom," Mercer said suddenly, "there's no dead guy buried in our basement, right?"

Rachel wheeled, the empty coffeepot in her hand. *"What?"*

Mercer chewed meditatively on a piece of toast. "There's no dead guy buried in our basement. Thornton said there was a dead guy here."

Rachel's jaw dropped slightly. "Thornton said that?"

Mercer nodded, dipping her spoon into her cereal. "But he's lying, right? He was just trying to scare us." She looked up, her brown eyes meeting her mother's blue-gray ones. "Right?" she repeated.

Rachel stared at her. Was that why she had awakened, yelling from the nightmare? Mercer, for once in her headlong life, needed reassurance.

"There's most *certainly* no dead man in the basement," Rachel said emphatically. "Exactly what did Thornton tell you?"

Mercer, surer of herself now, ate her spoonful of cereal. "He told us there was a guy murdered in Kip's house and hid in ours last year. And that if we told, the dead guy would come back and get us."

Rachel set the coffeepot on the counter and sat down at the table. "Who's 'us'? Who else did he tell this to?"

"To me and Evan McInery and Kip," Mercer said. "He made Kip cry. And he said we couldn't tell—ever."

"This is ridiculous," Rachel said angrily. "I'd never have expected this of Thornton. Tell the truth—is that what gave you the nightmare?"

Mercer shrugged nonchalantly. "I suppose. Yeah. It was about a dead guy coming out of the basement. He was totally gross, like in a horror movie."

"Oh, murder," Rachel said, unaware of the irony of her words. She ran her hand through her hair. If Thornton could reduce Mercer to nightmares, what had his tales done to the other children—solemn, serious Evan, and especially nervous little Kip?

She would have to call the other parents immediately. Explaining to Evan's mother would be awkward enough, but Jay Malone? She gritted her teeth. What would he do? Hang up on her if she called? Pierce her with his unearthly blue gaze if she tried to confront him, then walk away, snubbing her again?

And of course Minnie Crabtree would have to be informed—and Thornton's mother. It would all be extremely unpleasant.

Mercer wiped away a milk mustache. "Can I go out and catch lizards? I'm thinking of starting a lizard ranch."

"Brush your teeth first," Rachel said absently, and Mercer sprang off. She waited until the child had bolted from the house before she started phoning.

It was logical to tell the parents concerned first, Rachel thought, so they could ease their children's worry. She squared her shoulders, called information for the McInerys' number and was told there was no listing.

Damn, Rachel thought. Well, that was one reason people came to the lake, to get away from things like phones. She would have to find out where they lived and drive to see them.

She had no choice now except to call old ice eyes. She remembered a poem in which the poet called someone "a granite man, with flint and granite heart." That's how she thought of Malone. A flint and granite heart. Rude, cruel and insensitive. A jock with a chip on his shoulder.

But she got his number from information and dialed it. She was not surprised when he didn't so much as say hello.

"Malone," his voice growled. "What?"

The connection was terrible, Rachel thought with growing frustration. Interference crackled so loudly through the wires she could barely make out his words and wondered if he could understand hers.

Speaking as loudly and clearly as she could, she told him Mercer's story, and how Thornton had said the dead man would come get the children if they told.

"What?" Jay Malone yelled through the storm of static. "What?"

Oh, Lord, she could imagine him standing there, the phone clamped to his ear, his ferocious black brows drawn together, his free hand balling into a fist. She took a deep breath and tried once more to explain.

When she finished, he swore so forcefully she winced. Then he surprised her by saying, "I can't have a sensible conversation on this damned thing. Something's wrong. Meet me at McDonald's in half an hour."

"Pardon?" He hadn't asked her; he'd ordered her.

"Meet me at McDonald's in half an hour," he repeated curtly. "Did you hear?"

"Yes." She almost shouted to be heard above the crackles. "But—"

"Fine." He hung up.

Half an hour, she thought with resentment. She wasn't even dressed. Plus, she would have to round up Mercer, then drive like the devil, for she was much farther from the center of town than Malone was.

Flint and granite heart, she thought, practically running into her bedroom to throw on the first clothes at hand. *Rude jock,* she thought contemptuously.

She called Mercer, who was already muddy and had cockleburs sticking in her socks. Then she drove five miles an hour over the speed limit all the way to town, cursing both Jay Malone and Thornton.

Never, not even once, did it occur to her that what Thornton had said might be true, that a murderer had really struck and could strike again.

Chapter Three

Mercer chattered all the way. Would Thornton get into trouble? Could she and Kip have another breakfast at McDonald's? Would Thornton get into *enormous* trouble?

Rachel kept her answers short and stern. A poisonous knot squirmed, viperlike, in her stomach. Jay Malone was the last person she wanted to see, and Thornton was the last person she wanted to get into trouble, especially with someone as black tempered as Malone.

Entering town, she realized as always how torn her feelings for it were. The setting was lovely, and the town's quiet made it seem an ideal of rustic Americana.

But in her heart she also found it boring, self-satisfied and greedy. The town welcomed the money of summer people. But, more subtly, it did *not* welcome the summer people themselves.

She felt herself and Mercer locked out, excluded. The two of them didn't belong here, and therefore they didn't matter. They were transients, nonentities.

Ironically, Thornton was the one townsperson who was sincerely friendly. She still remembered him riding into their yard on his bicycle and introducing himself. "Hi. I'm Thornton. I got a whole shelf full of toys."

She shook her head unhappily. She truly didn't want to get Thornton into trouble. The knot in her stomach twisted nastily.

As she entered the city limits, she saw the sign that always startled her.

YOU ARE NOW ENTERING SANGRIA
POPULATION 21,030

Sangria, she thought. *Blood.* Why should such a dozy, peaceful town have a name that meant gore? No one she'd asked had ever been able to explain.

Well, she thought, today she would disturb the town's smug and dreamy peace. She gripped the wheel more tightly, hoping once more that the Malone man wouldn't make a scene, that he would be at least semireasonable.

Workers were hanging red, white and blue banners across the broad main street. Sangria was making ready to celebrate its new festival, Stokes Day. Every place of business was draped with flags, with the exception of the tall, palatial white funeral home, aptly named Berryman's.

When Mercer saw the funeral home, she began to sing:

"Did you ever think,
When a hearse goes by,
That you might be
The next to die?
They'll wrap you up
In a big white sheet
And throw you under
Six feet deep—
And the worms crawl in
And the worms crawl out—
And the ants play
Pinochle on your snout—"

"Hush," Rachel said, in no mood for that particularly gruesome piece of childish rhyme.

"When are we going to see the mortuary people?" Mercer asked. "Will they show us a body?"

"Hush," Rachel repeated, "I'm in no mood to talk about *that* today." Henry knew the woman who ran the mortuary, Vanessa Berryman. He'd encouraged Rachel to visit her, but Rachel felt too drenched in death already to drag it into her meager social life.

Leave it to Henry, she thought ruefully, to befriend a mortician. He said she was an invaluable source of information about rigor mortis and so forth. Rachel gave a small private shudder.

Mercer's attention had already darted elsewhere. "Why do they celebrate Stokes Day?" she asked, staring at all the bunting. "What did he ever do?"

"He was a politician or something. He was born here," Rachel said. "They're celebrating his birthday, that's all I know." She'd read in the newspaper that the town's most famous son was the late Honorable Albert Pike Stokes. Yet until Rachel had come to Sangria, she didn't recall ever hearing of Albert P. Stokes, nor did she know why such a great to-do was being made in his name.

"Sean Alan says his daddy's wrote a little book about Stokes and now is writing a big one," Mercer said. "But Sean Alan picks boogers, and he listens and tattles—"

"Don't say 'booger,'" Rachel said, "and don't—"

"There's McDonald's!" Mercer cried, pointing at the Golden Arches. "There's Kip's car."

Malone's black Corvette gleamed in the morning sunlight, next to the restaurant's playground. Rachel glanced at her watch and saw she was already ten minutes late. She set her jaw. Malone was not a man who would gladly suffer tardiness. She feared that it was going to take everything she knew about psychology to handle him.

When she and Mercer walked in the door and she saw him sitting there, his brow like a storm cloud and his eyes sheer ice, she knew she was right.

JAY MALONE WATCHED her enter. At her side was the kid, a smaller antic version of the mother, her dark hair wind tangled and her pointed little face smudged. "Where's Kip?" Mercer yelled across the room.

Frowning slightly, he nodded toward the playground area. With a whoop, Mercer ran out the side door to join Kip. Half kid, half tornado, Jay thought darkly.

His attention focused on Rachel Dale again. She was tall, slender almost to a fault, but her small rounded breasts were firm beneath her T-shirt, and her legs, slim in faded denim jeans, were excitingly long.

There was nothing flashy or glamorous about her face. The features would have been ordinary except for their amazing regularity. That regularity gave her an unusual, oddly classic beauty.

He caught himself watching her with something akin to hunger. Displeased, he fell back on the hostility that had grown so familiar to him in the past year.

She hadn't bothered to fix herself up for this meeting, he thought. She wore no makeup, and her hair was tousled, as if she'd barely run a brush through it. The T-shirt, which was well-worn, said University of Nebraska. She wore no socks, and one of her tennis shoes was coming untied.

Her face was pale and her jaw set as if she sensed his dislike but wasn't going to let it faze her. When, after looking her up and down thoroughly, his eyes locked with hers, she didn't blink.

She sat down across from him.

"You're late," he said, before she could speak.

"You didn't give me enough time," she said matter-of-factly. "I live farther from town than you."

Then she put her foot up on the bench and tied her shoe, quickly, firmly, in a double knot. It was such a simple, yet elegant gesture it took him aback.

She brushed her hair back from her face with the same economy of motion. "I just had time to throw on clothes and pull Mercer out of the mud."

He didn't smile. Instead, he stared out the window at the children. Before Mercer's arrival, Kip had drifted forlornly around the little playground. Unlike Mercer, his clothes were immaculate and his every hair in place. But now that she was here, swinging on the jungle gym like the world's wildest monkey, the boy looked happy.

A pang of failure and anger sizzled through Jay. "Let's get down to business," he said, his voice harsh.

"Fine."

"Do you want coffee?" The question was mechanical, without real kindness or politeness.

"No." She folded her hands together on the tabletop and gave him a long cool look. "Thank you very much."

He had a large cup of coffee and he took a swallow of it now. It was cold, nasty and matched his mood.

"Tell me again. What that weirdo told my kid—and why."

Rachel clenched her hands more tightly. "Thornton's not a weirdo, Mr. Malone. Let's get that straight. He's a human being, the same as you and I."

She was surprised at the range of emotions that played over the man's dark face. It was a rough-hewn face, square jawed with a cleft in the stubborn chin. His nose was not straight, and looked as if it had been broken and rearranged with a slight inclination to the left.

His eyebrows were black, and set at such an angle they gave him a perpetual brooding expression. He had a small raised scar on his left cheek, and another scar slanted across his full lower lip, drawing it down at one corner.

It was, Rachel thought, struggling to find the right words, not a handsome face, but a striking one, a masculine one, a *tough* one.

Yet when he spoke of Thornton, something like apprehension tightened his already controlled features. Resentment blazed in his eyes, contempt twisted the curl of his lip. The dark brows lowered in anger, but something more complicated glittered in his eyes.

This man's in pain, she thought with a jolt of surprise. *What could it have to do with Thornton?*

"I'll call him what I want," he said, turning to watch the children. "He's got no right to terrify my kid."

His blue eyes stayed trained on Kip, as if he could guard the child simply by the intensity of his attention.

"Mr. Malone—" she said his name carefully, sensing he was more complicated than she had anticipated "—Thornton's basically harmless."

His head snapped around to face her again. "That kid out there—" he pointed at Kip "—was so terrified he cried himself to sleep last night. Too scared even to tell me what was wrong. Your Thornton did that to him. You call that harmless?"

His tone scalded. Rachel straightened her back and struggled to keep her voice calm. "What he did was wrong. But I doubt he understood how much it would alarm your boy."

"He didn't 'alarm' my boy. I told you—he *terrified* him. Nobody does that to my kid. Nobody."

He swallowed the last of his coffee and tossed her an unfriendly glance. "Tell me exactly what Thornton told the kids."

Rachel took a deep breath. His shoulders were powerful, and he had a way of shifting them slightly. Even that small movement seemed charged with dangerous energy. She tried to make her story as spare and clinical as possible.

Jay Malone swore. His shoulders made one of their sinister shifts. *It's like talking to a panther in his cage,* Rachel thought. *Only he's built the cage himself.*

"I have to say," she hurried on, "that it was partly Mercer's fault. She's been ignoring Thornton lately. He wanted attention."

The twist of Jay's mouth became more ironic.

Rachel took another deep breath. "One of the reasons she ignored him is because her two other friends don't like him. Evan McInery and Kip."

His response was quick and vehement. "I don't want Thornton near my kid."

Rachel held his angry gaze and didn't flinch. "All I'm saying is the children weren't without blame. They left him out, he felt hurt, and he tried to make them notice him."

Disgusted, he turned from her and looked at the children again. Mercer was zooming down the slide, making faces. Kip laughed. Dammit, why did the kid like her so much? Jay wondered. All wild hair and mud stains today, she looked like some imp from the swamp. How could she, a mere kid, comfort his own child when he could not?

Rachel studied Jay Malone's craggy profile. He really seemed to care about his boy, and she sensed frustration and yearning under his anger. But she couldn't understand his prejudice against Thornton. Was it simple bigotry—or something deeper, more complicated?

"My suggestion," she said, trying to sound as reasonable as possible, "is that we talk to the McInerys, and then we all go talk to Minnie Crabtree. It's her responsibility to safeguard their play environment."

She bit her lip. Her last words had sounded all too much like a psychologist's jargon.

He'd noticed and turned back to her. His upper lip twitched into something resembling a sarcastic smile. "Safeguard their play environment?"

"You know what I mean."

He nodded. "I can understand big words. I know several of them myself."

For the first time she allowed a glint of anger to flash through her defenses. "I wasn't implying you were stupid. If I sounded stuffy, I'm sorry. Now—what do you say?"

He shrugged one shoulder casually. "Fine. But we also see Thornton's mother. She gives him too much freedom. He came creeping around our house when we moved in—"

"He's just *friendly*," Rachel insisted. "I asked a psychologist—a friend of mine who's stayed down here. He says Thornton's like a big puppy."

"Psychologists," Jay said with a sneer. He said it as an insult. Rachel had no choice but to take it as one.

Male chauvinist bigot pig, she thought in rising impatience, but only smiled coolly at him.

"Why, look who's here, Sean Alan!" burbled a familiar voice. Jay and Rachel looked up to see the plump figure of

Katherine Menander, another mother from the play group. With her she had her overweight and adenoidal seven-year-old son, Sean Alan.

Katherine Menander was a summer visitor, aggressively cheerful to all. Her motives, Rachel feared, were ulterior: the woman was desperate for Sean Alan to make friends. Sean Alan was not easy to like, especially when he snaked his forefinger up his nostril as he now did.

"It's Mr. Malone and Mrs. Dale," caroled Katherine Menander. "And look, Sean Alan, there're Kip and Mercer out playing by Mayor McCheese. Why don't you go play, too?"

Sean Alan grunted and made his way toward the playground, his finger still tunneling his nose.

"Are you two having a coffee date," Katherine Menander asked brightly, "or did you just run into each other?"

Rachel and Jay tried not to look at each other, and both mumbled that they had just happened into each other.

"Look at those three," cooed Katherine, pointing at the children. "Aren't they cute together?"

In actuality, Mercer and Kip played together. Sean Alan excavated something from his nostril, regarded it with scientific interest, then wiped it on Mayor McCheese's large shiny head.

Katherine's face lit as if a wonderful thought had just occurred to her. "You know," she said, "my husband's gone. He was called away just when his first book is coming out. *More* research—busy, busy, busy. You know how it is, Mrs. Dale, the world of scholarship."

She dimpled at Rachel. Katherine's husband, Tarquin Menander, was a loud, pretentious man who was also writing a dissertation. Rachel thought his field was political science and wondered if he had written about Stokes, as Mercer said. She didn't much care. The entire Menander family made her uncomfortable, especially the overeager Katherine.

"I thought I'd take Sean Alan down to Benton County. Somebody has a litter of purebred cocker spaniels, and Sean

Alan has been begging for a dog. I thought, well, if it's purebred... I don't mind telling you, living out as far as we do, I wouldn't mind having a dog, especially with Tarquin gone so much—we're all of us so isolated on that lake.''

Rachel nodded mutely, and Jay regarded the woman with wariness.

"Well," Katherine said in her bubbly voice, "why don't I take Kip and Mercer, too? All children love puppies. And each one is an only child. I think only children need to socialize, don't you? How lucky I found you—I only stopped to buy Sean Alan a milk shake. Isn't that a growing boy for you? Always eating!"

Rachel and Jay looked at each other with that peculiar discomfort couples feel when an unexpected third party appears, making an equally unexpected proposal.

"Sean Alan is unhappy today," Katherine confided, lowering her voice. "Our closest neighbors and best friends down here are little Evan's parents, the Rineharts. I try to see that Sean and Evan play together as much as possible. But the whole family left last night. Did you know?"

Rachel darted Katherine a look of astonishment, then glanced at Jay. Unreadable emotions chased across his face.

"They left?" Rachel asked, making sure she heard correctly. "I thought they were here for the summer."

"Oh, they were," Katherine said, her eyes growing round, "but Judy's father hasn't been well—he's an art dealer in St. Louis—and he took a turn for the worse. They had to leave. Such a shame. This was sort of a honeymoon summer for them, you know. They're newlyweds. Just like Tark and me. Judy and I are both on our second time around on the marriage-go-round.'' She giggled, then sobered. "But then, her father... well, I'm afraid it's serious."

"I'm sorry to hear it," Rachel said. *So that's why I couldn't find their phone number,* she thought. *Evan's mother's remarried, and now her name is Rinehart, not McInery.*

"I told her that Tark and I'd look after the place for them—check it, pick up the papers and mail every few days.

We summer people have to stick together. Be good neighbors, don't you think? Tark has an ideal about being a good neighbor. His parents were very standoffish. It hurt him. He doesn't want to see Sean Alan hurt the same way."

Rachel nodded helplessly.

"I know Mercer and Kip will miss Evan as much as Sean Alan will," Katherine said rather slyly. "Maybe they can make up the loss to each other. You know—become three little musketeers for the rest of the summer. What do you say? Can the children go see the puppies? I think it'd be so good for them *all*."

Rachel and Jay exchanged another charged glance. It would be easier to confront Minnie Crabtree without the children along. As for playing the three little musketeers with the Menander family, they would cross that bridge later. She and Jay held a silent dialogue of perhaps thirty prickly seconds.

At last Jay said, "Sure. Let them go."

"I'll have them right back here by three o'clock," Katherine promised. "I swear." She held up her hand as if swearing in court, and giggled at her gesture.

"We have to talk to Kip and Mercer first," Rachel said, tossing Jay another look. "A little something in private. Do you mind?"

"Of course not," said Katherine. "I have to buy Sean's milk shake. I may get one myself. Anything for your kids?"

"No," Jay refused immediately, and Rachel said, "Thank you, but no."

Katherine bounced off to the counter to place her order.

"Ready?" Rachel asked him. He nodded curtly. She rose and so did he. They went to the door and called the children. Sean Alan played on alone, lying back on a swing, seeing if he could drag his hair in the gravel.

Quickly Rachel explained to Kip and Mercer that they were going with the Menanders to see some puppies. Kip seemed excited, Mercer dubious about spending that much time with Sean Alan.

Jay said little, so Rachel plunged on. "Listen," she said, kneeling and putting an arm about each child. "We know what Thornton told you, and it isn't true. Do you understand? He made it up because he wanted attention. There's no dead person, there never was, and you don't have to be afraid. Not at all. Do you understand? We love you and we wouldn't let anything happen to you. Not ever."

Kip looked solemnly into Rachel's eyes. "I understand," he said. "My daddy said so, too. In the car."

Jay reached down, awkwardly gripping the boy's shoulder. "Everything's okay," he said. "Nothing to be afraid of. He won't tell you anything like that again."

"That's right," Rachel said, putting her finger on Kip's nose and almost making him smile. "He won't. And if he does, why, then he'll have to deal with your daddy and me—because we intend to take care of you. Very good care. The best ever. All right?"

Kip glanced nervously up at his father, then back at Rachel. He nodded.

"I explained that to him already," Mercer said impatiently. "Thornton is a major bore."

Rachel squeezed each of them, then stood, taking Mercer by the hand. "And you, young lady, need to wash up and comb your hair before you go anywhere. Come on. Before somebody plants radish seeds on you."

She dragged a reluctant Mercer into the ladies' room. Jay watched them disappear behind the door. He looked down at his son.

Kip swallowed hard and didn't look up to meet his father's eyes. "I'm sorry I cried last night," the boy said at last, a quiver in his voice.

Jay wanted to pick him up and hug him till it hurt and say, "Don't be sorry. It was fine. I'd have cried myself." But he was not bred to do or say such things, especially in a public place. The impulse seemed frozen within him, permanently trapped.

But still he felt a wave of relief so intense it was almost sickening. Kip seemed almost his familiar self again. The

Dale woman had said all the right things to the boy. But she had said so little, really. It didn't seem fair that it was so easy for her, so difficult for him. It had even come easy for that wild little hellion of a girl.

He allowed himself a grim smile. Nothing was fair, of course. That was the whole point. There was no justice. When he thought of that, his smile, cynical as it was, faded.

JAY INSISTED on driving the two of them to the Crabtree house, which was on the other side of town. At first, an uncomfortable silence swelled between them, filling the Corvette, making Rachel feel crushed by its bulk.

She tried to deflate it. "What do you do, anyway?" she asked. "Somebody said you were in sports. Baseball?"

She'd guessed baseball because, although he was a powerful man, he didn't have the height of a basketball player or the bulk of someone who played football.

He shook his head, keeping his eyes on the street.

"Then what?" she asked in frustration.

"Hockey," he said between his teeth. "I played hockey."

Oh, Lord, Rachel thought. Growing up in Oklahoma and Nebraska, she knew little about hockey, except that it was fabled for its roughness. Hockey was a contact sport, physical, violent, and fights were apt to break out between players. She found it mindless and distasteful.

Still, the idea almost made her smile. Here she was, Ms. Straight-*A* Student, riding around town in, of all things, a black Corvette, with, of all people, a *hockey player*.

She slid him a sideways glance, understanding now about the scars, the nose slightly rearranged to the left. His black hair tossed in the breeze, playing over his brows, which looked, as usual, locked in unhappy thought.

"Do you still play?" she asked. "In winter, I mean?"

"No," he said shortly, not bothering to look at her.

She shrugged at his brusqueness. Mr. Charm he was not. What did she care? Her business with him would soon be over.

They rounded a corner, and the Crabtree home came into view, a small house distinguished only by the high wooden back fence that signaled a swimming pool lay within the yard.

Jay shook his head and spoke out of the side of his mouth. "I don't like it," he said unexpectedly. "What she said about Evan's parents leaving."

She stared at him openly this time. He wore a pale blue shirt with short sleeves. The tanned and bared muscles of his arms played intricately as he did something to the car's gears, halting it before the house. He tossed her a glance bluer than the hot Missouri sky above them. She suddenly realized some women might find him attractive.

"The Rineharts? Why?" Rachel challenged. "If her father's sick, then they had to leave."

He only shrugged. He surprised her by getting out of the car and opening the door on her side before she even had her seat belt unfastened. He further surprised her by reaching out his hand to help her out of the low car.

She took it and had the same sensation as the day before, as if the charge of a live wire swarmed up her arm to seize her spinal chord. She tried to ignore it and keep her face blank.

"Why?" she repeated. They stood on the grassy verge between street and sidewalk. He was tall enough so that she had to look up into his eyes.

Meeting his deep-set blue gaze still came as a shock to her. It reminded her again of electricity, the cold blue of sparks that tingled and tautened the marrow. Twice she'd asked him the same question, and twice he hadn't answered her. It was unnerving.

She repeated it, more emphatically. "*Why* does it bother you that they left—Evan's parents?" Her mouth was so dry she had the desire to lick her lips. She resisted because his eyes were fastened so steadfastly on her face.

"Look," he said, unsmiling, "you wouldn't understand. There's just...something about this whole thing. I get... feelings."

Rachel tilted her head slightly in puzzlement. He kept staring at her. Then impatiently he tossed his head to shake the hair off his brow. He didn't smile, didn't let her see any expression on his face whatsoever. She said nothing, because she could think of nothing to say.

"Feelings," he repeated almost angrily. "I said you wouldn't understand." He paused, regarding her as if she were an adversary. "They aren't exactly scientific," he said, his mouth crooking downward. "Come on."

He turned and led the way toward the Crabtrees' front door. Rachel discovered that for a moment he had made her stop breathing. Now her heart and lungs raced to catch up, and she struggled to exorcise the foreign emotions he had sent flying through her, jumbled and swift.

Feelings, she said to herself with stern irony. He got *feelings.* On top of everything else he was superstitious, which offended all her rational principles. Or, worse yet, perhaps he imagined himself to be psychic.

She cast a furtive glance at his back, how the width of his shoulders tapered to the hard narrowness of his waist. Then she looked away, as if she'd done something wrong.

A bad-tempered jock who thinks he's psychic, she thought. *He believes in muscles and magic. The original primitive man,* she thought. But she followed him.

Chapter Four

Jay Malone punched the doorbell three times in a row, as vehemently as if it were the enemy.

He waited all of ten seconds for an answer, and when it did not come, he hit the bell again, as irritably as before.

"Look," Rachel said between her teeth, "I want to be civil about this. I want to make sure—"

"I want to make sure it never happens again," he said, his brows lowered. "Not to my kid. Not to anybody's."

"Of course," she said, hoping she could keep him relatively calm. "But—"

The door swung open abruptly, and there stood Minnie Crabtree. She was, Rachel had been told, a minister's widow, a short, stocky woman with sharp green eyes and graying hair so curly it was almost frizzy. She wore a brightly flowered housecoat that seemed at odds with her dour expression.

"Yes?" she demanded, eyeing them unsmilingly.

Rachel saw the woman every weekday and had thought their relationship politely cordial. Why did Minnie Crabtree now seem so unfriendly? Did she sense trouble?

"Hello," Rachel said with false heartiness. "Sorry to bother you on a Saturday, but—something's come up."

"We've got problems," Jay said so harshly that Rachel flinched. "*You've* got problems."

Minnie Crabtree drew herself up. "I beg your pardon." Her tone was grudging, suspicious.

"You should." Jay's eyes glittered icily. "The problem is—" he began, but Rachel interrupted him.

"We didn't want to bother you, but we thought this should be resolved as soon as possible." She tried to smile calmly. But the smile, she knew immediately, was a failure.

Minnie Crabtree cocked her head in distrust. "What's this about? The play group?"

"Yes." Jay's voice was an angry hiss. "Our kids. Your group." He pointed at Minnie Crabtree with accusation. "Your nephew."

His Irish was up, Rachel thought with dismay, and Mrs. Crabtree's unexpected coldness did not take him aback. His anger was controlled, but he made no attempt to hide it.

Minnie blanched. "My nephew?" Her hand moved to grip the halves of her collar tightly together. She kept her face stony, but something in her demeanor changed. She looked wary, almost frightened. "Who? Thornton, you mean?"

"Thornton, I mean." Jay spoke through clenched teeth. "He's been lying to our kids, scaring them. If he can't behave, then keep him the hell away. I don't want him around my kid. I won't have it."

Minnie, still pale, seemed to reach deep inside herself to rally against Jay's ire. Her face stayed as rigid as before. "Thornton's harmless. He's no more than a child himself. I won't have you discriminating against him."

Rachel took a deep breath, getting ready to try to smooth things over. But Jay gave her no chance.

"Telling my kid somebody was murdered in our house last year isn't *harmless,* dammit." He pointed at Rachel. "Telling her kid that a body's buried at her house isn't *harmless.*"

"Murdered? Buried?" Once more Minnie was quick to recover herself. Her tone became frostier than before. "Well, of course, the boy lies sometimes. Like any child. For attention. Sometimes he doesn't even *know* true from false. He doesn't even have any conception of time. A week is like a year to him. He gets things mixed up, he makes things up. It's nothing to be upset about."

"My kid was scared out of his head," Jay snapped back. "It was something to be upset about. And Thornton's no child. If you people can't control him, then you better damn well keep him away from my kid—or else."

Minnie glared at Jay in disdain. "What do you mean, keep him away? This is my house. The group meets on my premises. I'll have my own sister, my own nephew on my premises any time I want. If you don't like it—"

Rachel interrupted. "Mrs. Crabtree, please don't take offense. Mr. Malone's understandably upset. Thornton did frighten the children. I'm certain you're right—he did it just for attention. But he...caused problems. We thought you should know, so you can help put a stop to it. I'm sure you don't want this sort of thing happening, either."

"Of course not," Minnie said righteously, still fidgeting with her collar. "Nobody wants it happening."

"Precisely." Rachel nodded. "All we want is to make sure it doesn't happen again. We didn't mean to upset you. It's just that the incident has unfortunately been disturbing. It's been...emotional."

Minnie Crabtree looked Rachel up and down coolly, as if taking her measure. Jay did, too, with the same watchful thoroughness, which made Rachel self-conscious. A wave of prickliness, first hot, then cold, crept over her. She tried to shake it off as she smiled apologetically at Minnie.

Minnie did not smile back. At last she nodded. "I'll talk to my sister."

"Thank you," Rachel said. "That's all we want. We didn't come to make trouble. We came to try to prevent it, that's all. Isn't it, Mr. Malone?"

She reached out and lightly touched his bare arm in a friendly way, to emphasize she wished no hard feelings.

Immediately she wished she hadn't touched him. The strange prickliness swam over her again, startling her like an electric shock. His ice blue eyes widened slightly, as if at her audacity. Instantly she drew back her hand.

Although he made no physical movement away from her, he somehow seemed to put more space between them. He crossed his arms stubbornly, without further acknowledging her touch, so she was surprised when he nodded in agreement with her.

"Will that be all?" Minnie Crabtree said pointedly, her hand moving to the doorknob to close the door.

"One more thing." Rachel tried to sound as reasonable and friendly as she could. "We need to get in touch with Evan's parents. To let them know about this. Thornton talked to their boy, too. But they've left town. I should have asked Katherine Menander, but I forgot. Could you tell me where to find them?"

"I have no idea." Minnie's manner seemed even colder than before. "None. I don't see the Rineharts socially. Where they go is no concern of mine. I shouldn't have taken on their boy. I have too many children to handle now."

"Do you know who'd know?" Rachel asked. She was struck by sudden inspiration. She remembered that Minnie Crabtree's son, Powell, was a realtor who handled many of the lake-property rentals. He might know how to reach the Rineharts. "Do you think Powell might—"

"My son and I are estranged," Minnie said flatly. "We have been for years. I prefer not to discuss him."

"Oh," Rachel said, feeling awkward. "Well, thank you for your time. I'm sure we'll smooth all this out."

"Yes," Mrs. Crabtree said, unsmiling, as she closed the door. "Goodbye."

The door shut in their faces. At least it shut gently, Rachel thought with relief.

Wordlessly Jay strode back to the car. He swung the Corvette's door open for Rachel and waited for her to climb in, shutting it after her.

He got in on the driver's side and pulled his own door shut. He started the car and stepped on the accelerator. "Old bat," he muttered darkly.

Rachel clinically noted the hostility of the remark, but let it pass. "She didn't seem to want to be bothered."

"Too bad," he said, narrowing his eyes against the noon sun. "I'll bother her, all right."

He swung the car back onto Main Street, and she looked at the red, white and blue banners that announced the approaching Stokes Day.

"Who exactly was Albert Pike Stokes, anyway?" she asked, trying to change the subject.

"You're asking me?" he asked, never taking his eyes from the road. "A dumb jock?"

"I didn't call you a dumb jock," Rachel said emphatically. "I never thought of you as one. That would be... thinking in stereotypes." *Fine,* she thought in self-disgust. *He sees right through me and now I'm lying to him.*

He nodded as if to himself. "Right. You'd never think in stereotypes. So stop looking at me as if I'm a grenade you think's going to explode, all right?" His voice was sarcastic. "Albert Pike Stokes was a senator, then an ambassador. To Belgium or Bolivia or Bulgaria or someplace like that. He was born here. Native son. Local boy makes good. He died last year. Now the town consecrates his name. So it can bask in his reflected glory. It wants to partake of his greatness. A typical case of small-townitis."

Chastised, she looked at him in surprise. She hadn't been aware her attitude toward him had been so evident, nor had she expected him to talk the way he did. "How do you know so much about him?"

"I live in the house that used to be his. I rented it through Powell Crabtree—he gave me the whole lecture."

Powell had sold Henry his condo, as well, Rachel knew. It was Powell who had seen that the utilities were turned on when she arrived. He had visited her to make sure things were all right. She had found him unpleasantly hearty and more than a little flirtatious, an unlikely candidate for Minnie Crabtree's son.

Jay continued bitterly, "But he didn't say anything about bodies." He swung off Main Street, taking a side street that led to the east-west highway.

"Where are you going?" She had thought he was driving her back to McDonald's, where her car was parked.

"To Thornton's," he said grimly, his eyes still straight ahead. "To talk to his mother. Get to the root of this."

"Oh, no," Rachel protested, shaking her head. She didn't want to risk another scene. Jay Malone's temper was too formidable. "I'd rather phone her. Really. Mrs. Crabtree took us for a hostile posse. No."

"Yes," he said firmly. "This should be done face-to-face. Besides, the old bat's right. I *am* hostile. And you're the posse." He tossed her a glance and flashed her the ghost of a crooked grin. "Keeping law and order."

He turned his attention back to the road. His smile had astonished her and made an odd sensation ripple down her spine. "I don't want another confrontation," she insisted.

"I do." He said it simply and with conviction. "So I need you. To keep law and order."

"What?" She stared at him, puzzled.

He swung the Corvette onto the highway. This time he didn't smile when he looked at her. "You're a steadying influence. I can use one."

For a moment his ice blue gaze pierced her through. "Look," he said gruffly, "this mess has me hot under the collar. The past year, I've been ... volatile, all right? Talking to these people—it's got to be done. You're better at it than I am. So I'd like you along. Okay?"

He said it quickly, harshly, with no pleading in his tone, then turned his attention to the road. But Rachel was oddly touched that he would say he needed anyone for any reason. She had never imagined him making such a statement.

Almost against her will, she nodded. Perhaps he was right. It was best to confront Thornton's mother in person and soon.

"All right," she said, smoothing her blowing hair. "But try to keep your temper. You weren't exactly Mr. Sweetness-and-Light back there."

He gave a mirthless laugh. "I've never been Mr. Sweetness-and-Light. Besides, she reminded me of a ref."

"A what?"

He frowned in concentration as he headed the car out of town. "A hockey referee. She's even built like one. Same rock head—doesn't want to hear a word you say. You want somebody like that to listen, you get in their face."

Rachel smiled slightly at the thought of Mrs. Crabtree in a hockey mask. "That's hockey. This is the real world. You can't yell and bang somebody on the head with a hockey stick just because you disagree."

"Yeah? Well, I'm still learning," he said, his face grim. "And it used to be gratifying, banging somebody on the head. If he deserved it. Highly gratifying."

Rachel's smile faded. Jay Malone was a man who had lived in a world where violence was both allowed and expected. She was not used to such men.

"So what are you?" he asked abruptly. "Divorced, widowed, what? Or have you got a husband hidden someplace?"

"Divorced," she said just as abruptly. She didn't like talking about Damon. Remorse still filled her for having been naive enough to have gotten involved with him. At least, she told herself for the ten thousandth time, she'd gotten Mercer out of it.

"What'd he do? Was he a *psychologist,* too?"

How, Rachel wondered irritably, did he always manage to put such a hostile sting into the word? "No," she answered. "He was a poet."

"A poet?" Once again he gave his humorless laugh. "I never met a poet. What was he? A mad genius? Isn't that what poets are? Mad geniuses?"

"Half-right," Rachel said, forcing herself to keep the bitterness out of her voice. "He wasn't any genius."

He cast her a speculative look, but she said no more and was relieved when he asked no more questions about Damon. He changed the subject.

"So what kind of psychologist are you? You make people lie down on a couch and tell about their potty training?"

"No," she answered. "I'm an unfinished psychologist. I'm working on my dissertation. It's on murderers. The psychology of murderers."

He frowned and stared at her, his mouth crooked with distaste, his eyes cold. "Murderers?" he said, as if he suddenly found her repugnant.

"They're very...interesting."

The line of his mouth grew more crooked still, his eyes colder. "Interesting," he repeated, his tone dead with disapproval.

"Yes," she said, and looked at the green countryside instead of him. "Interesting."

She wondered irritably why he seemed repulsed by what she did. There was nothing wrong with studying psychology. Her work was meaningful. Somebody who had chased a stupid hockey puck for a living certainly had no right to look down on her.

"I want to stop and see somebody before we go to Thornton's," he said in another of his abrupt conversational shifts. The tone of his voice had changed, too. He was suddenly cool, businesslike.

She gave him a questioning look, her face under careful control. His attitude about her work rankled.

"Up at the intersection," he said in the same distant tone. "Castor Bevins. A deputy. He's always parked up here this time of day. Pretending to watch for speeders. He's usually taking a nap."

"A deputy?" Rachel asked, frowning slightly. "Now, really—you're not going to file a complaint against Thornton, are you? That's going too far—"

"I'm not filing any complaints," he said with a sudden show of impatience. "I'm not nuts. I want to ask him a few things. About...this." He shrugged one shoulder, a gesture of disgust with the situation.

"What about it?" she asked, wishing that she'd never agreed to come. His moods changed like some slightly sinister black mercury, always keeping her off balance.

"About murder, for instance," he said. "For a woman who likes murders, you're showing damned little interest in this one. Me, I'm curious. I've got questions."

Rachel tried to smooth her fluttering hair. "I don't like murders," she said with asperity. "Curiosity about what? That there really was a murder? That's ridiculous. Thornton made it up."

He gave her a condescending look. "Well, we both jumped to that conclusion. But you're such an exceptionally intelligent woman, I'm surprised it hasn't occurred to you that maybe he *didn't* make it up."

"Oh, certainly," Rachel returned, letting her sarcasm match his. "There really is a body in my basement, and the police know about it, and this deputy will tell you. But things have been so busy, what with Stokes Day and all, that nobody's bothered to come over and dig it up."

He cocked an eyebrow. "Well. Look at that. You *can* show emotion. Impressive. You should do it more often. I kind of like you with fire in your eyes."

"I don't care how you like me," she retorted. "The point is that Thornton made up the story."

"You assume," he said smugly. "Did you ever ask yourself if he *could* make it up? If he's capable of a lie that complicated? A nice, sweet, totally harmless boy like Thornton? Could he? You're the psychologist. Tell me. And what happens if somebody just happens to be missing? And could be stashed in your basement?"

Rachel stared at him. He had reached into his shirt pocket, pulled out a pair of sunglasses and put them on. She could no longer try to read the expression in his eyes.

Minute chills snaked through her system, and for the first time, doubt entered her mind. Was Thornton capable of making up such a complex set of falsehoods and threats? The question disturbed her.

What if, just possibly, somebody *was* missing? She thought of her basement with its rough dirt floor. Anything could have been buried beneath that damp earth.

Anyone could be buried there. The thought made her slightly ill.

CASTOR BEVINS WAS a big man whose neck bulged over the collar of his uniform. Jay drove the Corvette up beside the deputy's patrol car and parked. The two men spoke to each other from their cars.

There was a slightly stilted masculine camaraderie between them, and from what was said, Rachel understood that Bevins often fished in the cove near where Jay and Kip lived. Jay introduced her perfunctorily to Bevins, but she felt oddly left out of the conversation.

No, Castor Bevins assured Jay, nobody was missing from last year, nobody was dead.

"Anybody got murdered around here," Bevins said cheerfully, "it was the perfect crime. An absolutely brilliant job. 'Cause nobody's heard a thing about it."

"Anybody missing?" Jay asked.

"Naw," said Castor Bevins, "nobody's really been missing for three years. And that was Ella Blankenship." He laughed. "She turned up safe and sound in Provo, Utah. Ran off with her first cousin who was twice her age and married to boot. Quite the scandal." He laughed again.

The only thing vaguely like murder on the books, Castor said, was one shooting that occurred after a drinking bout, and that charge was reduced to manslaughter.

"So nobody's gone?" Jay asked. "Nobody at all?"

"Oh, hell," Castor said, shaking his head humorously, so his jowls wobbled. "Nobody we ever missed. A girl over in Paradise City run off, but that didn't surprise anybody. She was the sort. Trashy family. And the fruit doesn't fall far from the tree. You know."

"Well," Jay said with a careless gesture, "what about Thornton? Could he make up something like that?"

"Hell, man," Castor said, laughing his fat man's laugh, "I don't know. Isn't that the psychologist sitting next to you? Ask her."

Jay smiled. Rachel blushed and hated herself for it.

"No," Castor said, "biggest thing around here is that kids've been putting garter snakes in the mailboxes along the rural routes. Scared some folks half to death. I've got to drive along in my spare time, check 'em out. No pleasure, opening one up, wondering if an old snake'll jump out. No pleasure at all. But it's about all the excitement we've got. Murder? No way."

THORNTON AND HIS MOTHER lived in a large mobile home almost nine miles outside of town. The home was in need of painting, the yard untended, but a nearly brand-new Buick sat in the carport. Thornton's familiar red bicycle, with its yellow streamers on the handlebars and yellow happy-face sticker on the back fender, was nowhere to be seen.

Ruby Fuller, Thornton's mother, was a nurse at the city hospital, but she worked only part-time because of her arthritis. Rachel had seen her before, at Minnie Crabtree's.

Like Minnie, Ruby Fuller was small, stout and graying. But Ruby, unlike her stern-faced sister, was usually animated, full of energy and talkative.

Ruby Fuller was also prettier than her sister, in spite of her plumpness. She always took special care with her hair and makeup, and her clothes, while not as expensive as her sister's, were more stylish and more flattering.

But Rachel was shocked when Ruby opened the door to Jay's impatient knock. Ruby was not her usual self at all.

She wore a faded bathrobe and rubber thongs. Her tangled hair looked as if she hadn't touched a brush to it, though the hour was past noon. Nor was she wearing any makeup. She looked far older and plainer without it.

Gone was her usual hectic liveliness, her skittish smile. Her face was drawn, as if she had slept little the night before. Her hand settled on the doorframe, and Rachel thought she saw a tremor in the fingers.

"I know why you're here," Ruby Fuller said, before Jay had a chance to speak. Her chin shook and her lips trembled. "My sister phoned. All I can say is I'm sorry. It'll never happen again. I can't tell you how sorry I am. It'll never, never happen again, I promise you. He's never said anything like this before. I was—shocked. But he does lie. Yes, he does. He does it so people notice him. It's a terrible habit, and I'm working hard to break him of it. He's not a bad boy. His imagination runs wild. Movies—I shouldn't let him watch those movies on television. That must be where he got it. These movies are terrible nowadays. They show terrible things. That must be where he got it. How else could he come to say such a thing? It'll never happen again. I promise you."

The words poured out in a nervous torrent. Even Jay seemed taken aback. He'd removed his sunglasses, and he frowned, regarding Ruby with coldness and surprise.

Ruby's eyes darted back and forth between him and Rachel. His frown seemed to unsettle her even more.

"Mr. Malone," she said, her voice shaking, "I swear to you by all that's sacred—I swear on my husband's grave— Thornton will never do anything like this again. I promise by everything that's holy. I—I'm taking him away for the summer. I never would have taken him to Minnie's if I'd thought anything like this would happen. But he loves children so—and Minnie's the only family we have. She's *all* we have. But I never . . . He didn't mean it. He was lying. He wanted attention. He . . . I . . . we . . ."

"Mrs. Fuller," Rachel said, reaching out and putting her hand over the older woman's as it clutched the doorframe. "We understand. We just want Thornton to know that it's wrong to tell such stories, especially to children, and that he mustn't do it again."

To Rachel's dismay, Ruby grasped Rachel's hand between her two and squeezed so hard that Rachel fought to keep from wincing. "Mrs. Dale," she said, "believe me, I'd die before I'd let it happen again. I mean it. I'm taking Thornton away. I just have to make arrangements. I . . . we . . . money's a little short with me only working parttime, but—"

"There's no need to take him away," Rachel said earnestly. "None. We don't dislike Thornton. We only—"

"No, no," Ruby protested, squeezing Rachel's hand harder. "This will teach him. He can't tell such terrible lies. This will teach him. It's best this way. And you won't have to worry. You won't have to worry at all."

Rachel felt Jay eyeing the two of them apprehensively. "You're taking this too hard, Mrs. Fuller," she said gently. "I realize we may have been . . . emotional when we talked with your sister, but you really don't have to—"

"No, no," Ruby said again. "I was planning to go away, anyway. Just a little later is all. It's no trouble. I know him. I know what teaches him. I know what works. He lied, that's all. I'm sorry. I am. Truly, truly sorry."

She released Rachel's hand as abruptly as she had taken it. "It won't happen again," she repeated. "I promise you. I promise you."

She took a step backward into the trailer and began to close the door. "It really won't," she said, the quaver stronger than ever in her voice.

The door shut, leaving them standing on her tinny little porch. They heard a lock click.

Rachel looked into Jay's eyes. His face was taut, and hers, she knew, was naked. She could not hide how deeply pained she was by the other woman's undisguised anguish.

"Come on," he said, his voice rough. When she didn't move, he reached out and seized her hand, the one Ruby Fuller had held so desperately. It still ached from Ruby's touch. Now it burned from his.

"Come on," he said again, drawing her down the rickety stairs and back to the Corvette. "Lord," he said, opening the door for her, "let's get out of here. Before she kills herself out of remorse."

He slammed the door behind her, got in on his own side, slammed his door even harder and started the car. He gunned out of the gravel driveway in a cloud of dust.

Rachel put her elbow on the window's edge and her forehead in her hand. "The poor woman," she said. "That boy must be everything to her."

She could understand that, she thought achingly, for Mercer was everything to her. What she could not comprehend was the depth of the woman's remorse, her obvious fear. "I don't understand," she said, once more feeling sick deep inside.

Jay wheeled onto the highway, heading back toward Sangria. "I only understand one thing," he said moodily. "She was terrified. She was flat-out terrified."

Rachel turned to look at him. "Well, you shouldn't have been so ferocious with her sister. Mrs. Crabtree probably told the poor woman to expect a fire-breathing dragon. By the time we got there, she'd worked herself into a state."

He gave her one of his looks in which fire mixed with polar ice. "Do you think she was scared of *us?* What could we do to her? Nothing. We're not threatening to put Thornton in jail or take him away or sue her or anything."

Rachel stared back, partly out of stubborn defiance. She knew what he was thinking, and she didn't want to think the same thing. She could not allow herself to think it. It was madness.

He glanced at the road, then his gaze riveted on her again. "All right," he said with an impatient shrug. "She knew I might yell. That shouldn't *terrify* her. If she was that frightened and knew we were coming, she could have left. She could have avoided us. She could have not opened the door at all."

"Look at the road," Rachel ordered, not wanting to listen. "You're going to get us killed."

He looked at the road. He fairly glowered at the road.

"No," he said, almost growling his words. "She wanted to face us. Whatever she's scared of, it wasn't us."

"Then what's she scared of?" Rachel demanded. She didn't want to ask the question or hear the answer, but she had to ask, had to hear. A strange, claustrophobic feeling of fate closed over her.

Jay paused. He put on his sunglasses again. He didn't look at her. The line of his jaw was grim.

He said, "Maybe you really do have a body buried in your basement."

CONFESSION

In school once, this teacher forced everybody to find a poem about "parent and child" in the library and memorize it. This is what I chose:

Lizzy Borden took an ax
And gave her mother forty whacks.
When she saw what she had done,
She gave her father forty-one.

The teacher made me stay after school. Years later, she woke up one morning to find her front porch drenched in pig's blood, gallons of it.

Did I do it? Maybe. Maybe not. Maybe I'm lying about the whole thing. I'm no fan of the truth. It's different things to different people.

See, for Malone, the one big truth was death. I under- stand these things. Death had hit so near him he couldn't see things the way other people did. That's why he acted the way he did. That's how he set things in motion. Maybe I wanted it that way.

They say at first the Dale woman thought Malone was crazy. She always tried to be so reasonable. That was her mistake. Neither of them knew that they were entering a realm where reason didn't matter. Lives were at stake. Mine. Theirs. Even the children's.

Such fine children. So loved. *Not like some I could name.*

Chapter Five

"What's the matter?" Jay asked, frowning. "You must have thought about it. You look sick."

"I'm fine," she said, her voice weaker than it should be. "It's just...I *know* there's no body. But...if somebody wanted to bury one, my basement would be a fine place. Ugh."

"Why? Why would it?"

She kept staring straight ahead, her hair blowing out behind her. "It's got a dirt floor. The dirt isn't even smoothed out. It *looks* like a grave."

His frown deepened. He knew the kind of place she described. Built on a steep. He and Cindy had looked at such a vacation house near Big Sur. Cindy had said it looked like a grave, too.

He'd laughed, although he'd seen her point. This time, with Rachel, he didn't laugh.

"I can't believe it," she said, shaking her head. "I won't. Something else is bothering Mrs. Fuller. They don't have money—maybe she's afraid she won't be able to keep him. Especially if he makes trouble. That must be it."

He'd put his sunglasses back on, and she couldn't see his eyes, but the set of his jaw was grim, stubborn.

"You don't agree," she accused. "I can tell. You think something's going on. You have *feelings*. Well, it's just a story. Mercer said Thornton even told them he had gold charms to protect him. And some nonsense that the body had green hair. It's nothing but an ugly fairy tale.''

He shrugged. He sensed trouble, and he'd learned the hard way to trust his instincts. He would do so now. "Gold charms?'' he said sardonically. "Green hair?''

"Besides, you live in Stokes's house. You think *he* was mixed up in something? The glorious native son?''

"He's dead. For over a year. Who knows who lived there last year—when the killing was supposed to have happened?''

"I won't even think about it,'' she said with finality. She rode beside him in silence until they reached the outskirts of Sangria.

They saw the first of the Stokes Day banners fluttering over Main Street. Red, white and blue streamers billowed in the wind. Every store window held a poster announcing, "The First Annual Stokes Day Celebration!''

Jay drove past it all, hardly seeing it. Rachel stirred almost imperceptibly beside him. He glanced at her and saw that her serious eyes were on him, studying. He looked away, not wanting to be studied.

"Your son,'' she said. "You don't want him to believe this nonsense. You won't tell him it's true, will you?''

She'd hit his weakest spot. For a few moments, he'd been so caught up by his intuition he'd almost forgotten Kip's problems. But, of course, Rachel was right.

He turned to her, glad for the sunglasses, glad for his years of acting tough, talking tough. Yeah, he wanted to say, his lip curled into a sneer. I want to say it's true. I *want* to scare him into hysterics.

He was suddenly too weary for sarcasm, too tired for dark suspicions. He wanted the world to be a place of safety and sunshine, where his son was happy and confident, a world where friendliness was again possible.

He was surprised to find himself saying, "Maybe you're right. Nothing happened. We've an hour before the kids come back. You want lunch or something?''

The invitation was not gracious, not polished, but she was surprised he'd issued it at all. She was equally surprised when she accepted.

"McDonald's okay?" he asked, unsmiling.

"McDonald's is fine," she answered. It was safe. What was more innocent, more mundane, than sitting in a fast-food franchise in broad daylight?

The Sangria McDonald's was perfectly ordinary, its only unusual feature the Stokes Day banner that fluttered between the Golden Arches. Jay and Rachel made small talk, mostly about the children. When the small talk ran out, they sat in awkward silence over their second cup of coffee.

"Look," he said abruptly, "I owe you an apology. Yesterday you tried to talk to me. I walked off. I shouldn't have. It's...an unusual time."

She looked at him with curiosity. He still wore the sunglasses, and he kept his handsome, slightly asymmetrical face expressionless.

"My wife was killed," he said. The unexpected statement shook her. "A year ago yesterday. Shot in a mall. By a kid that got off because of 'diminished capacity.' She's dead. But he's not considered 'fully responsible.'"

"Oh," Rachel said and stared into her coffee. Suddenly she understood. The darkness of Jay's moods no longer seemed like rudeness or affectation. The strain between him and the boy took on a poignancy it hadn't had before.

She realized, as well, that, fair or not, this was why Jay disliked Thornton. Every time he saw him, he must be reminded of the other boy, his wife's killer. Such a comparison might not be just, but emotions in turmoil were seldom just; they were too raw and powerful.

She bit her lip, ashamed of how she had judged him before knowing the facts. He no longer seemed a savage man, but a suffering one, trying his best to be strong for himself and his son.

"So don't mind me, okay?" he muttered, as if impatient with himself and the whole situation. "Like I said, I've been…volatile. A person like yourself, in your…profession, can understand, right?''

Rachel glanced across the table at him. The dark glasses stayed in place like a mask, and the controlled expression on his face told her little. She smiled a small, unhappy smile. "You don't like my profession, do you?"

Unexpectedly he took off his sunglasses. As always, the blueness of his eyes startled her. Only the most elemental things in nature were that blue: sky, flame, ice.

Although she had avoided staring at him, he stared at her, the slant of his mouth troubled. "I don't like—" he paused "—most of the ones I met last year. Especially in court, when I wanted justice for what had happened."

"Forensic psychologists?" she asked, holding his gaze now, determined not to let hers waver. "Ones who specialize in evaluating sanity? In court testimony?"

"Yeah," he said bitterly, the muscle jerking in his cheek. "See, there was disagreement about the competence of this person. They got him off. Five years in some high-security hospital. He'll never serve all five. He'll be walking around free any day. But my wife's dead. She's going to be dead forever."

The steady, almost hypnotic blueness of his eyes disoriented her, as if they could throw all her inner compasses off course. It gave her an uneasy hollow feeling.

"That's what I'm studying to be." She wished she didn't feel so vulnerable as she said it. "A forensic psychologist."

The corner of his mouth curled downward. He frowned. It was odd, she thought with a start. She was getting used to his frown, the way she might get used to another man's smile.

"I don't get it," he said, shifting his wide shoulders. "It's an old line, but what's a nice girl like you doing in a job like that? Why?"

She shrugged in self-deprecation. He had been surprisingly open with her. She supposed she might as well tell him about Henry, his stellar reputation, and how he had chosen her, trained her to follow in his footsteps.

But before she could speak, the door opened, and Mercer rushed in, Kip faithfully following. All trace of orderly adult conversation vanished as the saga of Sean Alan and the puppy was recounted.

Rachel gathered up the whirlwind that was Mercer and prepared to leave. But first she wanted to speak to Kip again. She knelt beside him and ran her hand over his fair hair, smoothing it. "You're not going to worry anymore, are you? Your daddy's been to see Mrs. Crabtree and Thornton's mother, and everything's fine again. He made sure everything's fine. You have nothing to worry about, and your daddy's here, taking good care of you."

She cupped his chin in her hand and rubbed her nose against his. He smiled shyly. "So you won't worry, right?"

"Right," Kip repeated in a small voice.

"That's my good boy," she said.

She stood and glanced at Jay, who watched her, his expression unreadable. "Goodbye, Mr. Malone," she said. She smiled down at the boy. "And Kip." She led Mercer out the door and into the afternoon sunshine.

Jay, too, rose and nodded gruffly to Kip that it was time they, too, left. He stood and looked out the window, watching as Rachel and her daughter drove away.

He looked at the empty space where their car had been.

He felt an unaccountable and unexpected emotion. It was loneliness. He looked down at Kip. Kip was staring at the empty space, yearning on his face.

When Rachel pulled into the gravel drive beside her condo, she forgot all her rational, sensible answers to the problems of the day. Instead, she remembered Ruby Fuller's inexplicable fear and Jay's words: *Maybe you really do have a body buried in your basement.*

Her heart seemed to shrink with foreboding. She stared at the woods behind the house—such an isolated place. Such a lonely house.

It really was a good location to bury a body, she thought. *Nonsense,* she told herself.

Ruby Fuller had been fearful and had overreacted, for reasons Rachel didn't understand. That proved nothing. Jay Malone was suspicious and had "feelings." That proved even less. Thornton had lied. That was the end of it.

But still, only yesterday the condo had looked peaceful, picturesque. Now it seemed different. Today the place looked somehow—although she hated the word—haunted.

She whistled with false bravado as she made her way up the stairs of Henry's half of the condo. Mercer had already darted off to the shore to retrieve her minnow bucket and begin her evening ritual.

"I scream, you scream," Mercer sang in her off-key voice. "We all scream for ice cream."

Rachel hesitated on the porch, almost unwilling to enter the house. But her telephone rang, and she pushed aside her eerie thoughts and unlocked the door.

When she answered the phone she was surprised to hear Henry's voice. He was calling from Madison, Wisconsin, where he had been invited by authorities. He had been too busy to phone her much of late.

"Great news," Henry said with enormous cheer. "He's killed again."

"What?" Rachel said, disoriented. *Murder,* she thought, *There's too much murder in my life. It's like I move through a fog of it. No wonder I started seeing it even here.*

"He's killed again," Henry repeated. "This time in Fond du Lac. Only three counties away from the last one. Only a week apart. He's getting desperate. He's getting careless. We're going to nab him before long."

Rachel's head had started to ache. She realized that Henry was talking about Mr. Fixit. Mr. Fixit was a serial killer who seemed to be working his way up from north Texas toward the Great Lakes.

His nickname, Mr. Fixit, was grim tribute to his preferred tools in the murdering trade.

Henry had been gleefully following Mr. Fixit's progress for four years. That was why, when it seemed Mr. Fixit had reached Wisconsin, authorities called in Henry to help predict what the murderer might do next.

"He's cracking," Henry said with relish. "Just like
Bundy at the end. Do you know what this means?"

Rachel's head throbbed worse. "It means women can
stop dying."

"Of course," Henry said, "but if they grab him before
the end of the summer—and they will—then you can have
him for your dissertation. A nice little present, eh? It's too
late for him to be included in your main text, but he can
make a hell of a footnote."

A nice little present, Rachel thought, closing her eyes and
rubbing her forehead. Mr. Fixit had killed at least eleven
women. He would make a hell of a footnote.

"Henry," she said, wanting comfort, "sometimes I get
tired of this. I'm developing a very gallows-type sense of
humor. And suspicions. I'm so suspicious lately."

"Dear, we all get tired of it," he said. "You've just got
the dissertation blahs. How's it coming?"

"Lousy," she said with total honesty. She no longer
wanted to look at her dissertation. She hated it.

"Good," he said heartily. "That's how you're supposed
to feel at this point. Very typical."

"I don't want to be typical. I want to be exceptional. I
want to move forward with confidence. And possibly even
joy. Except it's hard to work up joy over serial killers."

"To know them is to love them," Henry said. "How
would I make my living without them?"

She frowned. In her mind's eye, she could see Henry's
seamed, confident face, his silver hair, and knew he was
joking as usual, teasing. But she was not amused.

"How's Mercer?" he asked companionably. "How's the
place? Is it still working out for you?"

"Mercer's play group is about to elect her Most Likely to
Become a Terrorist. And I want to talk about this place."

"Oh, Mercer's fine, don't worry about her," he scoffed.
Then his tone grew more serious. "What about the condo?
Is something wrong? It's not termites, is it?"

She paused. She opened her eyes and stared out at the lake where Mercer was already half-covered with mud, happily catching minnows.

"No, it's not termites," she said, unaccountably irritated. "Thornton—you know him—"

"Yes, yes, of course, I know Thornton. Known him since he was a boy. Back when I just had the fishing cabin. He's harmless. Good boy. Good fellow."

Rachel squeezed her eyes shut to block the growing pain in her head. "Well, the good fellow told Mercer that there's a body buried in this house. That somebody was killed in another child's house last year and buried in this one."

There were several seconds of silence. The line hummed. "Poppycock," Henry said at last.

"Henry," Rachel persisted, "you only bought this condo last fall, didn't you? Do you really know much about it? I mean, it does have that dirt floor in the basement—"

"Tut, tut," Henry said in his most professorial tone. "Would I buy a house of sinister repute? Yes, actually, I would. But I've never been offered one, alas. It's just a boring condominium."

"Who owned your half before?"

"An absentee landlord. He rented it out until he got bored with it. Then I bought it. My birthday present to me. I was tired of giving myself neckties."

"Who rented it before you bought it?"

"I haven't the foggiest. I'm sure they were boring."

"What about the other side?" she persisted. "Was that rented, too? It's empty now."

"A boring old lady owned it. She was always in the hospital with some boring illness. Finally she got so bored she died. Last winter I think. That, of course, rendered her boring forever. Then a real-estate speculator bought it. From Des Moines, I think. Boring fellow."

She wished he would stop being facetious. "Mercer was upset. It was hardly boring."

As usual, Henry derided her worries. "It doesn't hurt a child to be frightened once in a while. It has therapeutic aspects. Anxiety is a survival tool."

Oh, Henry, she thought wretchedly, *please don't lecture me now.*

"You've got dissertation fever," Henry soothed. "You're inventing distractions for yourself. It's normal. There's nothing to worry about."

That was Henry, she thought tiredly. He always had all the answers. Everything about herself and Mercer was always "normal." There was never anything to worry about.

She thought suddenly of Jay Malone, who had no answers, but was full of questions and anger. He knew what suffering was; he was a man with a slow fire inside, consuming him. To Henry, suffering was merely a clinical problem.

Why, she wondered, was she comparing the two men? Why should she think at all of Jay Malone, with his dark-browed frown and blue eyes, his angry mouth and his sad child?

Henry would undoubtedly have a pat answer to that, too. She opened her eyes, weary of thinking. Outside, Mercer waded in the lake as the sun settled nearer the horizon.

Henry droned on about how it was time she overcame her own fear of water, a sermon that no longer registered because she had heard it so often. Her thoughts drifted. Suddenly she grew alert again. Something had moved at the edge of the woods.

She blinked and looked again. A shadow had moved strangely, and now a dim form materialized.

She narrowed her eyes, took a step closer to the window.

Thornton, she saw with shock. Thornton was hiding among the trees at the edge of the woods. He was standing there among the shadows, spying on Mercer.

What is this? her mind screamed. What was he doing now? Why was he lurking in the woods, watching Mercer?

"Henry, I've got to go. Mercer needs me." She hung up so fast the receiver crashed against the cradle.

She threw open the doors of the deck, ran out and grasped its railing. "Mercer!" she cried. "Mercer, get up here right now—this instant! Do you hear me? *Now.*"

Something in her voice caught Mercer's usually elusive attention, and for once she obeyed without hesitation. Rachel ran down the stairs.

"Go into the house and lock the doors," Rachel ordered. Again at the edge of the woods, she saw movement. She hesitated, then sprinted toward it.

She was certain it was Thornton. She intended to confront him and demand he stop acting this way. She would threaten to see Ruby Fuller again, no matter how painful such a visit might be.

She raced toward where she had seen his form, shadowy among the leaves. "Thornton? Stop. Don't you dare run—I mean business."

But when she reached the spot where she had seen him, no one was there. A branch stirred, as if someone had passed there only a moment ago. But the place was empty and, except for the fragile twitter of the sparrows, silent.

She stood staring into the woods, heart beating hard.

THORNTON FLED to where his bicycle was hidden. From childhood he had played in these woods, and he could slip through them effortlessly.

By the time he reached his bicycle, he was panting, his breath coming in raw, painful gulps. He snatched up the bicycle, wheeled it to the dirt road, then mounted it.

Dark woods towered on each side of the road, but the sky was still light. Thornton looked at the lengthening shadows with despair.

His mother was mad at him, and she had scared him so badly he had run away. He was afraid to go home.

He had done the bad thing, said the bad thing.

That long-ago unreal night with the dead person had become real again. It had become so real that sometimes Thornton just hid and cried. He couldn't help it.

He had told. Now the dead person would come back for him, try to make him dead, too.

He pumped hard to make it up the steep hill. Sweat dampened his hair and dripped, burning, into his eyes, making him cry again. He clamped his mouth shut and cried silently, his body shaking. He pumped the pedals harder.

He had magic. He kept telling himself that it would protect him from the dead person. He believed that.

But he was still afraid. The dead person might chase him forever. The dead person might always be waiting for him to lose his magic. Then the dead person would catch him and take him to hell. Hell would hurt all the time. Forever.

Thornton knew he must take good care of his magic, or he would die. But that was not the scariest thing.

What scared him most was that he had made the badness spread. If you told about the dead person, you would die—unless you had magic.

Now Mercer had told, too. And Kip must have told. So now the dead person would kill Mercer and Kip. If Evan told, the dead person would come back and kill him, too.

Three children dead. Because of him.

He had to save them. He didn't know how. He was trying to watch them, to keep them safe, but they were so far apart—how could he do it? And Evan had gone. Thornton knew where Evan's summer house was, but he didn't know where his real house was, or even what city it was in.

If Thornton watched Mercer, he couldn't watch Kip. If he watched Kip, he couldn't watch Mercer. He didn't know where to find Evan at all. It all made Thornton crazy.

Worse, the bad kept spreading. It was becoming an ocean of badness. Mercer's mother and Kip's father had talked about the dead person. Now they, too, would die.

HENRY CALLED Rachel back. "What's wrong?" he asked. "I wasn't through talking."

She explained as calmly as she could, because she didn't want to alarm Mercer, who was sitting within hearing distance.

Henry said Thornton was probably going through a difficult time and not to be judgmental. The boy's father had died two years ago this summer. Rachel was trained; she should know that the anniversaries of deaths were difficult for people. His words made her remember Jay Malone, the grim set of his jaw, the angry blue of his eyes.

Henry told her to wait until morning to call Ruby Fuller, that Rachel wasn't herself tonight and shouldn't talk to the other woman until she was more rational.

Rational, she thought in frustration. She was beginning to think that reason had nothing to do with this.

"I wish I could come down and be with you," Henry said, but the statement sounded perfunctory.

"I know," she said. She supposed she wished he was there. She was suddenly hungry for adult companionship, someone to lean on, even briefly.

"But I can't," he stated briskly. "I've got Mr. Fixit on my hands. They need me here."

"I know," she repeated.

"Later," he murmured. "After this summer. After your dissertation's done. Then we can be together."

"I know." *God, I sound like a parrot,* she thought with inexplicable irritation. *I may marry this man. Why can't I talk to him?*

"We'll talk specifics later," he went on. "When I'm not your dissertation adviser anymore. I wouldn't want anybody to accuse me of not being objective about your work. For my sake, as well as yours."

"I know." *Damn,* she thought. She sounded as if she knew only two words. And Henry explained what he had explained a dozen times before. He was of the old school; he made a practice of never being emotionally involved with his students. It was a good policy, even though he had broken it in her case. Still, they must observe the formalities.

Sometimes Henry's formalities struck Rachel as a complicated form of hypocrisy. After all, everyone at the university knew they were involved. It seemed foolish to pretend they weren't.

"By the way," Henry said, "I did hear of something possibly criminal down there last summer. Heard it from one of the FBI men here. But not murder. Not even close."

Rachel's attention quickened. "Criminal? What?"

"Well," Henry said with a laugh, "remember, it has nothing to do with bodies in my humble basement. This is far more a genteel crime—art theft."

Rachel paused, savoring the information. "Art theft?"

"Or smuggling," said Henry. "I can't remember the details. Anyway it's not important. Art thieves are effete. I'd rather have a nice juicy killer on my hands any day. Wouldn't you? By the way, have you met my mortician friend yet? Nessa Berryman?"

"No," Rachel answered absently. She stared out toward the lake, stretching silvery in the darkness. She didn't want to meet Vanessa Berryman because she couldn't bear to think about death any more than she had already.

"Ah," said Henry, "what that woman taught me about decomposition."

RACHEL WAITED until Mercer was engrossed in her video game, then dialed Katherine Menander's number. Nobody answered. She sighed and dialed Powell Crabtree's home number. She had to find some way to get in touch with the Rineharts. "Well, pretty Mrs. Dale," Powell said in his ever-cheerful voice. "To what do I owe this pleasure?"

Rachel squared her shoulders. Henry had warned her from the first that Powell was a womanizer, and Rachel had always been careful to keep her distance.

"I was hoping you had some information," Rachel said. "Something's come up. I need to get in touch with the Rineharts. I hope you might know how to reach them."

"They're not here," Powell said. "They had to leave town. Her father's ill. What's the problem? If it's a little one, I'm sure it can wait."

Rachel drew in her breath. The situation did, after all, involve Powell's cousin and his mother, and he wasn't on the best of terms with his mother. She paused, wondering how much she should say.

"Mrs. Dale?" Powell said. "What's the matter?" A beat of silence pulsed between them on the phone line. "Is it serious? Do you need me to come over?"

Oh, Lord, no, Rachel thought. She didn't want the conceited Powell Crabtree to think her call was some sort of invitation. She must make her purpose clear.

"No," she said hastily. "It's nothing for you to concern yourself about. It's just that . . . someone told my child, the little Malone boy and Evan a scary story about someone being killed in the Malones' house. He also said they couldn't tell or they'd die, and of course it upset them. I thought the Rineharts should know. Evan may be particularly upset by a story about death—with his grandfather ill. I thought I should contact them."

For once Powell Crabtree didn't sound cheerful. He sounded resentful, annoyed. "A body? In the Malones' house? Somebody told these kids a story about a body? Now that *is* upsetting, Mrs. Dale. Maybe I should come over. Set things straight for you. Now who would tell innocent children a story about a body? I don't blame you for being disturbed. I'll be right over. Who said this? That's a libel. That's a slander on a property I handle—"

"No," Rachel said emphatically. "I'm not disturbed. I don't want anybody coming over. If you have to know, it was Thornton—and I've already spoken to his mother about it, so the mistake won't be repeated—"

"Thornton?" Powell's voice vibrated with scorn. "Surely you don't put any stock in what that . . . that lummox says . . . ?"

"I don't consider him a lummox, but, no, I don't put any stock in it. It's a very silly story he made up with . . . with green hair and gold charms mixed up in it, and nobody but the children would ever believe it. I just want to know how I can reach the Rineharts—and that's *all* I want."

"Gold charms?" Powell demanded, sounding more incensed than before. "Now what sort of *contumely* is that?"

Finally, reluctantly, Powell Crabtree gave her a number in St. Louis at which he said the Rineharts could be reached. Rachel thanked him and hung up. She didn't wonder that Powell and Minnie had clashed; he was pleasure loving, pushy and suggestive, his mother so straitlaced as to be almost puritanical.

She sighed and dialed the number Powell had given her. It rang nine times before someone picked up the receiver. A man.

"I'm trying to reach Judy Rinehart," Rachel said. "I'm calling from Sangria. It's about Evan."

There was a pause long enough to be awkward. "She isn't here," he said at last. He had a raspy voice, hard and low-pitched.

"Well, is Mr. Rinehart there? I think his name is Cleve."

Another pause, longer than the first. "This is Cleve Rinehart," he said at last. She could tell by his voice that he begrudged her the information. "What do you want?"

Rachel took a deep breath, then launched into her story again. Unlike Powell, Cleve Rinehart never interrupted her or asked for more information. When Rachel paused in her narrative, only silence greeted her. She felt as if she was imposing on him by telling the story.

"So you can see," she finished gamely, "that I was concerned about Evan. I wanted you to know what happened—in case he'd been frightened."

Cleve Rinehart might have said a lot of things, but the reply he chose both surprised and angered Rachel. "How did you get this number?" he demanded.

"Powell Crabtree," she said, puzzled. "But I mean, is Evan all right? He hasn't been acting scared or having nightmares?"

"He's fine. Thanks for your concern. I'll take care of the situation. Please don't call again. My wife is upset enough. She doesn't need any more problems."

"I can understand that," Rachel said. "Perhaps when you get back to Sangria, she'll feel more like—"

"No. Please never attempt to mention this to her again. My wife has a complex about death. Never mention it. I've already said thank-you. Goodbye." He hung up.

Rachel stared at the receiver in dismay. Cleve Rinehart had been curt to the point of rudeness. Was it simply the stress the family was under? Or was it something more? Why had he reacted so oddly?

Troubled, she scarcely heard Mercer, who was playing Nintendo and cheerfully singing to herself:

Did you ever think
When the hearse goes by
That you might be
The next to die?

Chapter Six

The moonlight glittered on the water. Kip, worn out, had fallen asleep early. Jay sat alone on the deck, nursing a glass of tonic water.

He wondered how the woman and the little girl were doing. He knew where they lived, toward the south end of the lake. It was an isolated spot. Some crazy developer had been going to crowd that section of the shore with condos, but he'd finished only the demonstration model before he'd run out of money. An unpaved road led to the property, but there were no neighbors nearby.

The other side of her condo was empty, he knew. Powell Crabtree had shown it to him when he'd come to Sangria to house hunt, but it hadn't appealed to him. An older woman had died there last winter, Powell said. When Jay looked, her son had yet to clear out her things.

The cluttered rooms had given him bad vibrations. They seemed to announce, *Death's been here.* Jay couldn't take it. He'd had too much death lately. He'd rented this more expensive house farther north. It, too, was isolated.

Now, in spite of all the extra money he'd paid, he was getting strange vibrations about *this* house. It filled him with uneasiness, as if from time to time an army of ghostly ants swarmed over him.

Rachel hadn't approved of his intuition, hadn't believed in it. She'd looked down her pretty nose at him as if he'd been a savage. It just showed one more thing she didn't know, her in her tight, scientific little world. Science made mistakes all the time. His ghostly ants, hardly ever.

He wasn't superstitious, but he had strong instincts and trusted them. When he didn't, inevitably he found trouble.

On the day Cindy died, he'd had the strange urge to go straight home. If he had, he'd have taken her shopping, not to that cheesy little mall, but to a better one, farther from home. But Cindy didn't like driving in L.A., so she always shopped as close to the house as possible.

At the time, he'd laughed at his impulse, thinking he was going soft. The intuition had struck him as stupid, sentimental. Now he would have given his life's blood to have obeyed it.

There'd been a contract negotiation, a good one, and afterward three of his teammates wanted to celebrate. He was a macho guy. He couldn't say, "I've got a funny feeling I should get home." He'd gone with them.

He'd gone, and so Cindy had died. He figured that in remorse and grief, he had died, too, in a different way and too damned many times to count. At best he just felt numb.

But not today.

He swore and took a long pull of the tonic water. Today he hadn't been numb. He'd had feelings, floods of them running in contradictory directions. He'd been a storming maelstrom of feelings.

He remembered Rachel Dale beside him in the car and how he'd found himself stealing glances at her perfect profile, her straight nose, her firm chin and graceful throat.

He'd noticed, as well, that her profile was lovely all the way down. Alone in the darkness, he remembered too well.

The breeze had stirred her T-shirt against the sweet, pointed thrust of her breasts; her waist was slender, her stomach flat, her legs long and slender in her faded jeans. He even liked the way her bare ankles looked above her tennis shoes. They were chiseled, slim and elegant.

He finished his drink, flexing his shoulders uneasily. The business with Thornton and the children kept troubling him.

Maybe, he thought darkly, his instincts had finally slipped and run amok, and he was going truly crazy at last.

But the woman troubled him, too, bringing out a different set of instincts, the kind he didn't want, the kind he wasn't ready for.

Her unpretentious beauty bothered him. So did the cool, graceful motions of her tall body. So did her kindness, which seemed deep, genuine and admirable.

She had a warm and easy rapport with her own child; she dealt more surely and gently with Kip than he himself would ever be able to do. He envied her that. He envied her, and it awoke an odd hunger in him.

He'd watched her carefully the whole time, with an almost predatory intensity, and had felt a foreign emotion churn his heart, the strange hunger in him quicken.

She appealed to him. The longer he was with her, the more strongly he felt the stir of desire. He had come to believe that desire, like most other things within him, was dead. To learn it was not unsettled him.

Her appeal both confounded and angered him. She was too cool, too controlled for his tastes, too *reasonable.* Being reasonable was her profession, and he found her profession noxious, rank.

And for her to be a psychologist who specialized in murderers embittered him like gall and wormwood. How could she dedicate her life to the sickness of killers? Nobody ever cared about victims. No, to hell with victims. It was always the killers that fascinated people.

He couldn't deal with it. He didn't even want to try.

No, he couldn't think of any sort of woman he wanted less than a goddamn forensic psychologist. She'd been kind to other people all day, even his son, especially his son, and that was what was maddening.

With Jay himself, she was different. She looked at him as if she saw the wildness deep inside him. Saw it and disapproved, saw it and was both superior to it and fearful of it. He didn't need that. He didn't need her.

Jay rose from his chair on the deck and found himself staring down the shoreline toward Rachel's house. He was about to go inside, but paused, looking at the dark water.

The woman and the child were isolated over there. Alone. The bad vibrations went rippling through him again, along with the hunger he didn't want to feel.

"Oh, hell," he said miserably.

He wanted to feel nothing, nothing at all. He just wanted to get on with life, a nice, numb, dumb, meaningless life and raise his kid. Kip. His kid. How would he ever raise his kid?

He said it again, with more vehemence. *"Hell."*

Then suddenly, his intuition quickened ominously.

Someone was out there in the darkness. He knew with certainty.

Silently he stepped to the railing. The evening wind tossed his hair, fluttered his shirt, stirred the leaves. The crickets chirruped peacefully, as if nothing could be wrong. His skin prickled.

He listened and strained his eyes against the darkness, for the sky was swathed in clouds and no moon shone. He heard nothing. He saw nothing.

His certainty ebbed. But still he stood, listening and watching. His shoulders were taut, his fists clenched atop the rail, ready. He held his breath.

Still he heard nothing, saw nothing.

He released his breath in a harsh sigh. He must have been mistaken.

Maybe the woman was right to look askance at him when he said he had "feelings." He supposed it was possible Cindy's death had made him a little crazy. Hell, he supposed it was *probable* he was crazy. Hurrah for the lady psychologist.

He turned and went inside, locking the deck doors behind him. In his bedroom, he stripped off his clothing and climbed into bed, naked, restless. He switched off the light and lay staring up through the darkness.

He thought of Rachel Dale, which made him feel guilty and somehow deprived and angry. He thought of Cindy, instead, and that grieved him. He tried to think of nothing at all.

OUTSIDE, HIDING AMONG the swaying branches of the willow tree, Thornton began to breathe again, his heart hammering.

The man, he was sure, had *known* he was there. This man could somehow see things other people couldn't. It was one more thing to terrify Thornton, until he felt completely sick with fear.

Thornton had sat beneath the willow for hours, ever since it had gotten dark enough to steal there. He hadn't moved, he hadn't made a sound, even when bugs bit him or climbed in his shirt, or when his legs fell asleep.

He sat watching Kip's house, *guarding* it. Earlier in the evening, on the way to Kip's, he'd stopped in the woods. He had sat on a big fallen branch, put his head in his hands and wept. He'd felt empty, helpless, stupid.

Then he forced himself to be braver. He had to. He had to do whatever he could to protect Kip. So he'd made his way silently here. And he watched and guarded. He kept watch over them both, the father and the little boy. But at the same time, he had been frantic for Mercer's safety, and her mother's, and Evan's, too.

Now, with all the lights in Kip's house out, darkness was everywhere. Thornton felt as if he had fallen into a well of blackness and was sinking all alone.

He hadn't been home in hours, and his mother would be angry and frightened. She would be so scared that she would cry, which Thornton always hated.

He had to go home sometime, he thought tiredly. He had to eat. He had to sleep. He couldn't sleep on the ground, where the bugs would bite him all night long. He couldn't keep watch forever.

And, he thought, his skull throbbing with weariness, he still had to figure out where Evan was. He had to find a way to help him, to guard him. He'd done nothing to keep the dead person from getting Evan. Nothing at all.

Thornton pulled his numbed legs up and hugged them hopelessly. He buried his forehead against them, trying to think, but he was afraid he was only going to cry again.

He had to think in a smart way. If he didn't, so many people would die. But he wasn't smart. He hugged his knees harder.

Mercer was smart, he thought, his head throbbing. She always had ideas. What would Mercer do? What?

Suddenly, even though his eyes were squeezed shut, he saw Mercer standing before him, her hands on her hips. She wore her blue shorts and her shirt with Daisy Duck on it.

"Share the magic, Thornton," she said, shaking her head in impatience. "Share it."

He raised his head, blinking in surprise. The moon slid from behind a cloud, silvering Kip's yard. Thornton had seen and heard Mercer so clearly that he was astounded to find she wasn't really there.

What a smart idea, he thought, awed. He had more than one piece of magic. He had five. He could give one to each child. Then all three would be safe.

He would keep two pieces for himself and his mother. The other big people, he decided, would have to take care of themselves. Or maybe the children's magic would guard them, too. Yes, Thornton told himself. Of course it would. Then everything would be fine again.

But then another idea loomed and struck him, and his happiness sank. *How* could he give the magic to the children?

He couldn't just walk up and hand it to them. There was something secret about the magic, he understood that. Big people shouldn't see it. They mustn't know about it at all. It would cause trouble, all kinds of trouble.

And he *couldn't* tell Mercer. She was too brave. Kip might keep a secret. Evan might. But never Mercer. No matter what he said, it wouldn't scare her enough to keep quiet.

Thornton banged his head against his knees in frustration. What could he do? He could *hide* magic at Mercer's house. But at the end of the summer, she would move away and leave it. Then she'd have no magic, and she wouldn't be safe any longer. The dead person would kill her.

No, no, no, he thought, banging his head rhythmically, not caring that his forehead ached and his teeth jarred. The children had to have the magic, keep it close. But they shouldn't know it was there. Then they couldn't tell on him. But how? How?

He shut his eyes and bit his thumb. The problem was too great for him. How could he get the magic to the children, but still keep it secret? How could he make them *keep* the magic?

He was ready to cry again, but all his tears felt gone. His eyes burned with dryness. This was what hell was like, he thought desperately; hell must be feeling this helpless, this hopeless, this guilty. His eyes burned harder.

He wished the dead person would come and get him right now, if only the children could stay safe. Because there was no secret way he could give them the magic so they would keep it. There was none. None.

Once more he tried to sob and couldn't, so he hit his head against his knees again in a fury of hopelessness.

Pain crashed through his forehead, but as if by a miracle, Mercer appeared to him again. This time her arms were crossed over her Daisy Duck shirt. "Thornton," she said in disgust, "think. Children always keep their toys, you dweeb. Their *toys.*"

She vanished as swiftly as she'd appeared.

Thornton sat up straight, then went still with wonder. His mouth fell open. The tears he'd thought were gone welled in his eyes. This time they were tears of gratitude.

His mouth trembled and he almost smiled. Toys. Children always kept their toys close. Thornton had toys at home. He had many toys, a whole *shelf* full. Some toys were made so that you could put things inside them. Nobody would even know you had done it.

He would leave a toy for each child.

He might even think of a way to get a toy to Evan. He might. Mercer was helping him lately. She was helping him to be smart.

He stood, his legs weak from lack of circulation. For the first time in almost two days, he felt hope lifting him up. Perhaps everything would be all right, after all.

RACHEL SLEPT LATE Sunday morning, trapped in tangled dreams. She was awakened by impatient knocking at the door. Her eyes fluttered open, but her heart froze. Who would come calling on a Sunday morning? She prayed it wasn't Powell Crabtree.

She wore a flimsy nightgown of pale yellow and, rising, she struggled into the robe that matched her gown. Though the knocking grew more insistent, she paused long enough to give her teeth a quick brushing and smooth her tumbled hair. She hunted in vain for her slippers.

"Damn," she muttered and headed, barefoot, for the door.

She didn't welcome people who came calling before she had her morning coffee. She would not be glad to see anyone this morning, nobody, not even Henry.

She swung the door open. She was astonished to see Jay Malone standing on her front porch. His black hair gleamed almost blue in the morning sunlight; his short-sleeved shirt was so white against the hard coppery flesh of his arms that it dazzled. He wore, amazingly, a tie, gray and blue.

At his side stood Kip, his blond hair slicked down, his little shirt as white as his father's. He, too, wore a tie. Behind them, the black Corvette glittered in the drive.

For reasons Rachel couldn't begin to explain, she was happy to see them. Happy, but embarrassed that Jay should see her so. She pulled the thin robe more tightly about her, pushed her hand self-consciously through her rumpled hair.

Jay Malone's eyes looked as hot and blue as the sky behind him. They examined her with such thoroughness that she felt herself color. She dropped her gaze to Kip and said with counterfeit heartiness, "Why, Kip! Good morning. How are you?"

"Fine," Kip said shyly. He stared down and wiggled the toes of his shiny black shoes.

"Good." She crossed her arms over her breasts and nodded with animation. "Good." She did not want to meet Jay's fire-and-ice gaze.

She was saved by Mercer, who came out of the bedroom whooping in delight at seeing Kip. Her pajama top was buttoned crookedly, and her hair was wild.

"Kipper!" Mercer cried. "Come see where the minnows live. Yesterday I caught a crawdad. He pinches!"

Mercer had on mismatched thongs, and she went flippity-floppity down the stairs, dragging the enthralled Kip behind her. Rachel was left alone with Jay, her heart a swift, irregular drumbeat that sent her mixed messages.

She forced her eyes to meet his. "I'm sorry," she said. "We overslept."

She felt like a slattern next to Jay's shining neatness. She wished fervently that she could have walked to the door and opened it decorously, fully dressed, and greeted Jay like a lady.

"Did you have a hard night?" Jay asked, unsmiling. He, too, stood with his arms crossed, a stance that looked both militant and tense.

"No," she said, staring down at her bare feet in embarrassment. Then she raised her eyes to his again. "Actually, yes," she admitted. "I did. Strange dreams. I can't remember. Probably about this house."

He nodded. "I thought we should check on you. I kept thinking about you—I mean, you're isolated. I didn't know if you'd worry. Or not. You seem the 'or not' kind."

The frown line appeared between his eyes, so familiar that Rachel found herself almost smiling. "I usually am the 'or not' kind. Come in. I'll make coffee. Do you guys need breakfast?"

She held the door open for him. He paused, looking her up and down. "Yeah. We could use breakfast, I guess."

She led him in, tightening the belt of her robe self-consciously. "Where have you been?" she asked as lightly as she could. "Church? You're both spiffed up."

"Yeah," he said. "Church." He stood by her kitchen table, his eyes moving up and down her body again.

Rachel felt more unsettled than before. "Funny. I didn't take you for the church type."

"I'm not," he said shortly. "His mother was. His grandmother, too. I take him for them."

He turned toward the glass doors that opened onto her deck. He nodded at Kip and Mercer on the shore. "I don't believe in much anymore," he said, his back to Rachel. It was a flat statement of fact, with no trace of self-pity.

She bit her lip as she measured the coffee. "No," she said. "I didn't think so."

"It helps him," he stated, no emotion in his voice. "To think she's in heaven. You know. You do what you can do."

"Yes," she agreed, biting her lip harder. "You do what you can."

"So," he said, turning to her, "you're okay, the two of you? No more nightmares for your kid?"

Rachel was grateful for a change of subject, but would have liked a more neutral one. "Mercer was fine. I was the one who tossed and turned."

"But everything's all right?"

She considered mentioning Thornton. She decided not to. Jay was, by his own admission, volatile. Thornton was in enough trouble without Jay launching a second attack.

She gave her most businesslike nod. "Just fine."

There was a moment of silence. He turned from her to stare out the glass doors again. "Good."

Rachel bustled about the kitchen, feeling more foolish every moment. "I hope eggs and bacon and toast are all right—we don't always look like this on Sunday, really. I'm usually up."

"Don't apologize." His voice was gruff. "You look fine. Both of you."

She was surprised that his remark pleased her. It felt odd to be in her robe, her hair still tousled, cooking breakfast for a man. She hadn't done it since the first years of her marriage to Damon. She'd never done it with Henry. It had an oddly warm, familiar feel to it, a Sunday morning sort of feel, a family feel.

She started cracking eggs. "And I hope you like scrambled," she said, her heart beating too fast. "I never mastered anything else."

She put the bacon on to fry. "Let me go jump into some clothes," she said.

His back was still to her. "Don't change. I told you. You look fine."

"No, no," she protested and slipped into her bedroom. She thought he turned and followed her with his eyes, but she wasn't sure. She dashed water on her face, changed into clean jeans, a pink-striped blouse and white sandals. She brushed her hair again and swiped a dash of lipstick across her lips.

"Stop being goosey," she murmured to her image in the mirror. "You act like a high school freshman who's just had the school hero sit down beside her. You're ridiculous."

She sobered immediately. She *was* ridiculous. Her heart had hammered and her hormones had done cartwheels once before in her life, when she was little more than a child. All it had gotten her was a bad marriage to a crazy poet.

That was long ago. She was mature and sensible now, her hormones were under control, and Henry was about to speak for her. Cool, knowing, wry, unthreatening Henry.

She returned to the kitchen to find Jay still staring out at the children and the lake, his back to her, his legs slightly apart, his arms crossed.

She checked the bacon and turned it.

"I didn't know you had a motorboat," he said. "It's big. I was going to invite you two over to take a ride on mine. You'd probably think you were slumming."

Rachel looked at him in surprise, uncertain how to take the remark. "It's not my boat," she said in confusion. "I don't own this place. Or the boat. I just start it up every few days. And that's about all I can handle. I don't like the water."

He turned and gave her the barest hint of a smile, one dark brow lowered. "A phobia? You?"

She only glanced at him and kept on working in her coolest way. "A phobia. Me. It can happen to anyone."

She opened the freezer and pulled out a can of orange juice. She started to open it, but he stepped to her side and took it from her. His hand brushed hers, and she felt as if she'd been brushed by lightning. There was a tightening in the pit of her stomach.

"I'll do this," he said. "You tend the other stuff. Breakfast is always a juggling act. So. Why are you afraid of water? Care to lie on the couch and tell me about it?"

He was taunting her again, although gently, about being a psychologist. She fiddled with the frying pan. "My father took us on a canoe trip when I was little. Everything was fine at first. The river was wide and peaceful and pretty."

She frowned at the recollection. "But he didn't really know the river. All of a sudden it narrowed. Everything got very fast. There were rapids. We tipped. I nearly drowned."

He finished mixing the juice, set it on the table and crossed his arms again, regarding her. "I see."

She had half expected him to make some gibe that she ought to see a good psychologist.

"So if I asked you and Mercer to go with us, you'd say no?" he asked, one brow drawn down.

Good Lord, she thought in consternation. *The man isn't asking me out, is he? What a pair we'd make.* She despised herself for the thrill of excitement that rippled through her.

"She'd love it. I'd hate it." Rachel stepped to the deck doors, pushed them open and called. "Mercer—come wash up. Bring Kip."

She turned and almost bumped into Jay. The kitchen was small. She took a step backward, her arm burning where she had accidentally touched him. He didn't draw back. He held his ground and watched her.

"Come over to my house after breakfast," he said.

"What?" She didn't know if he was issuing an order or an invitation. Confusion constricted her chest.

"Come to my place. I want you to look at it. The kids can play."

"Look at it? Why?"

"Because I've been looking at it. I woke up early this morning. I couldn't sleep. There's something funny over there. Something . . . odd."

Rachel stared at him for fully half a minute. She shook her head. "You're not still thinking about what Thornton said?" she asked, her expression wary. "That somebody was killed over there? You don't believe that, do you?"

His frown line deepened. "I told you. I don't believe much. But I get feelings. And now certain things over there seem odd."

The children rushed in. "Go wash," Rachel ordered automatically, still staring up at Jay. "Mercer, change your clothes." Mercer and Kip disappeared into the bathroom, and Rachel heard splashing and giggling.

"Why should I look at it?" she asked. "If you think something is strange, have your friend—Castor Bevins—look. He's a policeman."

"No," he said, his expression more somber than usual. "You. You're smarter. And women see things differently. I should know. I lived with one long enough."

She looked away, hurriedly stirred the eggs, dropped slices of bread into the toaster.

"Besides," he said, "the kids can play. It wouldn't hurt. They're both alone too much. It'll do them good."

Rachel still didn't answer. She scraped the eggs onto a platter and set them on the table. She looked up and directly into his almost supernaturally blue eyes.

His mouth took on the same half troubled, half angry curl she'd seen the day before. "Please," he said, although there was no pleading in his voice. "Please."

She realized, suddenly, that he wasn't asking her so much as challenging her, as if he didn't wish her to come, but rather dared her to.

Mercer came flying into the room, wearing blue shorts and her Daisy Duck T-shirt. Her face was clean, at least in the major spots. She threw her arms around Rachel's knees.

"Kip says we're going to his house. Are we?"

Rachel's gaze held Jay's. *Why are you asking me to do this?* she demanded silently. *Why?*

But he gave her no answer. He was waiting for hers.

"Yes," she said as casually as she could. "I suppose we can. For just a little while."

OUTSIDE, HIDING CAREFULLY in the shadows, Thornton watched. He had been dismayed to find Kip and Kip's father at Mercer's house.

He stood, shifting from foot to foot, his eyes burning with unshed tears. He had to hurry. He'd run away from his mother again, who was almost crazy with fear, so he was in even greater trouble than before.

His mother had forbidden him to leave. She said she was taking him away, but she wouldn't tell him when or where.

The news terrified Thornton. Time was running out, everything kept going wrong, and he hadn't saved anybody yet. He hadn't even come close.

He gnawed his lip until it hurt. He should have gone to Kip's house first. But how could he know everyone would be here? With so many people, he could do nothing here.

And he had things to do.

He had the toys, had them ready. They were in his Ninja Turtle backpack. The toys could save the children.

Each toy had magic hidden inside.

A magic bunny. A magic duck. And a magic clown.

But he had to get to the children before the dead person did. Soon. Fast.

Time was running out for all of them. He could feel it. He knew it by the hopeless way his mother cried.

He stood in the shadows, waiting. It seemed he waited forever, his throat choked with fear. At last they left, all of them. Kip and his father got into the black car. Mercer and her mother got into the green car.

Relief washed over Thornton. He waited until the sound of the cars died away. Taking a deep breath, he stole to the deck. He would leave the bunny on the deck, next to Mercer's beach ball and bucket. She would find it and keep it.

He stood on the deck nervously, praying his plan would work. It would be better if he could put the bunny inside with her other toys. It wouldn't be so noticeable then. But the doors to the house would be locked.

He pushed hesitantly at the sliding door that opened into the house. It moved. He was amazed and delighted.

Mercer's mother had forgotten to lock the door! What luck! He stepped inside, flooded with fresh relief.

It took only a moment to find Mercer's room. His heart hammered. She had a big box filled with stuffed animals, some new, some worn.

He was so thrilled by his luck that his hands shook as he opened the backpack. He took out the white bunny and carefully buried it deep in the box, beneath the other toys.

Then he stood, his heart galloping. One child was taken care of now. Mercer was safe. As safe as gold and magic could make her.

Next he would ride as fast as he could to Evan's house, for he had finally thought of a way to save Evan. Thornton had lain awake worrying and agonizing last night. Then it came to him, in a bright flash of truth.

He didn't *have* to find Evan. The mailman would. It didn't matter where you moved, the mailman could always find you. His mother had told him so when they moved to the trailer after his father died.

In his backpack now was the clown for Kip and the duck for Evan. He had wrapped the duck up in brown paper and taped it with brown tape. He had put all his mother's stamps on it, to make sure he had enough. He had written Evan's name on it with a magic marker. The package said, ''To EVIN at his NEW HOWS.''

Thornton would put it in the mailbox of the house where Evan had used to live. The mailman would open up the mailbox and find the package and take it to Evan.

Then two children would be safe.

And only Kip was left in danger.

Chapter Seven

Jay was right, Rachel thought, disturbed. There were strange things about his rented house.

It was a beautiful house, with glass doors facing the lake and a huge fireplace of native stone. The decor was lovely, marred only by the surface clutter of a man unused to living alone and picking up after himself.

She glanced at him. They stood together in the kitchen. Through the window, they could see the children playing in Kip's sandbox, building a castle.

"How old is this house?" she asked.

"Six years. That's what Powell said."

He undid the knot of his tie and left it hanging loose around his neck. He unbuttoned the top button of his shirt.

He had a strong column of a neck, and Rachel could glimpse the curling black hair of his chest, just visible in the vee of his opened collar. She looked away, embarrassed. He was a well-built man, and it was too easy to imagine him bare chested, his muscles cleanly sculpted and powerful.

Sex is a dirty trick that nature plays to keep DNA alive. She remembered Henry's wry joke. *Think of the trouble it causes.*

Right, she reminded herself, she should think of the trouble it caused. She remembered all it had caused her, culminating in the hellish time with Damon. She forced her mind back to the house.

"This floor looks almost new," she said, trying to sound as cool and detached as possible. "Why would anybody put a new floor into a house that's already almost new?"

"Right," he said. "Look under the sink. They didn't replace it there."

Rachel knelt and swung open the door of the cupboard beneath the sink. She frowned. The floor of the cabinet was carpeted with a patterned gray kitchen carpet that looked expensive. The rest of the kitchen floor was done in polished squares of gray tile. The grout between the squares looked pristine, almost new.

"Maybe somebody just didn't like carpet in the kitchen," she said, standing again.

He shrugged and cocked one black eyebrow. "This way," he said, and took her arm. His touch made her nearly leap from her skin. She tried to mask the effect he had, to look unconcerned, unfazed.

He led her to the living room. "Look at the carpet here," he said, nodding at it. His hand stayed on her arm, filling her body with tingles so strong they were uncomfortable. *Look at the carpet*, she ordered herself.

"It looks new, too," she said. The carpet was pale gray, the same color as the tiles.

"This way," he said, guiding her down a hallway.

"This is new, too," she said uneasily, eyeing the hall carpet.

He swung open the door of a bedroom, obviously unused. The floor was carpeted in gray, but a slightly different shade. Rachel knelt to examine it and partly to escape Jay's touch and what it awakened in her, the unwanted awareness of his sexuality—and her own.

"This isn't new," she said, biting her lip. "It's good carpet—very good. But it's older."

"Right. Now look at my room."

She stood up, taking a step away from him so that it would be awkward for him to reach for her arm again. He gave her a quick piercing look that told her he understood.

She tensed herself. It seemed they were having some primitive physical conversation that ran beneath the spoken word.

"Lead the way," she said with false heartiness.

He gave her the same penetrating glance, then turned, going down the hall to another door. He opened it and nodded for her to step inside.

Rachel moved into the room and was conscious of him when he stepped to stand beside her. She took a swift inventory of the place. Glass doors, curtained in white, led to a long deck that overlooked the lake. A fireplace took up almost one whole wall.

The furniture gleamed, a lacquered black. The king-size bed was inexpertly made. She could see the corner of a black sheet hanging crookedly from beneath the gray comforter. The shirt Jay had worn yesterday hung from one of its black posts.

The carpet was new, the same as the living room and hall. She stared at it, trying to ignore Jay's nearness and the proximity of his bed.

"It's new, too," she said, "but the one in the other bedroom was fine. If it was all the same, why replace it?"

He shrugged again. He stepped toward the bed. He threw back the comforter and the top black sheet. He peeled back the corner of the bottom sheet, revealing the mattress and innerspring. He pulled the corner of the mattress cover off.

"And this," he said grimly, nodding at the mattress.

Rachel swallowed, a new uneasiness filling her. The mattress was blue and striped. The innerspring was beige, sprigged with small flowers. "They don't match."

"And the walls," he said. "Notice anything funny?"

She stepped closer to the nearest wall, examining it.

It was painted white, thickly, but rather ineptly.

"Whoever did it didn't do a very good job."

"Right." He crossed his arms and stared at her, his frown line deepening. "Everything else in this place is top of the line. But an amateur paint job. Here. In the hall. And living room. And kitchen. The other paint is fine."

He pointed to a place low on the wall where a small piece of paint had been chipped away. A tiny stain, flecked with white, marred the original coat beneath it. The stain was brownish, the color of dried blood.

"I took a penknife and scraped some away—where it was particularly thick. Does that look like blood to you?"

Warm sunlight poured through the filmy white curtains, but Rachel shivered. The spot might have once been a drop of blood. But, she told herself, it might just as easily have been a dozen other things.

"No," she said stubbornly. "It could be anything. What are you trying to say?"

His eyes, always such a startling blue, held hers. "I'm saying I get a funny feeling about this place. Since Thornton talked to the kids, I started seeing it differently. I told you I couldn't sleep. I got up, started looking."

She made a helpless gesture, a useless gesture. "And?"

"I noticed things. What you've seen. And started trying to put the pieces together."

She knew what he was getting at, but she didn't want to let such morbid thoughts enter her mind.

"I found this in the woods this morning," he said, reaching for a manila envelope on his dresser. "There's a dump way back in the woods, a sort of burning place. I'd never paid attention to it before. But I started wondering. Why would a guy who could afford a place like this *burn* things? He didn't need to bother. He could pay to have them hauled off."

From the envelope he drew several small charred pieces of gray carpet, the smallest no larger than a playing card.

There was also a scrap of fabric faded and burned at the edges. It was hardly half the size of the smallest carpet scrap, but Rachel could see, in spite of weathering, that it was beige and flecked with faded flowers. It matched the innerspring.

"The old carpet was burned," he said. "The mattress, too. In the back of my mind, I'd always wondered about that burning place so deep in the woods. Why so far away?

And I found this—hooked onto a big piece of carpet lining. It was caught between two folds, kind of protected."

She stared into the palm of his hand. He held a pair of brown feathers, not half an inch long, slightly singed. She would have taken them for ordinary sparrow feathers, somewhat bedraggled, except thin copper wire wrapped their bases. The wire ended in a hook blackened by smoke.

"That's an earring," she said softly. She reached to touch the feathers, then decided she didn't want to. Against all reason, they frightened her. So did the burned carpet and mattress. She didn't want to think what they could portend or that there really might be blood beneath the room's paint. Her mind closed against such thoughts.

"Look at this," he muttered, turning the earring slightly. Rachel flinched. A hair, perhaps three inches long, was caught under the wire coiled around the feathers. The hair looked human. But it was an inhuman color, a strange, chemical yellow-green.

She sucked in her breath. *Green hair,* Thornton had said. She stared at it, stunned.

Jay put the objects back into the envelope, set it on the dresser. His eyes met and held hers. Rachel felt dizzy with foreboding.

"Somebody could have died here," he said.

"No," she said, shaking her head. "No."

"A green hair? It's too big a coincidence."

"No," she repeated. "It doesn't mean anything. It can't."

He stepped closer to her, still looking into her eyes. "Then tell me I'm crazy."

She tensed. "I didn't say that."

He moved an inch closer, as if in challenge. "Okay. Tell me I'm unreasonable."

Her heart slammed against her chest. "I didn't say that."

"Thornton said there was a murder here. He talked about green hair. You're the expert. You tell me that there aren't earmarks of something funny going on here."

She shook her head again. "I don't know what you mean. And I'm no expert. Not at something like this. I work with psychology. How people think, not the scene of the crime. I don't know what you mean."

He put his hands on her upper arms, gripping her. "I mean earmarks. When there's murder, there's liable to be blood. Maybe lots of it. Why rip out good floors? Slap paint on walls? Torch a mattress? Unless there's something to be hidden. Something like blood. And that stain looks like blood—admit it."

"No," she said, resisting his logic.

"Are you saying it's impossible?" he demanded.

"No," she shot back. "But it's . . . I don't want to think about it. I'm tired of murder, dammit!"

She was amazed to realize that there were tears in her eyes and she was struggling not to burst out weeping.

For months, weeks, day in, day out, she had been immersed in murder, hemmed in by it, smothered by it. It had seeped through her carefully controlled scientific viewpoint like radiation until it was poisoning her.

She had tried for a time to deal with it by treating it flippantly, as Henry did, but she could no longer be flippant. Her only remaining safeguard was that the terrible things she studied were distant from her real life; she did not want the actuality of murder entering her existence. Yet it already had entered, because of Jay's wife.

The woman he'd loved had been senselessly killed, and that made murder that much more unendurable, that much more real, that much more terrible. It forced her to deal not only with killers, but victims. And victims, she had come to see, included not only the dead, but the living, men like Jay, children like Kip.

Now Jay demanded that she let still more murder into her mind. An insane murder, involving a corpse with green hair. She couldn't. Suddenly her whole life seemed misdirected, unwholesomely askew.

Tears glittering in her eyes, she stared at Jay as if he were the author of all her troubles and the contradictory feelings that tore at her.

"I'm tired of murder, too." His voice was quiet, almost somber. "Rachel? Don't cry."

He raised a hand and wiped away a tear that had brimmed over and scalded her cheek. "Don't," he repeated.

His touch was so surprisingly gentle that another tear spilled over. He wiped it away, too, and stood gazing down at her face.

Damn! she thought in rage and shame and sorrow. She realized, to her despair, that she wanted him to kiss her.

He was young and handsome and complicated and burning with emotion, and he was so close she could feel the heat of his body warming her like a private sun. In a world full of death and logic, he stirred with life and passion.

Off in Wisconsin, Henry was confident of her devotion. Sensible, unsexual Henry with his file drawers stuffed with carnage, all cataloged and sterilized. Henry was right for her, right for the woman she had become. She didn't *want* to want Jay Malone. It was all too complicated.

She bit her lip, unable to draw away from him.

"Rachel," he said, "I just want to know I'm not crazy to think this. I didn't mean to scare you."

"You didn't scare me," she retorted, angry at him for making her feel as she did. "I didn't say it was crazy, but it's...it's improbable. Nobody died here. Nobody is buried in my basement. How could I live in a house built over a grave? It's too awful."

He raised one dark brow. "You're the one who's supposed to be used to this sort of thing." His eyes were on her mouth. His right hand took a strand of her hair, wound it slowly around his finger.

"I'm not used to it," she said contemptuously. "I'm sick of it. I'm sick of death. I want . . . life."

There. She'd said it. She felt so emotionally wrung out it dizzied her. She stood staring into his eyes, her lips slightly parted.

He studied her face for a long moment. Then he lowered his lips to hers, hesitantly, almost reluctantly.

But if his kiss began in hesitancy, it quickly changed, changed as soon as his mouth met hers. At first his lips merely touched hers, warm, firm, shockingly pleasurable.

Then something ignited, first in him, then in Rachel, and the kiss transmuted into one of urgency, one of questing hunger so great, so long-standing that it threatened to sweep them both away.

His arms encircled her, crushing her against him covetously, and his mouth bore down on hers as if she were something he had been craving too long to resist.

She gasped, then gasped again with aching longing when she tasted his tongue and he tasted hers. One of his hands tangled in her hair, bringing her face closer still.

Somehow, then, both his hands were framing her face, holding her as if he could not set her free even if he wished, and his kiss grew more devouring. One of her hands gripped the warm hardness of his shoulder, the other helplessly clutched his loosened silk tie.

She found herself kissing him back desirously, voraciously, as full of unfulfilled hungers as he was. Her eyes were closed, but tears still burned them, and her whole body throbbed with yearning. She let her hand rise to touch his face, to guide his lips more intimately against hers.

Her breasts, aching with longing, pressed against his chest, and the only cure for that pleasant pain seemed more of his touch. His mouth moved hotly to the hollow of her throat, then downward, warming the valley of her cleavage, kissing the swelling roundness of her flesh.

The clatter of feet on the deck startled and alarmed her. *The children,* she thought, flooding with shame. She drew back from him instantly, but her hand still touched his face and both of his still framed hers.

His dark hair hung over his brow and he stared down at her, frowning, as if she were a stranger and he was amazed at the mere sight of her, there so recently in his arms.

The sound of children's feet stampeded past the doors, went rattling down the stairs again, faded.

Rachel and Jay looked warily into each other's eyes, still touching each other's faces. He was breathing hard. She was breathless.

Her hand fell away first. She stepped back from him guiltily. "This is a complication I don't need," she said, pushing her hair back from her shoulders.

He dropped his hands, clenched his fists, his expression inscrutable. "You acted like you need it."

Stung, she stepped farther away. "Look," she said, going to his bed and pulling the mattress cover back into place. "I'm engaged. Practically. I've been away from him a long time."

"Obviously." He kept his eyes on her as she tucked the sheets back into place, drew the comforter up to cover them.

She stood straight, facing him. "Don't get the wrong idea about this."

"It's hard to get a right one," he said between his teeth. "Isn't it?"

She looked away. It would have been one thing if he had kissed her. But she had returned his kiss with desire as famished as his, and that was another thing altogether.

"The boyfriend," he said, a bitter smile crooking his mouth. "Is that whose place you're staying at?"

"Yes." And what a rotten way to show her gratitude to Henry, she thought dismally, wishing the burning sting of Jay's lips would vanish from hers. But she could still taste him, and the taste was haunting.

"I noticed you," he said. He drew his tie from his neck and threw it carelessly onto the bed. "Right away. I noticed you from the first."

"It doesn't matter," she said.

"No." He wiped his mouth meditatively with the back of his hand. "It doesn't, does it?"

"No."

"Let's see. I invited you here to discuss murder. Not sex. The sex seemed real enough—for a minute. But you think the murder's imaginary."

She nodded, not looking at him. "It's imaginary."

"It's possible," he said. "But not probable. Old Jay-boy's a little off his head. Been sitting out in the woods too long."

Rachel willed her self-control to return. A cold, artificial poise settled over her. "We've all been sitting out in the woods too long. I've got to go."

She squared her shoulders and left the room. In the living room, she slipped open the doors to the deck and called her daughter. "Mercer. Come on. We're going home."

She sensed Jay's presence behind her.

"Maybe you should put your lipstick back on," he said.

She shrugged, annoyed, and picked up her purse from the kitchen counter. Snatching out her lipstick, she uncapped it and hastily applied it. She put it away and stood clutching her purse awkwardly, her back to Jay.

She stared, unseeing, at the tiled kitchen floor. She could feel his eyes on her, making her nervous. Her blood danced with too many emotions, her brain with too many ideas.

She kept gazing at the floor so she wouldn't have to look at him. Why new tiles? Why new carpeting between here and the master bedroom? Why a new mattress? Why had the old things been burned? Why the thick paint, rolled on with such little skill and obvious haste? Did it really cover bloodstains?

And how, against all probability, could he have found a green hair?

Somebody could have died here, he'd said.

Impossible, she thought stubbornly. Then she corrected herself. No. Not impossible. Improbable.

As improbable as the fact that her lips still tingled from the touch of his and her body still swarmed with yearning. *No,* she kept saying mentally, over and over. *No.*

But she was no longer sure precisely what question she was answering.

THAT EVENING while Mercer caught minnows, Rachel tried to pore over the notes for her dissertation. She had finally reached the subject that bothered her most: the British serial killer Dennis Nilson.

Nilson's crimes were so unspeakable they were almost beyond the power of imagination. Rachel, for one, did not relish imagining them; they were far too beastly.

But Nilson was unavoidable. He was one of the few serial killers who had spoken and written freely of his crimes, describing them in almost loving detail. If she wished to understand the thought processes of such a murderer, she must enter Nilson's mind. It was, thought Rachel, a ghastly place to enter.

She read Nilson's words, she looked at his strangely abstract sketches of the murdered victims. She kept her material on him locked in a drawer when she wasn't using it. She never wanted Mercer to see it. She wished she had never seen it herself.

Nilson had killed fifteen young men. He hid their murdered bodies under the floorboards of his apartment.

Rachel shuddered. Every morning Nilson had risen and walked over his floor, beneath which dead men lay. Every night he slept above their concealed corpses.

Thornton had said that somebody died at Kip's house and was buried in this one. At Kip's house, there was new flooring and new paint and a mattress replaced. Why? And why had Thornton said the corpse had green hair?

No, Rachel tried to convince herself. There must be a logical explanation for the things at Jay's house. There could not be a body in her basement. She was not, like Nilson, walking, eating and sleeping over the dead.

She rubbed her forehead and stared at the list of Nilson's victims. Fifteen men. Why did the killing go on for so long? Why had no one suspected?

Rachel's mind went cold and hard. Nilson had followed the pattern of many classic serial killers. He picked victims about whom nobody cared, society's outsiders. He had no grudge against them. Chance brought them into his lethal path, and when they were killed, there was no one to miss them.

Feeling suddenly chilly, she rubbed her arms. Damn! she thought. The Nilson material had made her slightly sick to her stomach and given her goose bumps, as well.

She stood up, trying to escape grim realities for a moment. She went to the doors and stared out at Mercer's comforting figure. But the thought of murder wouldn't be exorcised.

It *was* possible to commit the perfect crime, Rachel mused. Often it involved little more than picking the right victim—one who had no connection to the murderer, one who didn't matter to society. If he or she vanished from the face of the earth, no one cared.

She leaned against the doorframe. Her stomach pitched queasily. She wasn't used to confronting the other sort of victim, like Jay Malone's wife. That kind of death shattered families, twisted the lives of the survivors, made a painful and visible hole in society.

It's not your job to think about the victims, Henry always warned. *The victims are a distraction. Think about the killer. The killer—that's your bread and butter.*

She turned back to her desk, feeling ill and angry. She put the material on Nilson back into its folder and locked it in the drawer. She picked up the phone and dialed Henry at his motel in Wisconsin.

She felt guilty and vulnerable because of what had happened between her and Jay Malone. She needed to talk to Henry, to assure herself that he was the man she belonged with, the man she was fond of and needed.

He answered on the third ring. "Dr. Bissell. Yes?"

"Henry, it's Rachel. It's nothing important, really. I'm just feeling down. I started the Nilson material today. You know how he always gets to me. And Henry... I'm afraid I'm getting lonely. I, ah, don't quite know how to say this...."

"Dear," Henry said, his voice rushed, "the state patrol's picking me up in about two minutes. We think there may be a break in the case. There's another dead girl up by Fond du

Lac. It's exciting. He's going to fall into our hands any-time. Then it's goodbye, Mr. Fixit.''

Rachel straightened her back, steeled her jaw. "How lucky. If enough women die, they'll lead you right to him.''

"Oh, you *are* in a bad mood.'' Henry laughed. "What's wrong with Nilson? He's one of my favorites. Definitely makes my top-ten list.''

"Henry!'' she said, hurt and angered.

"All right, all right,'' he answered. "I'm just excited, dear. I've never been in at the actual kill before. I'm sorry you're lonely. Make friends with somebody down there. Take a day off. Go visiting.''

"I did go visiting,'' Rachel said from between her teeth. "That's what I wanted to tell you. I don't think I ought to do it again.''

Henry didn't ask why. "Dear, my car's here. Gotta go. If you don't hear from me again for a while, it's because we're on to something. I'll call if I have time. 'Bye.''

"Henry?'' There were a hundred things she wanted to tell him, a hundred questions she wanted to ask, a thousand re-assurances she needed.

"Rachel,'' he said firmly, "I have to go. You're a big girl. You can have a crisis by yourself. If you need a break, take yourself to a movie or something.''

His indifference pained her and jolted her mind into changing gears. "All I wanted to know,'' she lied, "is more about that art smuggling down here last summer. Are you sure there wasn't any violence? I'm concerned—''

"I'll check with the federal boys.'' She heard a horn honk in the background. "Have to go. 'Bye. Don't ask for whom the bell tolls. It tolls for me. Kiss-kiss.''

He hung up.

"Kiss-kiss,'' she said into the dead phone. She set the re-ceiver back into its cradle.

She folded her arms on her desk and buried her face in them. "What a life,'' she muttered unhappily to herself.

EVENING FELL and faint wisps of mist veiled the lake. Restless, Thornton had watched Kip's house since late afternoon. He did not know how to get the clown doll to Kip.

Kip's father had spent almost the whole day on the deck, reading, then repairing something, then playing solitaire.

Kip stayed close to his father. He colored in a coloring book. He played cars. Twice he went wading, but his father was always on the deck watching.

Thornton stood among the cedar trees and scrub, clutching the clown doll. The clown doll was old, and flakes of paint had flecked off its heavy rubber body. It was perhaps a foot high. It had a big red nose, and its head would come off if Thornton pulled just right.

The clown was like the duck that way. The heads came off. Now magic was in the clown, but Thornton couldn't get the clown to Kip.

Thornton's head ached from so much worrying and waiting. His stomach hurt from hunger. He had not eaten since morning, and he did not dare go home. This time his mother would lock him up or maybe even take him away.

His stomach growled, his temples throbbed, and his legs were exhausted from standing so long. But he could not go home until he got the clown to Kip.

Perhaps, Thornton thought, he would have to stand, aching and hungry and tired in the shadows, until everyone was asleep. Then he would leave the clown on the deck. But the clown would look funny on the deck all alone. Kip was neater than Mercer. He didn't scatter toys everywhere.

Thornton was no longer scared for himself. He had come to believe in the magic with all his heart. He had shared the magic with Mercer. He had put it in the mailbox for Evan. He would be at peace if he could just get it to Kip.

Thornton's trust in his magic had grown so strong he kept a piece with him all the time now. He put it in a little bag that had once held marbles and tied the bag around his neck. He didn't want to take it off even for a minute. He left the last piece of magic hidden at home, to keep his mother safe.

At last, almost at sunset, Kip's father and Kip went off in their boat. As soon as they pulled away from the dock, Thornton ran across a little open patch of lawn, even though the boat was still in sight.

Then he cowered behind the big lilac bush next to the stairs up the deck. Maybe he would be lucky. Maybe Kip's father hadn't locked the door. Then Thornton could put the clown inside with the other toys, like at Mercer's.

But then something terrifying happened, and Thornton's hopes came crashing down. The boat started coming back. It hadn't even been away, but it was coming back!

Thornton froze. He watched Kip leap onto the dock and run toward the house. Thornton tried to draw further into the cover of the lilac bush. He closed his eyes and hoped Kip wouldn't see him.

Kip ran up the path to the house and up the stairs, right past Thornton. He tugged at the doors and dashed inside. Thornton squeezed his eyes shut more tightly. The house wasn't locked. Maybe Kip would run outside again and leave it unlocked. He prayed so. He prayed hard.

Then he heard Kip's footsteps again and could not keep his eyes closed any longer. He opened them just as Kip clattered down the stairs. He found himself staring directly into Kip's eyes, which went wide and frightened.

The boy's face was almost exactly even with his. Kip gasped and so did Thornton. Kip was carrying a pair of binoculars. He stopped dead and kept staring into Thornton's eyes, the binoculars swinging from their strap. His mouth fell open.

Thornton, panicking, looked at the lake. Kip's father stood at the end of his boat, looking away from them. Nobody but Kip had seen him.

He hurried to thrust the clown doll into Kip's hands. Kip's fingers closed around it reluctantly, fearfully.

"This is for you," Thornton said, breathing so fast it nearly choked him.

Kip held the doll and kept staring at Thornton with fright, tears rising in his eyes.

"No, no." Thornton shook his head so Kip wouldn't cry. "This is *good*. It's magic. It keeps people from dying. But you keep it secret. You can't tell *nobody*. Nobody—or it won't work. Understand?"

Kip's eyes got wider when he heard the word "dying." He looked at the doll, his chin trembling.

Thornton nodded. "It keeps you from dying. It keeps you safe. But it's a secret. Or it won't work. Understand?"

Numbly Kip nodded. Thornton was frightened to desperation. He was grateful that Kip's father still had his back to them. "Remember," Thornton said, turning away, "don't ever tell. And don't ever tell Mercer. Or your daddy. Or let go of the doll. Or you'll die."

He did not dare say more. He turned and ran across the lawn and disappeared into the shadows of the forest.

Kip stared after him, then down at the clown.

When he went back to the boat, his father looked at him oddly. "Where'd you get that?" He nodded at the doll.

Kip, remembering Thornton's warning, hugged the doll more tightly. He didn't want to lie, but he was far too frightened to tell the truth. He shrugged nervously.

Jay took the binoculars from the boy and glanced down at him. Where'd the crazy doll come from and why was Kip hanging on to it so hard? What went on in the kid's head? Would Jay ever understand? He decided not to nag about the doll. Instead he reached down and brusquely ruffled Kip's hair.

He tried to think of something to say to the boy, but somehow couldn't. The child looked too much like Cindy at the moment. Jay had to turn his face away.

RACHEL HAD TROUBLE sleeping again that night. Her dreams were of basements and bloodstained walls. Somehow her subconscious remembered a murder in Maine, a man who killed his wife. He'd tried to cover the evidence by ripping out the blood-drenched carpeting, painting the spattered walls. The scene replayed itself through her nightmares.

She awoke feeling burned out, used up and bone weary. She tried to find an optimistic thought, but with little success.

She made Mercer breakfast, drove her to the play group. When she did not see Jay, she felt, paradoxically, both grateful and empty, somehow denied.

Instead she met Katherine Menander, who was oddly insistent that Rachel and Mercer come to supper with her and Sean Alan that night.

"We're going to be alone *again* tonight," she said. "Tark's got to leave town. More research for his dissertation. You know how it is. He was even the one who suggested you come. Please do. Sean and I feel so abandoned out there, all by ourselves, since the Rineharts left."

"No—thanks very much," Rachel said, shaking her head. Katherine Menander made her uneasy, and she knew that Mercer didn't like Sean Alan.

Katherine looked so crestfallen that Rachel almost relented, but she did not. "No," she kept saying. "I'm afraid I've got work to do, too."

Then her curiosity stirred her to pry a bit about Tarquin Menander's work. "My daughter mentioned that your husband was writing about Ambassador Stokes. Is he?"

Katherine nodded glumly. "Oh, yes. He even visited him a couple of times down here during the summer. He's trying to write the definitive book on him. That's how he met Cleve Rinehart."

Rachel looked at her questioningly.

Katherine sighed. "Cleve was the ambassador's aide. They were very close—like father and son."

"I didn't know that, either."

"Oh, yes," Katherine sighed. "We're all just one big Stokes Appreciation Society. Sometimes I think Tark's married to that book instead of me. It's worse than his having another woman. It's such a passion with him. I mean I know his future depends on it," she said unhappily. "But sometimes I hate scholarship."

"I know the feeling," Rachel said, and tried not to shudder at the thought of going home to Dennis Nilson. But she thought it odd to discover both Tarquin Menander and Cleve Rinehart had such close ties to Stokes.

Her house seemed abnormally silent when she returned. She postponed opening the drawer with the Nilson folder by going to the dock and trying to start Henry's boat. *I must be desperate,* she thought. She hated them both, the dock and the boat.

The boat's outboard motor was stubborn and always took coaxing before it snarled into life, roaring and stinking of gasoline. This morning it stubbornly refused to start, and she felt doubly frustrated, for Henry was very particular that it be run regularly. She was almost relieved when a car came down her graveled drive, even though the car was Jay's.

He got out and came toward her with a swift, graceful gait that reminded her he was an athlete. He wore faded jeans and a long-sleeved white cotton sweater with a vee neck. He looked handsome, solemn and unhappy, as usual.

Oh, please, don't still be thinking of murder, she pleaded mentally. *You'll drive us all mad. Sometimes I feel half-mad already.*

He strolled onto the dock and stood watching her battle the motor. "Can I help?" he asked, still unsmiling.

She wiped her hand against the seat of her jeans. "As long as you're here," she said. She didn't smile, either.

He climbed into the boat, making it bob and tip more than before. Rachel placed her hand on her midsection, which also bobbed and tipped.

He bent over the motor, the muscles in his shoulders rippling under the white sweater. He took the cord in his right hand, pulled twice, short, powerful pulls, and the engine roared into life. He turned to her.

When she'd covered her ears against the noise, she reminded him of her daughter, standing there like that. Except he understood that, much as they might look alike, mother and daughter weren't similar at all.

The kid, Mercer, was a wild little creature, all enthusiasm and imagination and no fear. But the mother struck him as something else altogether.

She wasn't wild; if anything, she was overly civilized. She had enthusiasm and imagination—passion, too—but she kept it reined in. Tightly and with all her self-control.

And she wasn't fearless. She was afraid of many things. What frightened her most was her own emotion. But she was afraid of boats, too, and water, and the idea of a body in her basement.

She made him feel something unusual, a surge of sympathy for somebody besides Kip. She obviously hated the boat, even docked as it was.

"You've got it bad," he said, his voice harsh. "Come on. Get out. I'll take care of it."

At first she hesitated when he held out his hand to help her from the boat. Despite her attempt to control her expression—and she was good at it—he saw a phantom of wariness cross her features.

But then she took his hand, and her touch, as always, thrust through him in a surge of shock. He knew she felt it, too. He gritted his teeth, pretending as hard as she did that no such feeling shook them.

Wordlessly he helped her scramble to the dock. The wind was high, and it tossed her long, dark brown hair, fluttered her red gingham shirt against the shape of her breasts.

He remembered the softness of those breasts yielding against his chest, the feeling of her long legs against the muscles of his thighs, his maleness against her femininity, the hungry sweetness of her mouth beneath his own.

Now her mouth was set in its most sensible line, and she looked at him with professional blankness in her eyes. He knew now what the blankness hid: fear. Fear of the dock, the water, of him, of herself.

"Go back to shore," he said curtly. "I'll do this."

She swallowed, nodded, turned and made her way back down the gangplank to solid land. He watched her, the way her slender hips swayed, how her long legs moved.

Onshore, she walked away, her arms crossed over her chest. She went and stood by her deck, in profile to him, pretending to look at the flower garden.

At least he supposed she was pretending, just as he was pretending not to watch her. *What am I doing here?* he asked himself in disgust, turning his attention back to the motor.

He shook his head. He'd had to come. He had bad news for her. Very bad.

There was more to it, too, he knew. At first he'd resisted his attraction to Rachel; she was the most unlikely woman for him he could think of, given their backgrounds. But things about her, especially her way with his child and her own, struck something deep in him.

For the first time since Cindy's death, it seemed a door had opened, leading out of the prison of the grieving self.

Go to her, said his instincts, although his reason told him the contrary. He cut the motor and it rumbled to a stop. The scent of gasoline hung in the air.

Jay took a deep breath. To admit he desired Rachel would make him vulnerable in a way he never wanted to be again. It was foolish. She wouldn't want him. She had a man; she'd made that clear.

Yet, his instincts whispered. *Yet . . .* Somehow Jay sensed Rachel and the little girl might need him, foolish as it seemed. Everything he'd heard this morning made him suspect it more strongly.

He felt as if he were at the center of a cloud, and the cloud grew larger, darker and more sinister all the time. He felt it palpably, the way most people might sense the temperature change.

Feelings, he thought angrily. All he had to go on were a bunch of dumb hunches and crazy feelings.

He took another deep breath, leapt from the boat to the dock and headed for the woman.

Chapter Eight

She turned, her demeanor nervous, when he reached her. She glanced at him and then away. "Thank you," she said.

His heart drummed oddly, like a fist beating against his chest. "You may not say thank-you when you hear why I came," he said. He was a blunt man. He had little practice in putting things tactfully.

She looked at him questioningly, her hair fluttering in the breeze.

He said, "Thornton's missing."

She blinked hard. "Missing?"

"He's disappeared," he said, voice grim. "He hasn't been home since yesterday morning."

"Thornton? Gone?" Rachel sucked in her breath.

Jay crossed his arms. "I talked to Castor Bevins this morning. The police are ... concerned."

She nodded numbly. Police had to be concerned about someone like Thornton. He was too defenseless, too easy a prey.

She thought back to this morning, when she'd dropped off Mercer. Minnie Crabtree *had* seemed distracted, more tight-lipped than usual. "Do they think he ran away?"

"Bevins hopes that's all that's happened."

Jay shifted his shoulders uncomfortably. "That's all Bevins knew about it. There were ... other things." He hesitated, as if reluctant. "I asked him about the girl—the one he said disappeared from Paradise City."

Rachel sighed in frustration. Was he back on that track again? Obsessing about a murder that never happened?

Jay shook his head doggedly. "He said her name's Missy Proteus. Two years exactly this month she set off hitchhiking and as good as vanished from the face of the earth. Eighteen years old. Reputation as the town tramp."

Rachel frowned. Such girls often got into serious trouble. She remembered the Green River serial killings. Almost all the victims had been girls like Missy Proteus. Nobody noticed their absence—until their bodies started turning up.

"What about her parents?" Rachel asked.

"Her mother's dead, her father didn't give a damn. She lived with her grandmother, who drank and also didn't give a damn. Nobody bothered to file a report on her."

Rachel bit her lip, frowning. The news about Thornton had stunned her, and that of Missy Proteus had a familiar, sinister ring. She didn't like it.

She stood, staring at him. The breeze lifted his dark hair, let it fall over his forehead. His sky blue eyes seemed hard, but the twist of his mouth was troubled.

I don't want to talk about murder, she thought. Her stomach pitched as if she were back on the boat. *Maybe murder's driven us both mad.* It suddenly struck her as a very real possibility.

"Have you got a cup of coffee?" he asked, nodding toward her house.

"Of course," she murmured, trying to sound natural. "I didn't mean to be rude. But it's a shock. Thornton, I mean."

She would keep Jay on the deck, she vowed. She didn't want to be in the confines of the condo with him. His eyes were too blue, and she was too full of confusion. Perhaps even offering him coffee was a mistake.

She led him up the stairs. She'd put a pot of coffee on to brew just before she'd gone to the boat. "Sit," she said, gesturing at the wrought-iron table and chairs on the deck.

She slid open the doors, stepped into the kitchen and poured two mugs of coffee.

She glanced at a snapshot of Henry that she had posted on the refrigerator that morning. It was to remind her of her proper destiny. But her hands, she noticed, shook slightly when she took up the coffee tray.

Willing herself to be steady, she went back outside and sat down. Jay's eyes stayed trained on her, and she looked away in embarrassment.

"You don't really want to hear what I have to say, do you?" he asked, his voice rough.

She put her hands around the mug and stared out at the glittering lake. "You're going to talk about murder again, aren't you? Has it occurred to you that neither of us is in a position to be objective about the idea?"

It was true, she knew. Murder had ripped his life apart and his child's, as well. Murder was becoming her obsession. It haunted her, both waking and sleeping.

"Yeah. It's occurred to me."

She shrugged, still watching the sunlight play on the lake. "But you have feelings."

"Yeah. I have feelings."

She sighed and took a sip of her coffee. The silence throbbed between them. "All right," she said, squaring her shoulders but still not looking at him. "So you talked to Castor Bevins and a girl's missing. That doesn't mean anything happened at your house—or mine."

"Did you know there was talk of smuggling around here last year? Something about stolen art?" he asked.

She gathered her self-control, turned and looked at him coolly. "As a matter of fact, yes. My . . . friend told me."

His brow creased, as if he was angry she'd withheld such crucial information. "Did he tell you the place involved was this one? Yours?"

She was startled. "This place?"

"It's nothing but suspicion at this point. That's all—suspicion. But last summer, two art dealers from London showed up here."

"London, England?" she asked, surprised.

He nodded, took a swallow of coffee. "Right. Later, federal investigators came. It's got something to do with a big heist of pre-Columbian art. From Peru. Some of it's gold. Two men were killed over it in Lima. Thornton said something about gold, didn't he? Gold charms?"

The sun kept shining, but Rachel felt as if a cold shadow had fallen on her. She nodded numbly.

"Millions of dollars' worth of the stuff's been smuggled out of Peru—mostly gold and pottery," Jay said. "The Peruvian government wants it back. But it's hard to trace. Most goes to private collectors, and they don't announce they've got it—they know it's contraband. The feds are having a tough time tracing it. They got a tip and checked out Sangria. And Stokes, by the way, happened to be an art collector. With an interest in pre-Columbian art. Coincidence? Maybe. Maybe not."

"Stokes—an art collector?" She looked away from him, the sick, empty feeling in her stomach again.

Jay reached into his back pocket, pulled out a folded pamphlet, laid it on the table between them. "I've been reading."

She stared down at the creased booklet. It bore the familiar red, white and blue Stokes Day logo and a title in red: Albert Pike Stokes: A Life of Public Service. But it was the author's name that leapt out at her: Tarquin P. Menander, Jr., M.A.

She opened it and gazed at the dedication page: "To My Darling Mother."

"Tarquin Menander..." Rachel said. "He's a Stokes scholar. He's doing his dissertation on him."

"That's what it says in the introduction. This is hot off the presses—just came out last week. This is the miniversion of Stokes's life. The Chamber of Commerce paid Menander to write it."

"And he specifically says Stokes collected pre-Columbian art?"

"Yes. But Stokes got rid of it toward the end of his life and left the money to a Save the Rain Forest fund. But it sounds like he collected exactly the sort of thing the smugglers dealt in. And Stokes was the ambassador to Bolivia—which is right next door to Peru."

She shook her head. "I don't understand. I'm confused. I mean, he was *dead* before last summer. If he sold his art collection, it would have been long before any smuggler got here. If whoever lived in my house even *was* a smuggler."

"Right. Stokes died a year and a half ago—in January. The art dealers came six months later. People visited them off and on during the summer—some of them other dealers. That was before your 'friend' bought this place."

They stared at each other. The wind stirred the leaves of the trees, and the lake sparkled in the purity of the morning sunshine.

"But you can't connect that to Missy Proteus," Rachel objected. "Those art dealers were here *last* year. Missy disappeared *two* years ago. What are you getting at?"

"I don't know. I can't stop thinking about it, that's all. And now Thornton's gone. I tried to reach Tarquin Menander to ask him more about the art collection, but he's out of town."

"I know," she said. "I talked to Katherine. Did you know that Cleve Rinehart was connected to Stokes, too? He'd been Stokes's aide. Apparently they were close."

"No. I didn't know." He paused, studying her face. "I want you to come see Powell Crabtree with me."

"What?" Rachel demanded. "Why?"

"To ask him about the weird remodeling—if he knows anything. When it was done. Why."

"Why do you need me to go?"

"Because it involves you, too."

"No. Nothing involves me. Thornton told a story, that's all."

"Maybe, but now he's disappeared. And what about the smuggling business? That's no 'story.' I got it from Castor

Bevins. Your friend heard about it, too. Or don't you trust him, either?"

Rachel gazed down at the table, abashed. Of course, she had believed Henry immediately. And his source had been impeccable: the FBI.

A beat of silence passed between her and Jay. "Come with me," he said. "If he says something that shows I'm thinking crazy, then I'll give up the idea. I'll drop it, all right?"

She hesitated. Inside, all that awaited her were documents about Dennis Nilson. Here, outside, Jay had filled the once bright landscape with doubts and shadows. Perhaps Powell Crabtree could shed light that would force those shadows to flee. She heartily hoped so.

"All right," she agreed. As soon as she said the words she regretted them. Why go with him when everything about him disturbed her so deeply?

RACHEL HAD NEVER BEEN in Powell Crabtree's real-estate office before. All too clearly it reflected Crabtree's flashy, artificially sunny nature. His gleaming desk was the largest she had ever seen. Oddly, lined beneath his huge picture window were several brown grocery sacks, loaded with ripe tomatoes. The room was fragrant with them.

Myriad gold trophies glittered from the bookshelves, and the paneled walls were full of pictures of Powell Crabtree shaking hands with assorted personages. Rachel saw two signed with a flourish: "Best wishes—Albert Pike Stokes."

Powell was a tall man of about thirty-five, handsome in a fleshy way. He had crisp, tightly curled hair much like his mother's, and the same sharp gray-green eyes. But his manner, glad-handing and smiley, was as unlike Minnie's as possible.

He rose, beaming, when Jay and Rachel entered, pumped Rachel's hand with artificial enthusiasm, winked at her and threw an arm around Jay's shoulder. "Jay-boy! Good to see you. Hear Thornton's been telling some tall tales about your places."

Rachel was not surprised, but Jay cocked a dark eyebrow in a questioning frown.

"Sit. Sit, sit, sit," Powell ordered, gesturing at the deep leather chairs in front of his massive desk. He returned to his own chair and sank into it. "Miz Dale told me. So did Castor Bevins. Yesterday at the donut shop. He was laughing like hell about it."

Rachel and Jay sat, but neither smiled. "He's not laughing today," Jay said. "Thornton's disappeared."

Powell's grin vanished. "Disappeared?"

"Missing," Jay said. Rachel nodded unhappily.

"Well, that's not good," Powell said, shaking his head. "Not good at all. The trouble with somebody like Thornton is a bunch of good ole boys get drunk and want to beat somebody up—why, there he is, a sitting duck."

"It's happened before?" Jay asked.

"Hell, yes. I always said Ruby shouldn't let him run around like that. Should put him in a home—lock him up for his own good, where he'd be safe. I've always said it. And I never thought my mother should let him hang around those kids, either—it was bad business. She was *asking* for trouble."

"I take it that you and your mother don't agree about that," Jay said.

"My mother and I agree about very little," Powell said amiably. "The truth—which nobody wants to face—is that the older Thornton gets, the more unpredictable he is. This crazy story about your houses—"

"That's why we're here," Jay said, nodding at Rachel. "Why'd he say such a thing? I want to know that—and why the carpet and mattress have been replaced in my house. It looks like something *could* have happened there."

Powell ran a hand over his crinkly hair. "Why would Thornton say such a thing? That's my very point. Who knows what goes on in his head?" With his index finger, he made a circular motion near his temple.

"As for your carpet and mattress," he continued, "Stokes replaced it two years ago. Almost exactly two years ago. I remember. There was an accident."

"Accident?" Jay asked, his eyes briefly meeting Rachel's.

Powell sighed harshly. "I've always thought it was the beginning of the end. For poor old Stokes, that is. It was a stupid thing, really. A pair of squirrels fell down the chimney while nobody was home. Stokes had a little dog—a miniature poodle, I think it was."

Powell shook his head sadly. "Dog went after the squirrels. Got them, but got bitten up—badly. Blood from one end of the house to the other."

Rachel's stomach tightened at the mention of blood, and she felt Jay tense beside her.

Powell smoothed his hair again. "Had to shoot the dog. Put it out of its misery. Broke Stokes's heart. He loved that dog, he did. He had that first small stroke a couple of days after. He died five, six months later."

Rachel wished she could will away the image of the bloodied house. Jay had been right about at least one thing, after all: there had been blood, a lot of it. In all likelihood, the spot on the wall *had* been a bloodstain.

"You didn't mention any of that when I rented the place," Jay said.

Powell shrugged. "What's to mention? It was an accident. The damage was repaired. What's the matter? You're not satisfied with the place? Listen, that house is a palace. Nicest piece of property I've got listed. Stokes was not a cheap man."

Jay made a restless motion with his shoulders. "You never mentioned anything about suspected smugglers living in her place, either." He nodded toward Rachel.

Powell shrugged again. "Listen. I had to give those FBI boys the keys to the place with no questions asked. But as far as I know, they found zip—zero—*nada*—nothing. So, again, what's to mention? And furthermore, I'll tell you something."

Rachel and Jay waited, questions in their eyes. "I don't think those two old English boys were smugglers at all," Powell said with a smirk. "Oh, people *talked* about them, all right. Because they were a couple of sissy boys. Light in their loafers. Round here, something like that can start a lot of rumors. You know small towns."

Rachel squirmed uncomfortably. She knew precisely the kind of thing Powell spoke of; in some areas, to be different was automatically to be guilty.

"I see," said Jay.

"Those boys had a lot of company over the summer. Artsy types. Well, like I say, folks talk."

Rachel glanced away, embarrassed. She supposed she would be talked about herself soon if she kept being seen with Jay.

"Hey," Powell said, his usual cheer returning. "How about some tomatoes? I've got a bumper crop of tomatoes this year. Let me give you some. I'm trying to give everyone who comes in a sack. Especially the pretty ladies." He winked at Rachel again.

I was crazy to come here, Rachel thought. *Like an insane person, I came looking for clues to a murder that never happened, and I end up with a sack of tomatoes and a wink. How absurd does life get?*

Neither of them spoke for a long time after they left Powell's office. Jay, gloomy, seemed lost in his own thoughts, and Rachel felt chagrined that her suspicions had been so groundless.

When they turned down the dirt road that led to her house, she felt the urge to speak, to clear the air between them before they parted.

"Well, now that it's all explained," she said, "you don't have to think about murder anymore. There's a perfectly rational explanation for everything—especially for what happened at your house."

"Maybe it's *too* perfect," Jay challenged. "*Too* pat. Did you ever think of that?"

"Oh, no," Rachel said in disbelief. "You're not still saying somebody was murdered at Stokes's place? Just because you found one earring—and one hair? That hair might not even be human."

He pulled up before her house. "You really think I'm obsessed, don't you?"

She stared at him in silence, nibbling at her lip. "Nothing happened at your place. It's just not probable," she said at last.

"But what about that damned earring?" he asked. "And Missy Proteus? She disappeared around the same time Stokes changed the house."

Rachel shook her head. "Why keep dragging the girl into this? Because she's the only one missing? She's not even from around here. Your problem is that you *want* to believe something happened. You're grasping at straws."

"She *is* from around here," Jay insisted stubbornly. "Paradise City's only fifteen miles away. That's nothing in these parts. That's practically next door. Castor Bevins said she just . . . vanished."

Rachel had turned to open the car door, to end the conversation. But Jay was already out of the Corvette to open it for her.

"You should have asked Castor if she had green hair," Rachel said dryly as she got out.

"I did. He laughed. He thinks she had brown hair—he can't remember for sure. Here—you're forgetting your tomatoes. I'll carry them for you."

"I'll carry them myself."

"I've already got them."

Rachel spoke in frustration as she climbed the stairs, Jay at her side. "You can't really believe something happened to that girl at your house. If it did, it would have been when Stokes was alive. Then you'd have him—the town's most honored man—involved. Why? And somehow, you probably still want to think smugglers are mixed up in it. It's a mishmash. It makes no sense. And, excuse me, isn't it all a little melodramatic?"

He paused at the top of the stairs, waiting for her to open the door. "Yeah. It's melodramatic. So's life."

Rachel shook her head as she entered the living room. The scenarios Jay sketched seemed wild and farfetched—except for two troubling things. First, Thornton *was* gone.

Also, whether Jay knew it or not, Missy Proteus sounded like a perfect victim, a textbook case. But for her to be killed in Stokes's house? Then be brought here, to Henry's? It made no sense.

"What's wrong?" Jay asked, studying her expression.

"Nothing," she said wearily. "But you said you'd stop talking about murder."

He followed her to the kitchen and set the tomatoes on the counter.

"Let me divide those ridiculous things up," she said, glad for the distraction. "There's enough for an army."

"Thornton said there was a corpse with green hair at my house. I found that damned earring with a green hair in it. I can't shake it out of my mind."

Rachel shrugged, still unsettled. "But Thornton said a *man* was killed at your place—*last* year. Not a girl and not two years ago. Last year there *may* have been smugglers here. But that doesn't *prove* anything. It doesn't prove there was ever a murder at all."

"No. It doesn't. But Thornton could have the time wrong. Minnie Crabtree said his grasp of time was weak. And are you sure he said it was a man? Kids get things mixed up. Are you positive that's what he said? Truly positive?"

"Yes," Rachel said relentlessly. "And there's no proof that anything happened. Could we change the subject? I have to think about things like this all the time—I'm sick of it."

"Maybe you should change jobs."

"Please," she said impatiently. "Here. Take these." She pushed the bag of tomatoes across the counter at him. "Talk about something else."

Take them and go, she thought. He was a man possessed; his thinking wasn't healthy, and he kept trying to pull her into his fantasy. Worse, at times he almost succeeded.

He scrutinized her with disconcerting seriousness. Then he looked at the snapshot of Henry on the refrigerator door. "Okay, I'll make small talk. Your father? You don't look much like him. You must take after your mother."

Her spine stiffened. Nothing he could have said about Henry could have jolted her more. "That's not my father. It's my . . . friend."

A disbelieving expression crossed his face. He looked at the photograph again. Then he said, "Excuse me."

"He's a . . . learned man," she said, meeting his eyes. "I admire his maturity."

"Yeah. He looks mature."

Jay crossed his arms and leaned against the counter. The sunlight fell through the glass door and glinted on his blue-black hair. "So what is he—a psychologist, like you?"

"As a matter of fact, yes."

"And what's his specialty? Murder, too?"

She looked away. "Yes."

"Nice to have something in common." Sarcasm vibrated in his voice.

"He happens to be one of the nation's foremost experts on serial killers," Rachel said defensively.

"Charming," said Jay, more sarcastically than before.

She bristled at his contempt, but it also wounded her. "The study of murderers," she said, struggling to say it as carefully as possible, "is important and fascinating."

"Really?" Jay said with a sneer. "The only murderer I ever met was the one who killed my wife. He had an IQ of ninety, and his brains were burned out on pills. The only important and fascinating thing about him was his victim. But nobody else seemed to think so. She didn't count."

He was outwardly calm, but once again he reminded her of a man on fire inside.

"They gave him five years in some cushy hospital for the criminally insane," he said.

Rachel tensed more stiffly, but she forced herself to meet his eyes again.

"On the other hand," Jay said, "he killed only one person. So maybe he's not so fascinating. Maybe to you he's just small-time—nothing."

Her cheeks burned. "I'm sorry about your wife. I truly am."

"That's a platitude," he said, still eerily calm. "Somehow I'd expected more from you."

She stared at him, frustrated. What could she say about such a tragedy that wasn't trite?

He looked away, as if in disgust. He made an empty, angry gesture. "They all had their platitudes. Everybody. The worst was the minister. At her 'service' he said something about God seeing every sparrow that falls. That everything's accounted for. Ha!"

He stared out through the doors at the light dancing on the lake, as if looking for something far beyond. "I'll tell you something—nobody notices the sparrow that falls. Nobody gives a damn. Nobody's concerned about justice. Not really. It's a farce."

She watched him furtively. The psychologist in her told her he was still learning to deal with his anger. The woman in her knew only that he hurt, and she ached for him.

He turned to face her again. He smiled, but with bitterness. "So maybe there's a dead guy in your basement. Or a dead woman. Why should you care? Why should I? Why should anybody?"

She shook her head. "That's not the point."

"Isn't it?" he asked, his smile dying. "I think I bring up things you'd rather not consider. You try to act like you're in control. But there are things you don't like to face, aren't there?"

He's talking about murder, she thought in distraction. *He's talking about my work, and he's talking about Henry. And he's talking about himself and me, too. He's right.*

"All people have things they don't like to face," she said. "Don't try to analyze me. I don't like it."

His disturbing smile came back. "Why? Is that a game only you're allowed to play? You've analyzed me, haven't you?"

"No," she lied. "Why would I bother?"

"That's right. Why would you bother?"

The facade of her composure cracked. She looked at him in perplexity and despair. "What do you want from me?"

"I'm not sure," he said.

But she could feel something unbidden running between them, something undeniable, burning and dangerous, currents of desire.

The air between them seemed to ripple, to pulse.

Then he said something completely unexpected. "Look— how about if your kid comes over to play with mine this afternoon?"

"What?" she said, confounded. She should avoid all contact with this man, and she knew it. "I thought... I thought you didn't want your son to play with girls."

"I didn't," he said, meeting her gaze and holding it. "I was stupid. I didn't realize."

She shrugged nervously. "Realize what?"

"His feelings," he said. "And he seems to be having a harder time than usual. He seems scared again all of a sudden. She might help him. Because he loves her. He needs her."

Rachel looked away, embarrassed again. *He loves her. He needs her.* What a surprising thing for Jay to say. The word seemed foreign, coming from his lips. *Love.* At least he understood that much—that his son needed love.

"Will you let her?"

She shrugged again. She stared at the boat. The stupid, terrible boat. It was Henry's boat, and she must think of Henry. "She has a doctor's appointment right after the play group. She has to get a booster shot."

"Afterwards," he said.

No, reason told her. *If you do, something is going to happen between you and this man. And it can't. His mind's*

more bent by murder than yours is. Think of Henry. What-
ever you do, say no.
    "Yes," she said.

Chapter Nine

"Now," Rachel said, immediately regretting her answer, "I think you'd better go. I've wasted the whole morning when I should have been working. I don't mean to be rude, but..."

"I know," he said, unsmiling. "You're right. I'd better go." His look shivered her down to her heel bones. It seemed to speak volumes about what would happened if he stayed.

But all he said was, "I'll see you later." Then he left as abruptly as he'd come. He didn't say goodbye, and he didn't bother to take Powell Crabtree's silly tomatoes.

Rachel watched him go, her heart beating hard. Although nothing had actually happened between her and Jay, she felt compromised.

She knew he wanted to go to bed with her. It was naked in his eyes. Equally clear to her was the fact he didn't want to want her, but he did.

Worse, she felt almost the same about him. And she knew he could tell. What had she in common with such a man? Nothing. He was in a lonely rage, she was in a depressing quandary with her dissertation, and something meaningless had sparked between them.

She must be sensible. She would let Mercer play with Kip this afternoon, but only because the children enjoyed each other so much and Kip was going through another rough spot. But then she must sever her own relationship with Jay as completely as she could.

WHEN SHE WENT to pick up Mercer, she tried to take Minnie Crabtree aside. "I hear Thornton's missing," she said with concern. "Have you heard anything about him? Have you said anything to the children?"

Minnie looked distracted and unhappy. "No," she said shortly. "I don't want to alarm them. And I'd rather not talk about it." She turned her back on Rachel and walked away, pointedly ending the conversation.

Rachel retrieved Mercer from the swimming pool. She hustled the child into the car to take her to the doctor. She drove off quickly, grateful that Jay had not yet appeared at Minnie's to pick up Kip.

Mercer sat in the passenger seat, chattering about lizards. Rachel thought of Thornton and of what Jay had said.

"Mercer," Rachel said carefully, casting the child a sideways glance, "tell me exactly what Thornton said when he told you the story. That a *man* was buried in our basement? Or a woman? Did he say?"

Mercer paused, her dark brows drawing together in concentration. "No . . . he said a *person*. Yeah. That's what he said, a dead person. And he didn't exactly say buried. Not exactly. Or in the basement, I guess. He just said they took a dead person to our *house*. And that the person had green hair and Thornton had gold charms."

The child sneezed. "If you'd buy me an iguana—"

Rachel cut her off. Mercer's unexpected answer had startled her, upset all her safe rationalizations. "He said a dead *person* was *brought* to our house? That's all? You're sure? Why did you say he said that a dead man was buried?"

"Well, that's what I *dreamed*," Mercer explained. "It's what I thought he meant. Besides, it's a better story my way. Now, if you bought me an iguana . . ."

Rachel's thoughts, dizzied, had veered far from the iguana. She pressed her lips together and her hands tightened on the wheel.

Thornton hadn't said a man had been killed, after all. He might have been talking about a woman. With a sinking feeling, she thought of Missy Proteus again, gone but never reported missing. The perfect victim.

Oh, Lord, she thought, now he's got me doing it. *It's true—we're both obsessed. It's becoming a folie à deux—a madness of two.*

She had to stay away from Jay, she told herself again. And she had to shut out his ideas; she was too vulnerable.

She stopped at a rest room to change Mercer's wet bathing suit for dry clothes, to wash her face and brush her hair. She had hoped to do so at Minnie's, but Minnie had been too unfriendly and distracted for Rachel to ask.

There was always a long wait at the clinic, and the longer Rachel sat, the more restless she grew, thinking about what Mercer had said about the body. The child's few words had changed everything, filling Rachel's mind with new uncertainties. Beside her, Mercer sat, happily absorbed in a *National Geographic* pictorial article about sharks.

"Excuse me, Mercer," Rachel said, feeling foolish. "I want to make a phone call. Stay here and don't talk to anyone." She rose and went to the pay phone in the entryway of the clinic. All right, she told herself, she was obsessive and compulsive and also paranoid. So what? Wasn't that the stereotype? That psychologists were as mad as hatters?

She couldn't answer any of the questions that nagged her about Thornton's story. But if she didn't mind making a fool of herself, she could answer one: what color was Missy Proteus's hair?

She flipped through the regional phone book, looking for the Paradise City listings, then ran her eye down the column of the *P*s. There was only one Proteus; Jimmy Don, 411C Railroad Street.

Gritting her teeth at her folly, she fed the coins into the phone. *He won't be home,* she thought in disgust. *It's a weekday. He'll be at work. He won't even answer.*

He answered. He sounded ill-tempered. He also sounded drunk. "Whaddya you want?"

"Mr. Proteus," she said in her smoothest, most professional voice. "I'm sorry to bother you. I'm a psychologist.

My work sometimes deals with young women who are missing. I don't mean to bring up a painful subject, but I've been told a young woman named Proteus—''

"My daughter?" he asked scornfully.

"Yes." Her heart started beating swiftly, almost painfully.

"I don't have no daughter." Proteus's voice was somewhere between a whine and a snarl. "My daughter's dead."

Rachel blinked in surprise. If Missy Proteus was dead, had no one ever told Castor Bevins? She felt as if she had blundered badly. "I'm sorry—I didn't know."

"I don't have no daughter. She hardened her heart agin me, and I done the same to her. My daughter's *dead*."

"You have my sympathy," Rachel said. She cringed at having called at all. "You really do. You've experienced the most devastating loss—"

"I have experience many devastatin' loss," he said drunkenly. "I could tell you 'bout devastatin' loss. People ask me why I drink. I tell 'em—*my life*. Look at *my life*."

"I'm really sorry, Mr. Proteus," Rachel said, feeling more awkward by the second. "I misunderstood. Has your daughter been deceased long?"

"What? Who are you? You got a young voice. Pretty voice. What you callin' me for?"

"Mr. Proteus, I'm sorry I bothered you. My most sincere condolences about your daughter."

"What daughter? I ain't got no daughter. My daughter is dead to me. I don't know where she is, and I don't care. As daughters go, she's nothin' but trial and tribbletash—tribbletash—tribulation."

Rachel's head whirled as she gripped the phone more tightly. "Wait. You mean she's *not* dead?"

"To me she is. She's one wild thing. She got no respect for nothin'. She lies. She lies about me. Know what? She had a skull tattooed on her butt, and under it she got wrote, 'Daddy.' What sort insane child that?"

Rachel took a deep breath. "Mr. Proteus, could you describe your daughter? What she looked like? Her hair color and—"

"Hair color!" He snorted contemptuously. "She tried to dye it yeller and it turned green. Stupid child. Never did nothin' right. Looked like a nut. Wore feathers in her ears and cut holes in her jeans. Stole her own grandma's cigarettes. Told lies about me. What sort insane child that?"

Rachel's grip on the phone tensed so much that her knuckles whitened. His words seared through her brain like bolts of electricity. *She tried to dye it yeller and it turned green... wore feathers in her ears...*

Oh, God, she thought, remembering what Thornton had said. A corpse with green hair.

"She wore feathers in her ears?" Rachel asked, wanting to make sure she'd heard right. "Her hair had a greenish cast?"

So she wore feathers, so what? And she botched a bleach job. That proves nothing. Nothing. You don't build a murder case on two feathers and a single hair. It isn't done that way.

"She did. She did ever'thin' but put a gold ring in her nose. You sure sound young and pretty. I know how to make a pretty young girl happy. Sure do. Let me tell you what I'd do for you, sweet thing—"

"Thank you, Mr. Proteus, for your time. Goodbye." She hung up, her heart beating so hard she trembled.

"Oh, God," she said, touching her fingertips to her forehead. No wonder Missy Proteus had run away. What else could she do with such a father?

Rachel went back to the waiting room, and when she sat down beside Mercer, she put her arm around her little girl protectively.

CONFUSION FILLED Rachel's mind as she drove Mercer to Jay's.

She did not want to tell Mercer about Thornton's disappearance, or Jay about Missy Proteus. Nor did she want to tell him yet what Mercer had said about the body. She knew what he would make of such news. No, she vowed as she pulled up in Jay's drive, she would not say anything, not now. She had to be rational, to think things out. What the Proteus man had said still might mean nothing; it might only be another coincidence.

Kip, looking pale and worried, played in his sandbox. He brightened at the sight of Rachel's car, but Jay was right. Somehow the boy seemed even more withdrawn than usual.

Jay had been sunning and reading on the porch. He wore only swim trunks and sunglasses. He drew on a shirt when she came, but didn't button it.

His body was as muscular and bronzed as she'd imagined, and the hair that curled on his chest shone blue-black in the sun. It tapered to a thin line that ran down his flat stomach, disappeared intriguingly beneath the waistband of his dark blue trunks.

He walked to her car, frowning as usual. Mercer had already bolted from the front seat and joined Kip. She was chasing him through a patch of clover, whooping.

Rachel didn't get out of the car. She stared straight ahead through the windshield at the children.

"I was afraid you wouldn't come," he said, his voice surprisingly soft. One lean hand rested on her opened window.

"I said I'd bring her and I did," Rachel said, careful not to look at him. "I'll pick her up at five."

"I can drive her back. It's no trouble."

He smelled of warmth, sunshine and suntan oil. She didn't look at him, but imagined the breeze lifting his dark hair, the sunshine gleaming on his naked chest.

"I'll pick her up," she said stolidly. She didn't want him at her house again. She didn't trust herself or him any longer. She felt safer when she was in the car as she was now, as if it was a sort of armor that protected her.

"Why won't you look at me?"

Oh, God, thought Rachel, he never let her get away with anything. Why had she even come? Why hadn't she stayed away, as he'd expected?

"I don't have to look at you," she said from between her teeth. "I've already seen you."

"Have you?"

The question rankled. She wasn't sure she had really seen him as a person. She'd seen him as a sexual entity, and she'd seen him as a series of stereotypes: the jock, the angry young man, the father who couldn't communicate, the man driven by the idea of justice. Had she ever regarded him as an individual, complete and complex?

She glanced at him and wished she hadn't. He'd taken off his sunglasses, and his startling blue eyes looked at her with frank hunger.

"I have to go," she said curtly. "I have work to do." She tried to make her voice careless and light. "Something I never see you worry about. You're very lucky. Do you just get to lie around between hockey seasons?"

"I don't play anymore. I retired," he said out of the corner of his mouth.

She gave him a brittle smile. "So now all you have to do is sun yourself and loaf. Must be nice."

"All I have to do is figure out what to do with the rest of my life. And how to raise my kid. No, it must be nice to have your future all cut-and-dried and laid out in front of you. The way you do."

"Yes," she said. "It is."

She nodded goodbye and put the car into gear. She drove off, leaving him standing in the dappled sunlight, the breeze fluttering his opened shirt. Behind him, Mercer had Kip pinned down in the sandbox, tickling him.

She left the three of them behind and she tried to think of Henry. Instead, she remembered the morning's conversation with Jay.

He had such an intense manner that sometimes she had the eerie impression that what he might want from her was nothing short of everything.

That was absurd, she told herself. He might deride her for it, but her future was set clearly before her, sensible, orderly and predictable.

Henry's range of emotions was limited and cool, and that suited Rachel fine. Life with Henry would be smooth, reasonable, and he would make no devastating demands on her emotions. How did Jay Malone dare to mock such a haven? How dare he make her doubt it?

Jay was sexy and dangerous, she told herself darkly. There was nothing predictable about him, and that was what frightened her. That, and his stubborn conviction that a killing had taken place.

It had to be irrational; it had to be a delusion. She knew the intricacies of the laws of evidence. A verdict of murder demanded proof beyond reasonable doubt.

Thornton claimed someone had been killed—but a court would brand Thornton an incompetent witness. A reasonable person must doubt him.

Thornton said the body had green hair. Missy Proteus was gone, with feathers in her ears and a bad bleach job. Jay had found part of an earring and a single green hair.

One earring, one hair, didn't prove that Missy or anyone else had died. It didn't prove she had been in the house.

No, as circumstantial evidence, it was all laughably flimsy; no court could ever believe it proved, beyond reasonable doubt, that there had been a murder.

Besides, she kept telling herself, it wasn't a healthy way to think. Jay and his damnable *feelings*. He was trying to sweep her away, and at times he was so intent he almost did. She wanted reason ruling her life, not feelings.

And she didn't need anyone to make her think more about death. She was ready to call Henry and tell him she couldn't go through with the dissertation. She would have to change her subject. It was taking too great a toll.

She had reached the main highway and glanced up at the sky. Vultures wheeled and glided over the deserted ridge beyond the road that led to her house.

Vultures, she thought unhappily. Death again. They were black vultures, great hideous birds, and she couldn't get used to how many haunted the lake looking for carrion.

When the vultures filled the sky as they did now, it was a certain sign something had died. In fact, something very large must have died, perhaps a horse or steer, for she had never seen so many of the birds blacken the sky.

She frowned, watching them circle the ridge. They were beyond counting. But no horse or steer should be on the ridge, for no farm was nearby; the land was too steep for farming, and the road to the ridge itself had long ago been abandoned.

Hardly anyone drove to the ridge these days. The road was in disrepair, and nothing was there. Sometimes teenagers took advantage of the spot's loneliness to park, but that was all.

No, she amended, sometimes Thornton, indefatigable on his bicycle, rode up there. More than once she had seen him pumping purposefully to or from the place. Thornton bicycled everywhere; it was his main pastime.

Thornton, she thought, a queasy sensation squeezing her stomach. *Thornton's gone. And the ridge is a place he visits.*

She cautioned herself not to be ridiculous. Jay Malone and his determination that a murder had taken place had warped her thinking. She was becoming irrational.

Yet, almost against her will, she found herself heading the car toward the ridge. She wouldn't find anything, she tried to convince herself. Rather, all she might find was a deer.

She left the main highway and took the neglected dirt road that dead-ended at the edge of the ridge. The closer she approached the wheeling vultures, the more foolish and apprehensive she felt.

"This is insane," she said aloud. Then, in a grim attempt to cheer herself, she added, "And now I'm talking to myself. I have to call Henry. I need help. It's obvious."

Still, she knew she wouldn't rest until she'd looked. The suspicion was too sick, and she must prove to herself how unfounded it was. Thornton was probably already safe at home. In the meantime, she would act, simply for her own peace of mind.

The road grew rougher, more overgrown. When she reached its middle section, a cloud of vultures rose up from the grass. With their naked necks and heads, they were hideous birds, their beaks as sharp as scalpels.

Oh, Lord, Rachel thought bleakly, stopping the car. Whatever was dead was right over there, under the little grove of black locust trees, the buzzards gliding above in lazy circles. It probably *was* a deer, and she dreaded seeing the poor thing. Steeling herself, she switched off the ignition.

She opened the door and stepped out. The wind was high, whipping her hair and flattening her shirt against her body. The weeds grew tall between the road and the locust trees. She would probably get bitten by ticks or chiggers or worse on this fool's errand. Fine, she thought. A good reminder not to let her imagination run wild.

The ridge was silent except for the wind, and the isolation, the sheer loneliness of the place, oppressed her. Shuddering, she stepped into the tall weeds, hoping she wouldn't meet a snake.

She took five or six careful steps toward the trees, then stopped, staring. Her heart plummeted, and a sickening chill sprang through her veins. Her knees weakened.

"Oh, no," she breathed and began to tremble.

A red bicycle, badly twisted, lay among the nodding weeds. Its back wheel was so skewed it thrust up into the air, just clearing the earth. It turned, slowly, silently, in the strong wind.

"Oh, no," she said again. Tears stung her eyes. She recognized the bicycle. She knew from the sticker of the yellow happy face on the back fender, the handlebars with their yellow streamers fluttering in the wind.

Her vision blurred with tears, but she forced herself toward the locust grove.

There, beneath the trees, she saw a motionless form. She recognized the plump shape, the thick, wavy hair stirring in the breeze.

Thornton. Lying there with the terrible stillness that could mean only death.

CONFESSION

I'm telling you the absolute truth about this. I want my mother to know.

I should have killed him sooner. I should have killed him right away. I was trying to be careful. I was trying to be clever.

Then, that evening I opened the mailbox, I knew I couldn't wait any longer. I can tell you one thing: he never expected me to open that mailbox. But I did. And from that moment he was as good as dead.

A duck. Think of that. I twisted off its head because it didn't feel right. It felt too heavy for plastic. He'd tried to wrap the gold in an old sock, so it wouldn't rattle. My God, when I saw the gold, I was dumbstruck.

There I stood, the gold in one hand and a headless duck in the other. Up until that moment, I had never even suspected he had so much as an ounce of the gold. There'd been so much gold that night and so damned little time, who could keep track of it?

And what the hell was he doing, sending it to Evan? If he had one piece, he must have more. He had to. I knew it.

I found him up near the ridge, and he told me the truth: he'd stolen five pieces of it. Imagine that!

He'd left one piece in the duck in the mailbox for Evan. I'd found that. He had one piece in a bag, tied around his neck like a charm.

The other three I had to get. Oh, that was going to be fun. He'd left one piece in a stuffed rabbit for the Dale brat. He left another in a rubber clown with the Malone kid. And one he'd left at home for his dear old gray-haired mother. What a thoughtful son.

Then I told him to get on his bike and ride up to the ridge and get out of my sight, that I was letting him go.

But I drove after him, slowly at first, playing with him. He realized what was happening. . . .

I had to figure out how to get the rest of the damned gold back. Now, you tell me the truth: did I have any other choice but to kill him?

No, I had to get those toys.

I had to start stalking.

Chapter Ten

Somehow Rachel drove home from the ridge, somehow she called the sheriff's department. Deputies came and made her return to the scene. Her afternoon dissolved into a long blur of shock.

Hit-and-run, the officers said, staring down at Thornton's body. They bombarded her with questions, which she answered like an automaton. She watched a young deputy, his face grim, don gloves and carry the twisted bicycle to stow in the back of his car. An older deputy asked her to come back to headquarters and make a statement.

She nodded, although his words didn't quite register. *So this is what it's like from the other side,* she kept thinking. She'd read so much about violent death until often it seemed an abstraction, something not real.

This time it was all too real and it seethed around her, threatening to drown her. Every time she thought of Thornton, she wanted to weep and rage.

At the sheriff's office, she answered more questions and gave a statement. At last the questioning deputy seemed satisfied. He told a younger officer to take her home.

Her head began to clear slightly once she was outside the building. "Do...do you think," she stammered, "that it was an accident? Or that somebody . . . killed him on purpose?"

The young deputy shook his head. "No way to tell, ma'am. I can't think of a reason for anybody to kill the boy.

He was one of God's innocents. A sparrow that fell. No meanness in him. None.''

His words depressed her, because he was right. Why, of all the world's creatures, had Thornton been struck down? He truly was an innocent. The only bad thing she had ever known him to do was to tell his frightening story to the children, and that now seemed such a small thing, so unimportant.

But was it just a made-up story? Thornton had said somebody'd died in Jay's house. He'd said that anybody who'd told would die. Thornton had told. Thornton had died.

Her head ached from tears shed, as well as tears suppressed. She'd told the questioning deputy—in her rattled way—about Thornton's story. He'd seemed uninterested. He'd made a note, he'd drawn a doodle. He'd gone on to other matters.

Now the young deputy mused as he turned down the lane to the condos, "He was probably riding that lonesome road at night. That road, it winds. Somebody came on him real sudden, hit him, got panicky, drove off." He shook his head sadly.

"His mother, Ruby Fuller," Rachel said. "Do you think she's been told yet?"

"I imagine so, ma'am," he said. "She'll take it hard. She took it mighty hard that he disappeared. Like she expected the worst."

His words depressed her further. Ruby Fuller had expected the worst. Why?

At Rachel's place, the young deputy walked her to the door, asked if she would be all right. She nodded, thanked him and let herself in.

Henry had a bottle of bourbon in the cupboard, she remembered. She hadn't touched it all summer. Now she got out the bottle and poured herself a stiff drink. At least her hands had finally stopped shaking, and she wondered if she was too exhausted to shake. She drank, although the liquor made her cough.

The phone rang, startling her. She prayed it wasn't the sheriff's office again. She was weary to death of questions.

"Hello, dear," said Henry's bright voice. "What a day I've had. Spent it mostly with a dead body."

"So did I," Rachel answered. Her voice sounded foreign to her, changed.

He must have thought she was joking. "We found her last night. It was my first time actually at the scene of the crime while the body's still there. What's that word the kids use? Awesome."

"Really?" she asked. "I didn't think so."

"Spent most of the day at the medical examiner's. It's Mr. Fixit at work, all right. Perfect MO, what he'd done to her. Exactly what I'd predicted. Beautiful. In a grisly way, of course. Wow. I've dreamed of this."

"Henry," Rachel cried, appalled by the excitement in his tone, "will you stop? Will you listen? I found a body today—it was terrible."

There was a pause, a puzzled silence. "What are you talking about? This isn't that business about there being a body buried there, is it? Now, Rachel—"

"No!" she said. "Yes. I don't know. Thornton Fuller's dead. He was killed. By a hit-and-run driver. I found the body. The poor boy. I spent all afternoon with deputies. He was up on the ridge. I had to go back with them—see it all again. He'd been riding his bike."

"My God, Rachel," Henry said, suddenly sobering. "I'm sorry. That must have been unpleasant if you weren't expecting it."

"It would have been unpleasant if I *had* been expecting it," she answered angrily. "It was unpleasant, period. No, worse than unpleasant. Thornton's dead. Doesn't that mean anything to you?"

"Of course it does. And give my condolences to his aunt. It's unfortunate. But it's not exactly the same as if the president died. This is not a tragedy of major import. Try to put this into perspective. What's he to Hecuba, or Hecuba to he? It isn't as if a great intellectual light has been switched off. Get hold of yourself."

"I'm not talking about intellect, I'm talking about feelings," she said. "Will you stop being so flippant? Will you listen?"

"I *am* listening. You've been on edge lately."

"I've been drenched in death lately, now it's putting in personal appearances, and it's getting to me, Henry. I think I want out of this...."

"Dear, you don't know what you want," he soothed. "I told you. You're on edge. You've had a bad experience. But look at it this way: as bad as it was, you got your feet wet. Today we reached the same sort of spot by different paths. You've seen a real crime scene, you've seen police work. If you approach this scientifically, it can be a very positive, career-enhancing experience. Not on the same level as mine, of course, but very positive."

"Henry! Will you stop being so cold-blooded?"

"My dear, I have to be cold-blooded. It's my job. It's yours, too. All right. You're upset. That's perfectly natural. You're experiencing some self-doubt. Everybody does at the phase you're at."

"Henry, I'm experiencing doubt about *everything.*"

"Dear, please listen. That is perfectly normal. And if it'll put your mind at ease, I have more information on those 'smugglers.'"

Oh, Henry, Rachel thought tiredly. *I'm not a child who needs distraction. I'm a grown woman and I need... Oh, I don't know what I need anymore.*

"What?" she asked without enthusiasm. "What about the smugglers?"

"First, they actually did rent my place—now, there's a thrill. But second, nobody's proved they're actually smugglers. They're nothing for you to worry your lovely head about," he assured her. "One's under surveillance in London. The other's headed for Japan. If they're guilty, it's a matter for federal authorities, not a young woman in Missouri. Nobody's proved anything whatsoever happened in Sangria. And none of these people is near you. You're safe.

"Furthermore," he went on, "federal agents looked in the basement of the condo. With metal detectors and shovels only a few months ago. They were looking for hidden artifacts. It was wasted effort. There was nothing there. Certainly no body. But their poking around is probably what set the story off in the first place. There's *no* body."

"Thank you, Henry, that's very comforting," she said, but she wasn't comforted. After all the emotions that had raged through her this afternoon, she felt curiously empty, drained of all feeling.

"The feds are closemouthed, but I got that much."

"Thank you. I appreciate it."

"Rachel, dear, I have to go. I'm having dinner with the medical examiner. I wish you were here. I know what you're doing seems tedious and sometimes traumatic. I know that this business with Thornton is unsettling. I wish you could be here in the field with me. Everything would look different. If I were young again, I'd do this full-time. God, it's exciting."

"I'm sure it is," she said, the same hollowness filling her, almost choking her.

"I'm late. It's a circus up here. I'll call again when I've got more time. So calm down and take it easy. Promise?"

"I promise," she said without conviction.

"Kiss-kiss," he said, and hung up.

Rachel listened to the hum of the line for a moment, then hung up, too.

She sat on the couch, wondering if she was going to dissolve into tears again. No, she thought. She had no strength left to cry. She had no strength left for anything. It was as if Henry had somehow stolen the little she had left, leaving her desolate, used up and useless.

She pressed her forehead against the back of the couch, wishing there were someone to lean on, to hold her, to stroke away the horrors of the day. She had yearned to reach out to Henry, but he seemed unreachable. Purposely, years ago, he had distanced himself from the sort of things she was feeling.

She sat in the lengthening shadows, trying to regain her inner balance. Then she heard the sound of tires crunching on gravel. She sat up straight, startled.

For a wild moment, she thought that Henry had heard the need in her voice, after all, and come to her. But that was impossible; he was too far away to reach her this soon. She only prayed it wasn't the police again.

Then she heard the happy hoot of Mercer's laughter and a shy giggle that sounded like Kip's.

Heavens, she thought, leaping to her feet, the children. She had forgotten about picking up Mercer. She glanced at her watch in panic. It was seven o'clock. She was two hours late.

What kind of mother was she? she wondered in shame, to forget her own child so completely? Yet she was glad Mercer had been kept separate from these terrible events; unconsciously she must have wanted the child at a distance from what had happened.

Rachel hadn't been able to marshal strength for herself, but now it surged back to her for Mercer's sake. She'd have to be told about Thornton. And Jay must be, as well. And Kip. She winced. Telling Kip would be the worst; he would take it hardest and be most frightened.

She stiffened her back and moved to the front porch. Mercer flew up the stairs and threw her arms around Rachel's knees. "Where'd you go, you naughty mom? You didn't come, and we couldn't find you. We came before, looking. Your car was here, but you weren't. Kip was worried—but I wasn't."

Jay and Kip stood beside the Corvette, looking up at her. Kip's face alarmed Rachel. It was tense and wan, as if as soon as Mercer departed from him, most of his life force left him, too. He carried an odd clown doll. It was old and faded, and he clutched it to his chest rather desperately.

Jay, too, looked disturbed.

"I . . . I'm sorry," Rachel said, smiling as reassuringly as she could. "I got called away. I should have phoned. Have you eaten? You must all be starved." Mentally she made a frantic search of her cupboards and refrigerator, wondering what would make the children happy.

"A pizza," she suggested with forced cheer. "Mercer, you and Kip go catch minnows, and Mr. Malone can help me make a pizza. Would that be fun?"

She made eye contact with Jay, trying to smile at the same time as sent she him a frantic mental message. *We have to talk. Do you understand? We have to talk alone, you and I.*

"We ate," Mercer said. She tried to slide down the banister, but failed. "Mr. Malone took us to town. We went to McDonald's."

"Then," Rachel said, with the same false geniality, "why don't you catch minnows while it's still light? I'll fix Mr. Malone some coffee."

"Okay," Mercer said, and tried to get back down the stairs by turning somersaults. Jay snatched her up and set her on the ground. "You want to break your neck?" he asked.

"I'm immortal!" chortled Mercer. "Kip and me both!" She snatched Kip's hand and headed for the shore.

"'Found a peanut,'" she sang. "'Found a peanut just now . . .'"

Jay stood beside the Corvette, staring up at Rachel. He waited till the children reached the edge of the lake. "You really want me to come in?"

"I desperately want you to come in," she answered, her smile gone.

An unreadable look flickered in his eyes as he studied her face. "Something's wrong."

"Yes. Come in. I don't want the children to hear. I don't know how to tell them." She paused, biting her lip. "Especially Kip."

She turned and went inside, wanting the security of the house. He waited a moment, then followed her.

She kept her back to him, no longer able to keep up the smiling facade. Through the glass doors she watched the children play on the shore, Mercer with her minnow bucket and Kip keeping tight hold of his doll.

Jay stepped in front of her, blocking her view. "What's wrong?" he demanded, frowning. Then he frowned harder still. "It smells like you've been drinking. What in hell is wrong?"

She wiped her mouth self-consciously with the back of her hand. "I haven't been drinking. I had a drink." She took a deep breath.

He studied her with growing consternation, one dark eyebrow cocked. "Rachel?"

"Thornton's dead," she blurted. "It was a hit-and-run. Up on the ridge. He'd been on his bike."

She thought his face blanched. She backed away and leaned weakly against the counter, watching him.

He moved toward her, putting his hand on her shoulder. His hand was strong and warm, and she did not resist it. "Dead? When?"

She shook her head helplessly. "I don't know. But, oh, Jay... I found him. Coming home from your place. I saw vultures circling the ridge. I went to look. And I found him."

"My God," he said. He glanced at the glass deck doors, drew her away from them into the hallway where the children couldn't see them.

He put his hands on either side of her face, bent toward her intently. "Are you all right?"

She nodded, glad of his touch. His touch was like life.

"I don't know how to tell the children," she said. "It's going to scare them. It's just like Thornton said—he told and he died. We're going to have to think about this very carefully. Especially for Kip. He's a lot more vulnerable about this sort of thing than Mercer."

"You're shaking," he said softly. His hands moved to her arms again, running up and down them reassuringly.

"I've been shaking all afternoon," she said with chagrin. "I thought I'd be hardened to something like this. I'm not."

"Nobody should be," he said, shaking his head.

"Some people have to." She swallowed hard.

"No, not you," he breathed. He smoothed her hair back from her fevered cheek. "Never you. Thank you for caring about my kid. My God."

She drew in her breath sharply. What she had wanted from Henry she was getting from another man—touch, strength, comfort. It wasn't right. Not under Henry's very roof.

Abruptly she turned from Jay, walked back into the living room. Her face burned where his fingers had touched.

"Rachel?" He followed her. He came up behind her, putting his hands on her arms.

She shrugged away his touch. Slowly he let his hands drop, but her skin tingled wildly where they had gripped her. She stared out at the children with determination. "We have to think of a way to tell them that won't frighten them."

"I know." Jay's voice was a soft rasp.

"Kip doesn't want to let go of that clown doll," she said. "I never noticed him clinging to a toy before."

"He does. At home. It's usually a rabbit. With satin in its ears. The clown is something new. I don't know where he dug it up. He's been . . . funny since yesterday."

She turned to him. "Jay?"

"You're good with kids," he said. "You're good with my kid."

Don't look at me that way, she thought miserably. She turned her eyes away, once more watching the children playing at the shore.

"You were even always kind about Thornton," he said.

"It wasn't hard," she said. Tears stung her eyes at the mention of Thornton's name. "He was gentle. He was sweet. He really was."

"It was hard for me." He paused. "I...I could have been better with him. He hit a raw nerve in me."

"I know," she said, the tears smarting harder. "It wasn't your fault."

"I'm sorry he's dead. I'm sorry for his mother. I'm sorry you had to be the one to find him. Are you sure you're all right?"

"I'm fine," she insisted, but her chin quivered slightly. "But what do we tell the children?"

He moved closer to her. She could feel the heat of his body. "How about nothing—at least for now. Let them get a good night's sleep. Tell them in the morning."

She nodded. "I don't suppose Minnie will have the group tomorrow. Not with this. Thornton is—was—her nephew. But they should go back when it starts up again. All the children who knew him—they'll need to talk about it. To face it. I hope she can handle it."

"Maybe you could help her." His voice was gruff and his breath tickled her ear.

"Me?" She wiped her eyes and shrugged. "I can't even think of a way to tell our own. Do you suppose it'd be better if we told them together?"

He stepped more closely still, so that she felt his body brushing hers. He slipped his arm around her waist. He drew her back against him so that she leaned against his length. This time she was too tired to resist him, and he felt too good, altogether too good.

"Yes," she said, resting her head against his shoulder. "We probably should. Tell them together."

"Kip handles everything better when Mercer's there." Jay wound his other arm around her waist. His voice was rough, but his words were gentle. "I told you. He loves her."

He loves her. Again the words haunted her. But it felt good to hear of love after the long afternoon filled with death. She let him pull her nearer still. She closed her eyes.

"I seem able to handle everything better when you're there, too," he said in her ear. He kissed the side of her throat.

"Jay..." she said, feeling trapped, yet strangely languid, unable to fight, not wanting to.

He kissed her ear again. "I know. Not in another man's house. Come with me. You and Mercer. You shouldn't be alone tonight. Not in this house."

She shook her head. "No. Nothing's wrong with this house. Authorities searched it. They searched the basement."

His arms tightened around her. "Castor Bevins didn't say anything about *that.*"

She shook her head again, forced herself to open her eyes. "Maybe he didn't know. Or maybe he couldn't tell. The federal authorities are secretive. They like to keep things confidential. That's just the way it is."

His lips were so near her throat they seemed to burn her. "I keep forgetting." His voice was a ragged whisper. "You know things like that. Who told you about the search? Your friend?"

She stiffened in his embrace, but he held her fast, his lips still nearly touching her throat. "Yes. My friend. And this is his house. And I can't—"

He turned her to face him. "I know you can't. Don't stay here. Come home. With me."

"No," she breathed.

"Yes," he answered. "Both of you. Come with me." He bent so that his mouth took hers. He knew she needed gentleness, and he gave it to her. He was not used to being gentle, and the effort cost him a good deal of restraint. He and Cindy had always made love with high animal spirits, a youthful abandon. But this woman was different and so, now, was he.

Hunger for her burned in him, bright and fierce. He drew her to him tightly, not trying simply to take her, but trying to build a shelter for her in his arms, a shelter where she would feel safe and feel wanted because she was with him. A shelter where she would *be* safe.

"Come with me," he repeated against her lips.

"I can't," she said. "I can't."

But then he kissed her again.

KIP SEEMED shyly delighted and somehow relieved that Rachel and Mercer were coming to his house. Mercer looked knowing.

"Is this a date?" she asked, hanging over the back of the front seat, her head next to Rachel's. "Will you kiss and stuff?"

Jay laughed, but Rachel blushed. "Certainly not," she said. Coming with Jay seemed more rash by the second.

Mercer prodded her mother. "Can Kip come over to our house tomorrow night? And Mr. Malone?"

"We'll think about tomorrow night when it gets here," Rachel said, staring ahead so she wouldn't have to look at either Mercer or Jay.

Neither she nor Jay had said anything to the children about Rachel and Mercer's spending the night. Rachel was growing surer that she didn't *want* to spend the night, even if it proved to be a perfectly innocent night.

At the same time, after finding Thornton's body, she didn't want to be alone with only Mercer, isolated in the dark woods. She'd had a shock, and a kind neighbor was taking her in; that was all, she tried to tell herself. But that wasn't all, and she knew it.

"I'm too young for dates," Mercer said, then yawned in Rachel's ear. "Kip and I are plutonic."

"Platonic," Rachel corrected automatically. "Cover your mouth when you yawn."

"Are you and Mr. Malone platonic?" Mercer asked. She yawned again, this time covering her mouth.

"Yes." *This is a terrible idea,* Rachel thought.

"Are you and Henry platonic?" Mercer persisted.

Rachel leaned her elbow on the car window and her chin against her fist in frustration. "That's not a polite question. Now sit down."

"Why isn't it polite?"

"Mercer, sit," Jay said out of the side of his mouth.

Surprisingly Mercer sat, flopping into the tiny back seat.

"Did I show you my rabbit?" she asked, unfazed.

She thrust a well-worn cloth rabbit between the two of them in the front seats. It was a beanbag toy and had a large piece of duct tape mending its stomach. "I brought him to meet Kip's rabbit. If they were real, we might get little rabbits. But toys are platonic."

"Yes. You showed me." Rachel nodded, glancing absently at the toy. The rabbit was old, positively ugly, and for the life of her she couldn't remember where Mercer had gotten it. But she had too much on her mind to worry about a silly beanbag rabbit with duct tape on its stomach.

"This rabbit is from the planet Pluto," Mercer chattered. "Space aliens brought him. He just appeared. They beamed him down. He's Plutonic. And platonic."

I can't do this, Rachel thought, cradling her aching forehead in her hand. *I can't. What was I—crazy?*

When they reached Jay's house, it loomed silvery in the early moonlight. The children ran immediately to Kip's room to play, though Kip was slowed by fatigue, and even Mercer seemed tired. Rachel knew they would fall asleep within the hour, and then she would be alone with Jay. He'd made his intentions clear, and she had as good as agreed.

She stood uneasily in the middle of his large living room. He came to her side, pausing to pick up the engine of a toy train that lay on the carpet. His hair gleamed darkly in the lamplight, and his eyes were as blue as flames.

"Second thoughts?" he said.

She held his gaze. "Second, third and up to infinity."

He set the train down on the coffee table. "Because of your friend?"

"Yes," she said. "Primarily."

He nodded curtly. "I'll take you back if you really want. But sit for a while. Think it over. I'll get you a drink. You're still overwrought."

He went to the bar, poured her a glass of sherry. She took it and sat primly on the edge of the sofa, her jeaned knees together. "Aren't you having any?"

He cocked an eyebrow, shoved his hands into his front pockets. "I *can't* have any. I had a little problem with it. For a while. After she—my wife—died."

"Oh." She stared down into her sherry.

"Rachel?"

She kept her eyes on the sherry. "Yes?"

"I owe you an apology. About Missy Proteus." He paused. "This'll sound crazy to you. I called her father this morning. After I left your place. He told me she was dead. He said it twice and then hung up. I...guess he got word and never notified anybody. What I said to you this morning— I was out of line. I'm sorry."

Her head snapped up and she met his eyes. His expression seemed more weary than bitter. Thornton's death had driven all thought of Missy Proteus from her mind, but now memory of the girl rushed back to haunt her. She knew she had to tell Jay.

"No. She's not dead—or if she is, he doesn't know it," she said. "I called him, too. This afternoon." She paused, then plunged on. "And I talked to Mercer. She said Thornton didn't tell them it was a dead man, just a dead 'person' that was brought to my house—but not necessarily buried there. He might have meant a woman. But that still doesn't mean it was the Proteus girl, Jay. It can't."

"What?" The corner of his mouth drew down in disbelief.

She repeated her story, and Jay frowned. "Was Proteus drunk?" he asked. "When you talked to him? He sounded a little drunk when I did."

"Yes. Very drunk by the time I called," she said, remembering. "At first he told me she was dead, but then he said only dead to him. I don't think he has any idea where she is or what's happened to her. Or that he cares."

She shivered. She'd hated the way Proteus had talked.

She took a deep breath. She felt as if she were taking a step off a cliff, about to have a sickening fall. "He said she was wild. He said she dyed her hair, and it turned out greenish, and she had a tattoo—and wore feathers in her ears."

"She what?" Jay demanded. He got to his feet and stared down at her, his fists clenching.

Why am I telling him this? she wondered tiredly. *I'm telling him because I have to be honest with someone.*

"He said she wore feathers in her ears," she repeated, shrugging. "He must have meant feather earrings. He said she dyed her hair, and it turned green." She paused, then forced herself to go on. "Bleach can do that sometimes."

They sat in silence, both thinking of what he had found in the burning place: the two small feathers and the single hair caught in their binding copper.

Her eyes met his again, and she shook her head hopelessly. "But don't you see that means nothing? A single hair? A broken earring? None of it proves anything. It doesn't even mean she was ever in this house. It doesn't mean she's dead. Nothing proves anybody was murdered, let alone her."

They stared at each other, Jay's gaze unwavering and his face taut with some force she couldn't name: stubbornness, idealism, conviction—perhaps fanaticism. She couldn't say, and she was too worn to cope with it.

Irritation welled up in her. "Oh, don't look at me like that," she ordered. "I know what Thornton said, and I know he's dead, and I know what the children will think. But I'm not a child, and I won't believe it. Not because of some drunken lout or some burned carpet or one hair. Not because of some *feelings* you have. Isn't there enough death in the world? Why do you have to go looking for more?"

"I'm not looking for death. It keeps on finding me."

"I can't take any more," she said with passion. "And I shouldn't be here. You said you'd take us home. I want to go."

"Rachel?"

She looked into the dark depths of the sherry. "What?"

"I won't talk about it anymore, all right? I didn't mean to upset you. I would never want that. I'm sorry."

"I want to go back."

"Rachel?"

She bit her lip. "What?"

His voice was quiet. "I want to sleep with you. You know that."

She knew. She shook her head and shrugged without raising her eyes. "I can't. I told you. I'm engaged—or almost. Besides...the children. And I can't humiliate Henry. I was insane to come here. I'm sorry."

He was silent for a moment. "You didn't say you didn't want to," he said with the same quiet.

"No," she agreed. "I didn't say it. I'll say it now—I don't want to get caught up in something like this. I don't want a fling."

"A fling isn't what I had in mind."

She looked up at him resentfully. "I mean it. I don't want a one-night stand or a summer romance."

"I said that isn't what I had in mind."

"Don't say things like that," she said, setting the sherry down. She couldn't drink it. She picked up the toy train and spun its wheels uselessly. "I came here because...I was stupid. I just didn't want to be alone, that's all." She looked away, ashamed.

"I didn't want you to be alone. Either of you. I'd worry."

"Worry?" she asked uncharitably. "Why?"

"I want the two of you safe," he said intently. "I want you taken care of. Maybe I'm not going about it right."

"We don't need taking care of. *I* can take care of us."

"Yeah?" His mouth took on its cynical twist. "Then why are you getting married?"

She took a deep breath to give him an answer and found she had none. Why had she considered marrying Henry? It was no longer clear to her. It no longer even seemed right to her. In fact, it seemed impossible. Jay stared at her in challenge.

She was relieved when Kip appeared. He came trundling out of his room, the clown doll under one arm, his rabbit

under the other. He was barefoot and looked almost stupi-
fied with fatigue. He gazed at Rachel with weary hope.
"Mercer falled asleep on my bed," he said. "I'm scared to
sleep."

"Don't be scared," Rachel said with a sigh. "Come here.
Lay your head on my lap. I'll sing to you."

Wordlessly, he clambered onto the sofa beside her and
settled down, his old rabbit and the clown doll in his arms.
He snuggled close to her, laid his head in her lap, closed his
eyes and somehow managed to get his thumb in his mouth.

She gazed down at him. He was a beautiful little boy, fair
and finely boned. And he always seemed frightened, he always seemed sad; he needed so much attention. She stroked
his hair and started to sing a long, lulling song about an old
rocking chair.

Gradually his tense features relaxed, his small body went
still. He breathed deeply, and once in a while his mouth
twitched around his thumb.

Rachel kept looking down at him. She didn't want to raise
her eyes, because she knew Jay was watching her. "We
should put him to bed," she said.

Jay stepped toward them, but she didn't want to chance
even that much contact with him. She shook her head.

"I'll take him," she said quickly. Easily she wrapped her
arms around the child and hoisted him to her lap. He was
warm and limply heavy. She rose, holding him.

"I'll get the door," Jay said. His voice was husky.

Rachel tried to keep her attention on the little blond-
haired boy in her arms. He made something in her ache. She
had always wanted another child, at least one more. She had
always wondered what it would be like to have a son. With
Henry, she knew there would never be other children.

Jay pushed open the partly shut door to Kip's room. Toys
were strewn everywhere, and on one plaid-covered twin bed,
Mercer lay in a carefree sprawl, her hair spilling over the
pillow. The beanbag rabbit had fallen to the floor beside her,
its bandaged stomach in the air.

Rachel lowered Kip to the other bed as Jay drew the sheet and coverlet back. She tucked the sheet around the boy, then went to Mercer. She took off her child's shoes, tucked them beneath the bed, then managed to get Mercer, too, under the covers.

By the time she had finished, Kip was whimpering slightly. He had lost hold of his clown doll and was reaching for it ineffectually in his sleep. Rachel put it back in his arms and he stilled.

She rose and turned to face Jay. She felt odd, awkward, because they had just played out such a domestic scene together and it seemed an act of great intimacy. She had sung to his son, held the boy in her arms, and somehow it had felt right.

Jay stood watching her. Although one black brow was bent in a frown, she was amazed to see a strange glitter in his eyes, something like moisture.

He stepped quickly from the room. She did, too, her heart pounding. He reached back inside the room, switched off the light, pulled the door shut silently.

She stared at him in perplexity. Had a tear really glimmered in his eye, even for a second? The thought dismayed her.

He looked down at her almost angrily. "That's the first time I ever saw somebody sing him to sleep—since my wife died," he said. He made a restless, frustrated move with his shoulders. A muscle jerked in his cheek.

He clenched his fist and leaned it against the wall. He glanced up at the ceiling, his jaw taut with emotion, then down at her again.

"See," he said between his teeth, "I'm not like your friend. With me it isn't all reason and logic. I *need* you. I need you for a lot of things. For one, to teach me to take care of him. I'm not very good at it. In case you haven't noticed."

He nodded toward Kip's door. His face went hard, but he swallowed. "I need you—to teach me."

He reached out for her hand. "Please," he said, his harsh voice breaking slightly. "Besides, I want you so much. And you want me, too—a little—I think."

She could not help herself. She went into his arms.

Chapter Eleven

The first time they made love, it was wildly and with hunger. He took the time to make sure that sex between them was safe; it was the only instant of pause.

They had found themselves in his darkened bedroom, Jay shutting the door and locking it behind them as he held her to him with one arm and kissed her desperately. He kissed her until she was faint with desire, perishing with it.

Their clothes were strewn across the carpet, her body was bare, so was his, and they were lying in bed. He embraced her, pulling her as close as possible to him. She strained to be nearer still.

His hands ran over the smoothness of her naked flesh as he kissed her lips, her eyes, her temples, her throat. He kissed her breasts until they ached with pleasure.

Their hands touched all the secret places where pleasure is received and given, and when at last he entered her, he kissed her mouth again until both of them were breathless and mad with it.

She felt caught in a headlong and irresistible current of passion and seemed to die in it. Mind and body, she submerged in passion, let it close over her and take her. She reached its sweetest, most drowning depths just seconds before he did, and they shuddered together, clasping each other close and kissing as deeply as they could.

They lay in each other's arms. Rachel pressed her face against the thick silky hair of his chest, her eyes shut and her heart pounding. He held her against him, one arm around her waist, his free hand caressing the back of her neck. Neither of them spoke. They only held each other and touched.

The second time they made love it was slowly, deliberately, with a tenderness that made her weak.

"Do you like this?" he would ask.

"Yes, oh, yes."

"And this?"

"Yes, yes."

"What do you want? Tell me. Let me."

He was a man born to make love, she thought dazedly. He treated her body almost with reverence, yet with bold curiosity and daring. She felt herself blooming like a flower that could open only under the touch of his hands and lips; he made her want to smile and cry at the same time.

At last he swept her away again, this time on a lazier, more sensuous stream of desire, although it culminated in the same urgent whirl of need and delight.

Exhausted, she lay once more with her head against his chest, listening to the steady drumming of his heart. He was warm and moist with sweat, and if she touched her tongue to his flesh, he tasted of salt.

"I should go," she said at last. "I should take Mercer and go home."

"I want you to stay," he said, drawing her closer, holding her more tightly.

"No," she protested. "The children will know. They'll talk."

"Let them. I'm not ashamed."

She was silent. She placed her hand over his heart, felt its strong beat beneath the hair of his chest.

"I am," she whispered unhappily. "And I should be."

"No," he said, and kissed her. "You shouldn't. Is it about your friend?"

The shame swelled larger in her. She would have turned from Jay, but he held her fast. She had never made love with Henry like this. She had never made love with Henry at all. That was one of the things she liked about Henry, that he made no sexual demands. He never would. He joked he was past such foolishness.

She had almost been ready to promise her life to Henry. She had given him charge of her career and lived in his house and had planned to follow in his footsteps, continue his work.

"Listen to me," Jay said, taking her face between his hands. She could barely see his shadowy face in the darkness. "Listen. You don't love him. You couldn't and be this way with me. You had to find out, that's all. And this is how."

He kissed her again. Rachel's lips trembled when they parted from his. "It's not that easy," she said. "There are his feelings to consider. There are—"

"There are your feelings to consider. Consider them," he whispered in her ear. He wound one leg more closely about hers.

"It's too fast," she said to his shadowy face. She felt as naked emotionally as she was physically. "I need time. I can't be his fiancée one day and your...mistress the next. I don't want to be a mistress."

"You already are. You're mine." His fingers twined through her hair again, tangling in it.

"I can't. It's too fast. It's too much for the children to cope with at once. We haven't even told them about...about the other yet."

He was silent, holding her close.

"You know it's true," she said, hating that it was.

"The kids don't have to know about us," he said. "Not yet."

"They'll suspect. Mercer will, I know."

"I want to sleep with you. I want to know you're here, safe, in my arms."

"I'm not safe in your arms."

"It's the only place you're safe."

"No."

"Yes." He kissed her. "Believe me. Yes."

The third time they made love was bittersweet. Her guilt and fears tinged it. He was determined that she feel neither guilt nor fear, only pleasure, only love.

SHE AWOKE in the guest room, the sun pouring through the white sheer curtains. Her outer clothes and bra were stacked neatly on the dressing table. She wore her panties and one of Jay's T-shirts.

She had fallen asleep in his arms. At dawn he'd awakened her, kissing her ear. He took her to the guest bedroom, gave her the panties and shirt, told her he'd think of a way to explain her sleeping over. Exhausted, she fell asleep worrying.

Now Mercer pounded on the door. "Mom! Mom! Mr. Malone says to get up! He's got the car fixed."

Confused, heavy-headed, Rachel arose. She showered in the guest bathroom, brushed her hair and dressed. She didn't want to face the consequences of her own acts.

She squared her shoulders, held up her head and opened the locked door. She felt like an infamous adulteress, making her first appearance after the breaking of the scandal.

Jay stood in the kitchen barefoot, wearing white shorts and a white T-shirt. She liked him in white, she thought shyly. It made his hair seem darker, his eyes bluer.

Through the glass doors to the deck, she could see the children playing at the edge of the lake. Kip still carried the clown doll, even as he waded.

Jay smiled his rare smile, although one brow was drawn down in its habitual frown. "Are you all right?"

"It's ten o'clock," she said, dismayed. "Why'd you let me sleep so late?"

"Because you needed it. And you and I were up late trying to get the car started. Want some breakfast?"

She looked at him blankly. "We what?"

"Trying to start the car. I was going to drive you and Mercer home last night. I was going to move the car to the side door so we wouldn't have as far to carry her. But it wouldn't start. We were marooned. You slept in the guest room. I've 'fixed' the car. Gasket, it seems. Sit. I'll pour your coffee.''

Rachel sat. Guilt and confusion clouded her mood. Jay, on the other hand, seemed almost cheerful.

"Can I fix you breakfast?" he asked, setting a coffee mug before her.

"No, but the kids should eat."

"I've fed them. Even *I* can fix cereal. What about you? Surely you worked up an appetite last night. Or do I need to take you into the bedroom and ravish you again?"

"Don't joke about it." She stared at her coffee and pushed it away.

The cheer died from his face. His face went expressionless, his eyes hard. "Yeah. You need time. Or maybe you don't. Maybe you'd just rather forget it."

"I need time," she said unhappily. "Maybe you're the one who'd rather forget."

His gaze ran restlessly over her body. "Don't worry," he said. "I won't forget."

THEY DECIDED to wait until after lunch to tell the children about Thornton. Rachel wanted to return home to clean up Mercer and change her own clothes. After lunch she and Jay would sit down and talk with the kids, seriously and without condescension.

The children could spend the rest of the afternoon together. Mercer and Kip could sort out their emotions with both parents there to answer questions. Rachel and Jay talked at length about what they would do about the children. They talked not at all about what they would do about themselves.

MERCER WAS WILDER than usual this morning, Kip quieter. He had a troubled look in his eyes, as if his sleep had been filled with nightmares. He was just as uneasy at Rachel's house as his own.

"Why aren't we going to the play group?" Mercer demanded.

"Sometimes Mrs. Crabtree has other things to do," Rachel said vaguely.

"Like what?" Mercer challenged.

"Grown-up things," Jay said. "Your mother told you to take a shower. Take it."

Mercer gave him a long, measuring glance. "You give a lot of orders," she said sassily.

"Yeah," Jay said, putting his hands on his hips. "You got a problem with that?"

Mercer looked from Jay to Rachel and back to Jay. "Not particularly," she said, then made her way to the bathroom, but slowly, at her own pace.

"She minds you," Rachel said ruefully, starting to make a fresh pot of coffee. Kip drifted off to play in Mercer's room, clutching his clown.

Jay leaned against the counter watching her. He still wore his white shorts and white shirt and had added only a pair of well-worn deck shoes. He had extremely powerful legs, long, heavily muscled, his tan crisscrossed by an assortment of scars.

"Kids always mind me," he muttered. "I seem to have a fearsome aspect."

"Mercer's not impressed by fearsome. She's pretty fearsome herself."

"That's why she respects it," he said, studying the way the sunlight fell on Rachel's dark brown hair. It was funny, he thought. At first he'd disliked the little girl. But the longer he was around her, the more he saw something of his own wild childhood self in her. If she'd been a boy, she would have made a hell of a hockey player.

It made no sense, he thought gloomily. He understood Rachel's child better than his own. And Rachel dealt better with Kip than he could ever hope to do. Why? Why did the gods always deal everybody such damned strange hands?

Most troubling, Rachel really felt guilty, he could tell. Not just a little remorse; she was plunged into deep, old-fashioned, gnawing guilt.

Maybe she did love the older guy. Maybe he could offer her things Jay was incapable of giving: education, stability, coolness.

Jay moved to the opposite counter where she stood getting out the coffee mugs. The picture of the guy was still fastened to the refrigerator.

He took it off, scrutinizing it. The man looked dapper, sure of himself, maybe a little too sure. He also looked conceited, with cool gray eyes and a cool, thin-lipped smile. He didn't look like he could love anybody except himself.

Jay remembered Rachel's warm, naked body against his last night. He remembered her passion and sweetness. She wasn't meant for a man like the one in the picture. She couldn't be; he felt it in his marrow, but he damned his situation.

"Is this supposed to be a picture of the perfect husband?" he asked, holding it out for her inspection.

"It's just a picture," she said flatly. She took it from him and he felt a secret twinge of pleasure when she laid it on the counter facedown and pushed it away.

"Your career is tied up with this guy, too, I suppose."

There was mockery in his voice, daring her to talk about it, to admit the relationship was more professional than personal.

She refused the bait. "Maybe. I've been thinking of changing fields. But my sense of honor's tied up with him. And I've seriously compromised it. He's been generous to me. I don't like the idea of disappointing him. He's known in this town. He's come here for years. Or did before his wife died."

She poured the coffee, trying to suppress a frown of unhappiness. She had known Henry slightly when his wife had died. She had been in one of his classes and offered her condolences when she'd heard the news. He had smiled benignly. "She's better off," he'd said, still smiling. He'd patted her arm and walked away.

A month later he'd asked her out for coffee. His wife had suffered a long illness, but he didn't seem to grieve for her.

They'd had little in common after their first youthful attraction, he'd said; they'd had no common intellectual interests to bind them. His marriage had been moribund for years.

At the time she'd pitied Henry, thinking how long he must have been lonely. But now she didn't think Henry even knew what loneliness meant. When she compared the shallowness of his grief to the depth of Jay's ... No, she told herself, such comparisons weren't fair.

She shook her head in confusion and handed Jay his coffee.

"Quite the comfort to widowers, aren't you?" he asked sarcastically. His hand brushed hers, intentionally, she was sure.

She drew back, casting him a resentful look.

"We're going to have to talk about this, you know," Jay said, tenacity vibrating in his voice. "Unless you just want me to go away after today and not come back. Is that what you want?"

Rachel stared up at him, unable to say anything. She remembered being in his arms, in his bed. Tides of feeling she had held back for years had swept her away, and he was the one who had freed them. Yet, if she let him stay, he would sweep away her whole future, as well, and Mercer's, too—the future she had prepared for so long and so carefully. She could not make decisions that swiftly, that rashly. She simply could not.

"I ... I ... won't talk about it now. Not now."

They stared into each other's eyes. His expression was defiant, hers determined.

Mercer came pounding down the hall in her underpants and a green T-shirt. Her hair was damp and streamed out behind her like a mermaid's. Kip ran behind her, holding his clown and sucking his thumb.

Righteous outrage flashed in Mercer's eyes. "Somebody's been in this house," she declared. "In my room. Messing with my things."

She stood with her arms folded and stamped her bare foot for emphasis. Kip looked frightened.

"Oh, for goodness' sake," Rachel said, grateful for the distraction. "Of course somebody's been in your room. Kip. While you took your shower."

"Yeah?" Mercer said, cocking her head. "Well, he said he was looking at my Smurf books the whole time, and Kip doesn't lie. My toys are all put different than they were. In different places. And the door from your room to the deck is broken. And two of my toys are gone. So there."

Rachel stared down at her daughter in disbelief. It was Jay who acted. "Show me the door," he said.

Mercer darted toward Rachel's room, Jay and Kip on her heels. Rachel followed, telling herself that Mercer's imagination must be working overtime.

Jay examined the lock of the sliding door.

"It opened right up," Mercer said importantly. "And now it won't close. Somebody's broken it."

That's impossible, Rachel thought.

"She's right," Jay said, kneeling by the lock. He pushed the door open. "It's been jimmied. Somebody pried it open."

Kip moved against Rachel, as if seeking shelter. She put her hands on his shoulders, gave him a comforting squeeze. But she felt no comfort herself, only a cold, sinking fear.

The door's metal sash was dented, the weather stripping shredded, the lock itself bent out of alignment. The plate glass was fractured by a small crack snaking from the lock.

"See?" Mercer said with satisfaction.

Rachel pulled Kip closer to her, gripped his shoulders tighter. He was trembling.

"Was the thing this way yesterday?" Jay asked tersely, looking at Rachel.

Mutely she shook her head no, too stunned to speak.

Jay pulled the door shut and knelt in front of Mercer. "Okay, kid," he said, his voice grim. "You say your stuff's been messed with. How?"

"Nothing's where it was—exactly," Mercer insisted. "Things are shifted around. Especially in my toy box. And two toys are gone."

"All right," Jay repeated, nodding. He started to reach out to touch Mercer's shoulder reassuringly, then stopped himself. His hand fell back. "Okay," he said. "Listen. Tell me exactly what's different. Can you?"

"You bet," Mercer said, and ran to her room. "We've been burgled!" she chortled. "Burglars have burgled us!"

Jay rose and looked at Rachel. "How reliable is she on something like this?" he asked.

"Mercer? Frighteningly reliable," Rachel said, unable to take her eyes from the snakelike crack in the glass. "She's got almost a photographic memory."

They followed the children to the room and listened as Mercer dramatically explained the difference between where everything *should* have been and where it wrongly was.

Kip solemnly swore that he hadn't touched the toys. Jay looked at him in consternation. The boy seemed so incredibly worried for a child, so unhappy. "Okay, man," he said. "I believe you."

Rachel turned to Mercer. "You said toys were gone. Which ones?"

"My Raggedy Ann. Only Raggedy Andy's left. And my earthling rabbit," she said.

"Your what?" Jay asked, brows drawing together.

"My earthling rabbit," Mercer repeated. "The plush one. The boring one. It was white. With a pink ribbon."

"Earthling rabbit?" Jay frowned. "Explain."

"Not like this one," Mercer said, picking up the worn white rabbit by its ears. "This one's from Pluto."

"Mercer," Rachel said, "where did that rabbit come from? I don't remember it."

"I told you," Mercer said, "space aliens brought it. Come on—let's see if the burglars burgled anything else."

Grabbing Kip's hand, she raced off. Rachel stared after her, almost as frightened as when she had found Thornton.

The house seemed to throb around her, ominous with secrets. It had been invaded, and she felt violated.

She turned to Jay, who looked stormy. "What's this about?" She hugged herself against the chill shuddering through her.

His blue eyes seemed to gaze past her to a place she couldn't see. He shook his head. "Trouble. We've got trouble. I felt it from the start."

Feelings, Rachel thought fatefully, her lips parted. Had he been right all along? Had something once happened in this house, something as terrible as murder?

Her tangled thoughts were cut off by Mercer's cry from the living room. "Hey! The VCR is gone! This guy's a fiend!"

Jay took Rachel's arm and led her to the living room. The VCR was missing. So, from the hall closet, was Rachel's camera. A few other stray items proved missing, as well: Rachel's extra watch, a pair of silver earrings and some costume jewelry.

"It makes no sense," Rachel said, more puzzled than before. Why would a thief take an old VCR but leave her computer? Why her camera, but not Henry's binoculars, which were far more expensive? Why take cheap jewelry and a few toys, yet leave Henry's costly fishing gear?

"I'd better call the police," she said numbly. She dialed the sheriff's office, as she had done yesterday, feeling an unpleasant sense of déjà vu.

A man answered, and when she haltingly explained about the break-in, he took the information without enthusiasm.

"What'd they say?" Jay asked when she hung up.

She shook her head. "He said they'd send a man as soon as possible. He acted as if it wasn't important."

Jay swore under his breath, picked up the phone and dialed the sheriff's department again. "This is Jay Malone," he said, steel in his voice. "I'm at Mrs. Dale's. She just reported a break-in. I want somebody here *now*. I mean *now*. Call Castor Bevins, dammit. I just passed him up on the highway, half-asleep, pretending to watch for speeders. Tell him to get into gear. Or he answers to *me.*"

"Jay," she said between her teeth when he hung up, "do you have to sound so...aggressive? In front of the children?"

He gave her his tight, one-cornered smile. "If I want results. *You* sounded reasonable. You got the brush-off."

"Can we go outside and look for burglar footprints?" Mercer asked. "Can we take the magnifying glass?"

"Yes," Rachel said, "but stay in sight."

"And put your shorts on," Jay said out of the side of his mouth. Mercer was still dancing around madly in her underpants. She ran off to her room. "We're going to be detectives!" she caroled.

Kip stared after her, seeming lost in unhappy thought, his thumb in his mouth.

"Don't suck your thumb," Jay said automatically. Then he looked down and saw the hurt on the boy's face. The break-in had frightened Kip far more than Mercer, and the child's mood had already been mysteriously uneasy.

Jay glanced up, meeting Rachel's eyes. Her face felt stiff with pained worry, but she nodded at him, almost imperceptibly. *Go on,* she thought. *Go on.*

He leaned down and swept the boy up in his arms. He gave him a brief and awkward hug. "Don't be scared, kid. Your old man's here."

He set the boy down, looking embarrassed. "Try not to suck your thumb, okay?" Kip gazed up at him, uncertainty in his face. Then he ran to join Mercer.

Rachel was touched. It obviously wasn't easy for Jay to show the child affection. But he tried to do it, and she sensed the boy must know he meant it.

"You looked good doing that," she said softly.

He lifted one shoulder, his mouth crooked with displeasure. "Why's it so hard? Sometimes I think I have something missing in me."

"No," she said, resisting the urge to touch him, to comfort him. "I don't think so. For some people it's harder than others. It's the way they're brought up."

"Yeah," he said, looking away from her. "Well, I'll learn. I have to."

"Yes," she said softly. "But it's worth it."

IN LESS THAN fifteen minutes, Castor Bevins drove up in his deputy's car. When Mercer and Kip saw that it was only fat, stodgy Castor, and that he showed no curiosity whatsoever about Mercer's Raggedy Ann or stuffed rabbit, they went off to wade, looking for tadpoles and clues.

Castor's uniform shirt was already stained with summer sweat, and his neck, as usual, bulged over his collar. "Won't do any good for you to get upset, Jay," he said rather irritably. He took off his hat and mopped his brow with a handkerchief. His hand was bandaged, as if he had injured his fist.

"Truth to tell," he said, putting the handkerchief away, "we're shorthanded. I should be on traffic. And I got mailboxes to check. Somebody's still putting snakes in 'em. One bit me right on the knuckle. And all hell has busted loose. Yesterday it was Thornton, and the crime lab's still checking that out. And last night another terrible thing happened."

"I'm not interested in excuses," Jay said. "The lady's got a problem. I want it solved."

Castor's big face hardened, his eyes narrowed. "Oh, you'll be interested, Jay. You, too, Miz Dale. Like I say, it's a terrible thing. Thornton's mother killed herself."

"What?" Rachel cried. She remembered Ruby Fuller standing in her doorway, her face wild with fear. Rachel's knees suddenly felt weak, and she swayed slightly. Immediately Jay put his arm around her, drawing her close to his side.

"Ruby Fuller? Killed herself?" The frown line engraved itself more deeply between his eyes.

Castor watched their reactions carefully, as if they might prove themselves guilty of complicity in Ruby's death.

"Cut her throat. In Thornton's room," he said calmly. "Losing the boy made her crazy, I guess. Died on his bed. Terrible thing. Terrible."

Chapter Twelve

Rachel tried to shut out the image of Ruby Fuller, dead in her dead son's room. She could not.

"Oh...the poor woman. I was going to go see her—to tell her how sorry I was about Thornton."

"Only place you'll see her now is the mortuary," Castor said bluntly. "Alongside Thornton. When they bring him back from the medical examiner. It's a tragedy, that's the truth."

He glanced out the deck doors at the wading children. Both clutched their toys. "I didn't care to say nothin' in front of the kiddies. Kiddies are sensitive about death and such. Parents should always protect kiddies. Some don't."

He cast his gaze around the living room. "And I want you to know I came here fast as I could—*not* that we don't have other problems. Somebody broke into the Chamber of Commerce last night and stole almost a thousand dollars from the tickets for the Stokes Day Pageant. I *told* the committee members to put the money in the bank. But, oh, no."

"I'm sorry about Ruby," Jay said sharply. "I don't give a damn about the other. What about the break-in here?"

Castor looked at Rachel, narrowing his eyes until they almost disappeared. "You weren't here last night?"

"No," Rachel said, conscious of Jay's arm around her.

"You've got no idea what time this break-in occurred?"

She shook her head.

"Well, not much is missing." He sounded almost bored. "A VCR you say is old, some jewelry you say's cheap, a camera you say's not much, a watch you say's not valuable."

Her losses, next to the news about Ruby Fuller, seemed minimal, absurd. "And some toys," she added lamely.

"Toys," Castor said, hitching up his size fifty belt. "Well, ma'am, lookin' at the clumsiness of the entry, the hit-and-miss things taken, I'd say we're dealing with kids, most likely. They come along in a boat and see the house looks empty. That's the danger of living on the lake. People come up on you in boats. Maybe another boat comes along, the kids get scared off. That's how I see it. Not much to worry about really."

A petty act of thievery and vandalism, Rachel thought, that's how he saw it. Perfectly ordinary. Nothing sinister. His theory sounded logical, reasonable, sound.

But Jay attacked from another direction. "Castor, why the hell didn't you tell me this place had been searched before? That the FBI'd dug up the basement?"

Castor shifted his weight, eyeing Jay coldly. "It was only rumor to me myself. If you know for a fact there was digging here, you know more than me. The federal boys keep things quiet. They don't broadcast their business, and I don't do it for them."

Jay stabbed the air with his finger accusingly. "Castor, federal authorities think smugglers were in this house. On Friday Thornton said somebody was killed in my house and brought here. On Saturday we confronted his mother, and she was terrified. By Monday, Thornton's dead, now she's dead, too—and this house is broken into. Don't you think the coincidences are getting too thick?"

Castor stared at Jay sternly. "I think if Thornton heard about any digging here, he made up a story and scared himself with it. What happened is an unfortunate string of accidents, but it isn't any plot. It isn't any conspiracy."

Jay leaned closer to Castor, eyes flashing anger. "How in hell do you know Thornton's death was an accident? How in hell can you call suicide an accident? How can you call somebody breaking in here an accident?''

Rachel squeezed his arm, unsettled by his questions.

"I want all this noted,'' Jay insisted between gritted teeth. "I want it reported. I want to register an official complaint that I think something's going on here."

"Boy,'' Castor said, regarding him with greater and greater coldness, "I believe you got hit in the head with one too many hockey pucks. But I'll report it. You bet. And I'll say it's your idea, not mine, because I don't want to be the one they think is crazy."

"Listen—'' Jay's voice grew angrier "—I've got two kids out there.'' He pointed at the children wading in the shallows. "Thornton said anybody who told the secret would die. Now we've got to tell them Thornton and his mother are dead—and they know the house has been broken into. These kids could be terrified. But according to you, nothing is wrong. I say something's going on, and I want it checked out, starting now, dammit."

Castor kept his patience, but it seemed to cost him effort. "I told you, if anybody was murdered around here, it was the perfect crime, because nobody else has noticed it. To tell the truth, if some two-bit smuggler gets himself blown away, that's fine with me. Makes my job easier."

"Murder's murder,'' Jay said, his jaw clenched.

"Yeah, well, it helps prove murder if you got a body. Which you haven't,'' Castor said smugly. "It helps if somebody's missing. Which nobody is."

"What about Missy Proteus?'' Jay demanded. "She's missing. Not that you give a damn."

"She isn't *officially* missing,'' Castor said with emphasis. "To be missing, you have to be reported missing."

Jay narrowed his eyes. "She's gone, but she's not important enough to count?"

"I mean,'' Castor said with disgust, "that nobody reported her missing. Don't twist my words."

and I'd love to have you. And Tark has to go away
tonight.''

We're fine,'' Rachel said. ''We're staying with...
ds.''

Well, our door is always open, Tark's and mine. But I
imagine—finding a body. Ugh!'' She shuddered dain-
then lowered her voice. ''Did you hear about...his
her?''

achel nodded numbly. Katherine seemed unpleasantly
ted by the events.

Well, I don't wonder that Ruby did it,'' Katherine said
a *tsk*. ''Letting him ride all over on that bicycle! Irre-
sible is what she was. How could she live with herself?
should have cut her throat, I say.''

he nodded in righteous satisfaction, and the clerk named
lle nodded, too. Rachel blinked, shocked at the two
en's harshness.

It was a blow for poor Sean Alan not to have play group
y,'' Katherine said. ''He got so restless I had to bring
into town. I wonder how long Minnie Crabtree thinks
ll have to mourn? All week, I suppose, with it being both
sister and her nephew like that. Oh, I do wish you and
cer would come stay with us. It'd be so good for Sean
n.''

It's all too bad,'' Adelle remarked. ''But to tell the truth,
ornton used to frighten the tourists—if they didn't know
. It's been a problem. It has. Well, looks like he and
y are going to make up with Nessa at last. It all comes
nd. Me, I always said I'd never fight with Nessa—she
us all in the end.'' She shook her head.

achel felt her nerve ends prickle. She stared at the clerk's
nd, bland face. ''What did you say?'' she asked.

Vanessa Berryman,'' Adelle said, stifling a yawn. ''My,
y days make me sleepy. You know, she runs the funeral
ne. She was Ruby's sister, Thornton's aunt. Wonder how
els, laying out your own family like that. Brr.''

achel frowned. Ruby Fuller had said—more than
e—that Minnie Crabtree was the only living relative that

''Thornton said the corpse had green hair,'' Jay said.
''We've talked to Missy Proteus's father. He said her hair
was green—a bad dye job.''

''Oh, hell,'' Castor muttered, ''that old souse'd tell you
elephants are pink and porcupines are purple. He called up
the sheriff's department once screaming that big spotted
spiders were coming out of the cracks of his house.''

*Now Jay's going to tell him him about the earring he
found and the green hair,* Rachel thought. *And then he'll
believe we're crazy for sure.*

But instead, Jay's anger seemed to evaporate as suddenly
as it had gathered. He clapped Castor on the shoulder companionably enough, although he didn't smile. ''All right. It
gets to me, that's all. We've got an odd sequence of events
here.''

Castor shrugged, but didn't appear mollified. ''Life is
mostly an odd sequence of events,'' he said pompously.
''Your job isn't to invent mysteries. It's to raise those wonderful kiddies of yours out there.'' He nodded toward the
lake, where the children played, holding their toys.

RACHEL AND JAY agreed to tell the children nothing yet.
They feared that learning of the deaths of Thornton and his
mother so close after the break-in would be too much for
them to deal with, particularly for Kip.

Jay repaired the lock as best he could, wedged the door
into place with a block of wood and convinced Rachel that
she should return to his place. He didn't want her and Mercer staying alone in a house so isolated and vulnerable. To
his surprise, she agreed almost without argument.

She had become quiet after discovering the break-in, almost as subdued and troubled looking as Kip. He instinctively knew better than to press her about what she was
thinking; she was somewhere deep inside herself, mulling
things over. He had things to think over himself.

Rachel packed suitcases for herself and Mercer, and Jay
loaded her computer and files into her car. She drove behind him to his place. They passed Castor Bevins, back at

work, parked beside the road apparently waiting for speeders but looking suspiciously as if he was napping.

Mercer and Kip rode with Rachel. ''Will Henry get mad if you stay at Mr. Malone's house again?'' Mercer asked, hanging over the back of the seat.

''Our door's broken,'' Rachel said with artificial calm. ''We can't stay in a house with a broken door. I'll call Henry and explain.''

But deep within she thought, *I can't explain anything anymore, even to myself.*

THAT AFTERNOON, on the surface Rachel and Jay acted casual, confident and not deeply concerned about the break-in. Beneath the surface, he seethed with his feelings and she with a new set of fears and doubts.

Kip seemed especially nervous and anxious to stay near the adults. The day turned rainy, and the children stayed underfoot, leaving Rachel and Jay little privacy.

They learned to speak without speaking aloud, to communicate by a glance, the movement of an eyebrow, a slight shake of the head, a quirk of the mouth.

They knew the only sure way to keep the children from hearing about Thornton and Ruby was to keep them isolated from the outside world for the time being. When Jay realized food was running low, Rachel drove alone into Sangria to get supplies.

With an involuntary shudder, she passed the large Victorian house that was the town's funeral home, Berryman's. She swallowed hard as she drove past.

Ruby Fuller would be lying there now, pale and powdered. Soon, her only son would be at her side, the two of them dead within forty-eight hours of each other.

Over Main Street, the red, white and blue bunting flapped placidly in the breeze. Stokes Day balloons of bright yellow had appeared everywhere, bobbing and cheerful. The banners and posters seemed inappropriately jolly in light of the double tragedy the town had just suffered.

But when Rachel went to the little mall wi market and discount store, no face registe Shoppers looked caught up in their own worl happy or irritable. No sense of loss seemed to

As Rachel left the supermarket she paused paper racks on the sidewalk and bought a cop *gria Herald.* The lead story on the front page r robbery of the Chamber of Commerce. Anothe the events of the upcoming Stokes Day celebra

In the bottom corner she finally found Thornton: ''Local Youth Victim of Hit and R short paragraph followed. The story was contin eight. At the story's end, Ruby Fuller was name ton's survivor. The paper, too, caught up in the ities, hadn't had time to register news of Ruby'

She stuffed the paper into the nearest trash feeling angry and impotent. To Sangria, Thorn was not big news. And Ruby's death was not ne

She put the groceries into the back of her car to the big discount store on the corner to get Kip for swimming. The store windows were plas Stokes Day posters, and outside stood a ven Stokes Day buttons, T-shirts and booklets.

In the aisle of the sporting-goods section, Ra Katherine Menander talking to a plump, middle- with a name tag that said Adelle. Sean Alan stood mother, his finger exploring the interior of his n

''Why, Rachel Dale,'' chirped Katherine. ''Hov I've been trying to phone you—and where's Merc

''With a friend,'' Rachel said vaguely.

''Isn't it a shame about Thornton?'' Katherine eyes widening. ''And I heard you found him. Ick tossed my cookies. I phoned Tark right away, and should *insist* you and Mercer come over to spend But I couldn't get you. When Tark got home this he was *so* disappointed you weren't there. He's su passionate man, my Tark. Won't you come stay

Thornton and she had. Rachel didn't think Ruby had ever mentioned Powell. She was certain no mention had been made of another sister. "Vanessa Berryman," she said carefully. "She's Thornton's aunt. And Ruby's sister?"

"Umm," nodded Adelle, seeming to think it obvious.

"But," Rachel persisted, "Ruby Fuller never mentioned that. She never mentioned any relatives except Minnie."

"That's what I mean," said Adelle, shrugging. "They fell out—Ruby and Nessa."

"Fell out? But why?" Rachel asked, frankly curious.

The clerk shrugged again. "I don't know. It was about the time John Fuller was dying. Thornton's father. I believe it was about two years ago this month. It was some family thing. Well, Minnie and Nessa hadn't spoken for years, but Nessa and Ruby used to be thick as thieves. Especially after Nessa broke off with her own son. It was like Thornton took his place."

Rachel frowned, trying to digest this new information. Nessa Berryman, the mortician, was Thornton's aunt? And Thornton had another cousin besides Powell?

"These small towns," Katherine Menander said, shaking her head. "They seem peaceful. But every one's a book of secrets. And no outsider will ever read the whole thing. That's what Tark always says—no outsider will ever know."

Adelle rolled her eyes knowingly at Katherine. "Honey," she said, "you wouldn't *want* to read the whole thing. I could tell you where the bodies are buried, if I wanted to."

Rachel started so perceptibly that the clerk stared at her. "Where the bodies are buried?" she asked, voice tight.

"Oh, it's a saying," Adelle said with a superior laugh. "It means I know a few secrets about this town."

"Oh," Rachel breathed. "I'm sorry. The phrase . . . startled me."

"I forgot," Katherine Menander said, putting her hand familiarly on Rachel's shoulder. "Thornton told the kids that awful story. About a body. After all that's happened to you, you poor thing, I don't blame you for jumping."

Rachel started again. She had said nothing of Thornton's tale to Katherine. Was the story all over town now? "How did *you* know what Thornton said?"

"Why, Sean Alan overheard," Katherine said. "And I asked Mercer—when we went to see the puppies. Oh, she's a chatterbox, that Mercer!"

"I see," Rachel said, trying to sound calm. In truth, she had a strange, buzzing sensation in her head, like someone who suddenly finds the oxygen running too thin.

"Thornton was scaring the children?" Adelle said, narrowing her eyes. "That boy. I always thought he had the potential to be a menace."

Rachel wished Katherine would let go of her shoulder. The woman's hand was unpleasantly warm and sweaty. "I swear," Katherine said, "it's been like living in a whirlwind this summer. All this going on. Trying to keep an eye on the Rinehart place. Housebreaking a puppy. And Tark keeps having to go out of town—this dissertation's just driving him wild. He was so tired that he ran off the road the other night. He wasn't hurt, thank goodness, but he bashed in the whole front of the car. Had to rent a new one in Joplin."

"Keep an eye on the Rinehart place?" Adelle said skeptically. "Why? The Rineharts aren't gone."

"Yes, they are," Katherine said. "Her father's sick. We're watching their place. There's been vandalism lately. Snakes in mailboxes—have you ever heard anything so icky?"

"Cleve Rinehart isn't gone," Adelle insisted. "I saw him just yesterday. I was on my way to my sister's. I know it was him."

"Well, it couldn't be," Katherine argued. "He's in St. Louis. You must be wrong."

"I'm never wrong about things like that," Adelle persisted. "I've seen that man often enough. He was always hanging around Stokes every summer. If you saw Stokes, you'd see Rinehart, tagging right along. I know him, all right."

Katherine withdrew her hand from Rachel's shoulder and put it on her hip. "Well, I'd hardly say he was *hanging around* Mr. Stokes. He was the ambassador's aide. Cleve Rinehart was like a son to the man."

"Aide's not what *some* people called it," Adelle said with a sniff. "Some people called it something else."

"Now I won't tolerate that sort of talk," Katherine said sternly. "I know the filthy rumors that run through this town, but Tark knows the truth. Ambassador Stokes was as fine a statesman as this country ever produced. And Cleve Rinehart was his trusty right arm. Cleve has nothing but good to say about the man."

Rachel felt almost giddy trying to keep up with the conversation. She kept forgetting about Cleve Rinehart, but now the clerk named Adelle claimed she had seen him back in town, and Katherine, just as stubbornly, insisted he couldn't be. "If Rinehart *was* an aide," Rachel said, desperate to learn more, "what does he do now?"

"He's the dean of a small college outside St. Louis," Katherine said, still looking down her nose at Adelle. "He helps his wife run an art gallery on the side. He started that just since they got married. It's her father's."

An art gallery. The words ignited a blinding flash in Rachel's mind. *There were art smugglers in Sangria last year, and Cleve Rinehart is now in the art business.*

She tried to marshal the flood of new information. She had to keep it straight so she could tell Jay. "And you said Thornton has another cousin besides Powell? Nessa's son?"

"Oh," the clerk said dismissively, "he's estranged from the whole family. Nessa had such ambitions for him. He didn't care. They fought all the time. She wanted him to take over the funeral home, keep it in the family."

"He didn't want to?" Rachel urged.

"Oh, no," Adelle said, and covered another yawn. "Him? No, he's lazy. He's happy with what he's doing."

Rachel looked at the woman questioningly. The clerk smiled a bit superiorly. "He's gone from job to job. Let's see, he's with the police now—if he stuck with that. None of those sisters ever had much luck with their children, if you ask me.''

Nessa's son is a policeman. Rachel's flesh prickled. She opened her mouth to ask Adelle the son's name, but a voice reverberated from the PA system: ''Adelle, to the manager's office. Adelle, to the manager's office.''

''Who—'' Rachel began, but Adelle made a resigned face.

''No rest for the wicked,'' she sighed, cutting Rachel off. She scurried down the aisle and disappeared.

''Who's Nessa Berryman's son?'' Rachel asked Katherine Menander. ''The one she said's a policeman? What's his name?''

Katherine shrugged. ''Who knows? These small towns. It's scandalous. Did you hear the way she gossiped? I can hardly stand it. What? What?'' She glanced irritably down at Sean Alan who mouthed something at her. ''Again?'' she cried, sweeping him into her arms with effort. ''Oh, the curse of diarrhea,'' she said mournfully to Rachel and made her way swiftly down the aisle toward the rest room.

Rachel was left alone, looking after her. She wanted to know more about Nessa Berryman, the funeral director, and her son, the lazy policeman. She wondered, with a frisson of wariness, if Nessa's son could be Castor.

In an age when many people married more than once, his name might not be the same as his mother's. That had been the case with little Evan McInery, hadn't it?

She also burned to know more about Cleve Rinehart. After all, hadn't Rinehart's stepson, Evan, been one of the children who'd heard Thornton's story? Rinehart was connected both to Stokes and the art world, and he had acted oddly when she'd phoned him about Thornton. And now, he just might be back in town.

Suddenly all she wanted to do was get home to Jay. She snatched a pair of nose clips off the shelf, paid and hurried outside.

A dark instinct had captured her, an apprehension that Jay was, in spite of everything, somehow right. Perhaps something terrible really was happening, and they and the children were caught in its dark tides.

As Rachel drove out from Sangria, the rain increased. By the time she reached Jay's house the floodgates of heaven seemed to have broken.

Jay knew from her face that something had happened. Rachel managed to draw him aside and hurriedly explained what the clerk had said about Ruby's family: that there had been a mysterious estrangement between Ruby and Nessa two years ago, and that Nessa, like Minnie, had an estranged son—a policeman.

"I don't understand what it all means," Rachel said, running a hand through her damp hair. "And besides that, the clerk said Cleve Rinehart was connected to the art business through his wife. And she'd seen him back in town. But Katherine Menander insists he's in St. Louis."

She and Jay eyed each other tensely. But Kip was asking for his Smurf videotape, Mercer was begging that the four of them play Parcheesi, and both children needed to be fed.

It seemed to Rachel that she and Jay no longer had merely two children between them, but at least a dozen. The children dogged their heels the whole rainy evening, never straying far.

"I used to love the rain," Rachel said wistfully, just as Mercer was trying to do cartwheels through the length of Jay's house. "Mercer, stop!"

Rachel, curled on the couch, had been trying to read the booklet on Stokes that Jay had bought. Jay sat at the couch's other end going through a stack of old newspapers he'd found in the basement. He rubbed his forehead. "Somebody said once that having a family is like having a bowling alley installed in your brain. He was right."

She smiled wanly. Mercer crashed into something, and hooted with laughter. Rachel's smile faded. "Mercer, stop!"

Kip slowed, but Mercer didn't.

"Mercer, mind your mother," Jay ordered, rising and heading for her. He swept her up under one arm, grabbing a chair with another hand. With lightning speed, he planted the chair in the corner and Mercer on the chair, facing the wall. "Or you end up *here*," he announced.

Kip went suddenly still, and Mercer looked at Jay with blood in her eyes. "Mom? He can't do this, can he?"

"It's his house," Rachel said firmly. "Behave or pay the consequences."

"I never in my life had to sit in a corner," Mercer told Jay. A scheming look lit her eyes. "Henry would never make me sit in a corner."

Jay didn't seem impressed. "Welcome to reality. I'm not Henry. Mind your mother—or warm that chair."

Mercer gave him a resentful glance, but slipped off the chair and led Kip into the corner to play more quietly. Her transformation was sullen, but complete.

"Congratulations," Rachel said ruefully. Henry always let Mercer do as she wished, almost as if he secretly enjoyed her misbehavior.

Jay sat beside Rachel again. "What she needs," he said under his breath, jerking his thumb in Mercer's direction, "is a firm hand."

"I've got a firm hand."

"Firm enough for somebody like him." He nodded toward Kip. "But her? She needs somebody who'll butt heads with her. I was that way myself." He gave her a sidelong glance. "Your friend, I take it, doesn't butt heads."

Rachel curled more tightly into her corner of the couch. "No," she said softly. "He doesn't. He thinks she should go her own way. Express herself."

"Some friend," Jay said darkly.

She sighed and tried to concentrate on the booklet, but the words danced senselessly before her eyes. She should telephone Henry, she knew. It was, after all, his condo that had been broken into, his VCR that had been stolen. Besides that, he might be able to tell her something about the complex relationship between Nessa Berryman and her sisters, and who Nessa's son was.

But foremost, she must tell him she was at Jay's. She must also confess that her feelings had changed. She couldn't marry Henry; she didn't even want to continue working with him, but she dreaded telling him. Henry was usually flippant and cool. Would he be so over this?

Jay leaned over, his hand resting briefly on the back of her neck. She realized he had guessed her thoughts. "I'm sorry," he said. "I know how you must feel." He caressed her neck, touched her cheek, then drew his hand away. He nodded in the children's direction. "It's like being surrounded by spies."

She smiled in frustration. "Exactly."

"And you're more worried than you were before."

She nodded, casting a glance over her shoulder at Mercer and Kip. They seemed deep in play and Mercer was singing her "Found a Peanut" song, loudly and off-key.

"It's because of the break-in. And what you found out in town," he said, watching her closely.

She nodded again. "It's so...complicated. I can't wait for the kids to go to bed."

"Me, either." She saw the hunger flash deep in his eyes.

She turned away. She hadn't meant it that way. She shook her head. "I...I'm worried."

"Yeah," he said, solemnly. "Yeah."

SHORTLY BEFORE eight-thirty, just when Rachel thought the children at last might be growing tired enough for bed, the phone rang. Jay answered it in the kitchen, then came into the living room.

"It's for you," he told Rachel. His taut expression told her trouble was in the air. "It's a man. Maybe you should take it in the bedroom."

Henry, she thought, her heart sinking. Who else would call her? Yet how could he know she was at Jay's house? Uneasy, flooded with guilt, she went into Jay's bedroom.

The phone was on the bedside table. She hesitated, then sat on the edge of the bed. In that bed last night, she had made love to a man. Now, sitting there, she must talk to another man, one she had once thought she might marry.

"Hello?" she said.

"Rachel?" Henry's voice snapped in her ear. "What's the meaning of this? I've had calls. Two anonymous calls—I couldn't even tell if it was a man or a woman—saying vicious things. About you. I didn't believe it. I phoned my place and no answer. But I phone here, and there you are. The calls said you were with some...some hockey player. Explain, please."

Resentment trembled in Henry's voice, resentment mingled with wounded pride. Rachel's mind whirled dizzily. Who could have told him? And why?

Jay's line rattled with static, and Henry's voice seemed far away. Its strength faded, then surged, then faded again. But the force of his indignation was unmistakable.

"I heard you spent last night with him. You just brazenly spent the night with him. Is that true?"

She paused before replying, the blood beating in her ears. The phone line crackled and buzzed. "Yes. It is."

"And now you've actually packed your suitcases and moved in with him? Is that true, too?"

Her mouth seemed cottony, her tongue thick. "Yes. But...but it's not...that simple. Things have happened. Your place was robbed."

"Robbed?" Henry almost screamed. "Robbed?"

"Yes. Somebody broke the deck door to the bedroom. They took your VCR. And some of my things. The police said it was probably kids."

"When?" Henry demanded, his voice rising. "When did this happen? They broke my door?"

"Last night but, oh, Henry, listen, things have been so awful here. Ruby Fuller—she killed herself. Over Thornton. And then your place was broken into, and there's been so much dying and so—"

"I don't give a damn about Ruby Fuller. What about my place? Did you call the police? What else was taken? And why weren't you there? Is this true? Are you actually two-timing me for the whole town to see? After all I've done for you? Do you want to make me a laughingstock?"

Henry's anger pushed her into a defensive position. "I came here last night because I was upset. I'd found a *body*, for God's sake. When I turned to you for comfort, all I got was condescension and not much of that—"

"Don't you *dare* try to shift the blame," Henry retorted. "Just what kind of 'comfort' did you get from this man? Sexual? Is that true? You always claimed you weren't a sexual person. Well? Well?"

She took a deep breath. "I never claimed that. I said . . . I said its power scared me. It still does."

"Answer the question," Henry ordered. "Did you sleep with him? Did you? And the whole town knows?"

"The town *doesn't* know." She ran her fingers through her hair, bit her lip. "I'm sorry, but something happened between us. Between him and me. It just happened."

"I didn't hear you," Henry shouted, determined to overcome the bad connection. "I said, *Did you sleep with him?*"

"Yes," she shot back.

"Now you're going to say you find me sexually inadequate," he accused. "You never complained before. Not when I could open doors for you. Not when I was introducing you to the inner temple of my knowledge. Thank God I never formally proposed to you. Were you sneaking around before, too?"

"No! Never—"

"I thought you wanted intellectual companionship," he went on, his voice bitter. "I thought you wanted professional companionship. My God, I had you living under my *roof*. On my *charity*. Do you realize I hold your future in my hands? What if I decided to be as malicious as you've been? You'd better thank God that I am a rational, objective man."

She took another deep breath, her heart hammering. She listened to the static and crackle of the line. "Henry," she said, "I was going to tell you. Immediately. I wouldn't deceive you. I tried to tell you before—"

"Stay with your stud as long as you want. See if I care," Henry hissed. "But keep out of my house. I'll call the police and *see* that you're kept out. As for your dissertation—"

"Henry—"

"As for your dissertation, I hope you know you're at my mercy. And my mercy is just what you'll have to pray to get. You know what happened today, Rachel? They caught Mr. Fixit. *I* helped catch him. Not only that, he's confessed. I've talked to him. He's an intelligent man. He likes me. We have rapport. He wants me to work with him to tell his story. It'll be an extremely important book. I'd hoped to share the joy of working on it with you. I saw you working with us, the three of us, a splendid team. Instead, you *ruin* the most perfect day of my life."

"Henry—"

"I regret wasting my learning and trust on an ungrateful, sex-crazed—"

She hung up, smashing the receiver back into the cradle. Then she curled up on Jay's bed and wept angrily into a pillow, burying her face in it to muffle the sound.

Part of her mind said that Henry had every right to be furious. But another raged that he had no right to insult and degrade her, to want vengeance. All summer he had ignored her, too excited about his favorite killer to listen to her problems, recognize her needs. All he wanted was for her to be his disciple and to love death as he did.

Well, she couldn't, she thought, her anger mounting. She had always unconsciously flattered his vanity before. And that seemed the only part of the man she'd hurt—his vanity. Now he had turned mean, judgmental—even threatening.

She supposed she had put her degree, her whole future, in jeopardy. She hardly cared. She'd rather go on without Henry's help, independently, in some direction far removed from his.

In the meantime, Thornton was dead, his mother dead, and her own house—no, Henry's house—broken into. She had a headful of fragments and theories that scared her far more than they enlightened her.

Finally, drained, she rose, went into Jay's bathroom and washed her face. She couldn't repair all the damage her tears had done, but did her best.

She straightened her clothing, assumed the calmest expression she could, then walked back into the living room. She still had to play the game she'd played all day: *Don't let the children know anything is wrong.*

But Jay was alone, lounging on the couch, frowning as he thumbed through another newspaper. The kids were nowhere to be seen. She glanced at the kitchen clock. It was a quarter past nine. He must have put them to bed.

"Well?" he said, looking her up and down. "Was that your friend?"

She gave a pained laugh. She sat on the other end of the couch because her knees suddenly felt weak.

"He doesn't want to be my friend anymore," she said, trying to sound unconcerned. "Somebody told him about—" She almost said *us.* But with Jay, she was not sure there was or could be an *us.* "Somebody told him about this," she finished lamely, with a gesture indicating the house.

He scowled. "What?"

She nodded wearily. "Somebody called him. Anonymously. Twice. They said I was here last night. And tonight. That I'd brought suitcases. He's furious. I can't blame him. I hurt his pride badly."

Jay's eyes flashed with angry disbelief. "Pride? He'd let you go because of lousy pride?"

She sighed. "He's got a lot of it."

Jay moved closer to her, slid one arm along the back of the couch. She looked away. She didn't feel she deserved any ease or consolation, especially from him.

"Rachel," he said, his voice low, "I know you're not the kind of person to take this lightly. But believe me, we've got more important things to worry about than him."

She looked at him resentfully. "That's easy for you to say. This wasn't just a personal relationship. It was professional, too. I've probably loused up my entire future and

Mercer's, too. Oh, how *stupid*. Why did I ever get involved with him?''

''You're not stupid,'' he said, urgency in his voice. ''But you're not thinking clearly, either. Rachel, who told him you were here? Who knew? Nobody but you and I and the kids knew. Unless . . .''

''Unless what?'' she asked miserably.

''Unless we're being watched.''

It took a moment for his words to sink in. Then their significance chilled her with a cold rush of terror. He was right. Who could know about them unless they were being watched? Who would watch them? And why?

''Rachel.'' He spoke as gently as he could, although the muscles of his jaw were clenched. ''Rachel, *think*. Nobody except the four of us knew you stayed here last night.''

''Castor Bevins suspected. . . .''

''But nobody *knew* you'd come back here with suitcases . . . unless we're being watched.''

She stiffened slightly, went paler than before. Henry fled from her mind like an irrelevant ghost.

Instead she remembered all the strange and separate pieces of information that had come her way that day, the things she desperately wanted to talk over with Jay and for which there had been neither privacy nor time.

''But why would anyone watch us?'' she asked, her gaze clinging to his.

''Because Thornton was right,'' he said emphatically, taking her by the arms. She shivered in spite of the warmth of his touch. ''Somebody died here. Thornton knew.''

They stared at each other a long, charged moment. She saw the fervent conviction in his eyes.

''You started believing today,'' he said, his jaw still tensed. ''Didn't you? After the break-in. After what happened to Thornton and Ruby. And what you heard in town.''

She nodded numbly. She had to face it now, what she had avoided facing all day. The moment had come.

"Yes," she said, feeling almost surreal when she said it. "I think somebody died here. It scares me. And somebody must be watching us. But who?"

"I don't know," he said, drawing her into his arms. For the first time in months he wished he had a gun. Cindy had never wanted one in the house. Then with Cindy gone, he knew he didn't dare have one; his mood had been so black a gun would have been too tempting.

But now, with Rachel in his arms and the children in their beds, he wished he had an arsenal of guns.

"Who? Why?" she asked again.

"I don't know," he repeated. "I just don't know."

He held her tighter.

CONFESSION

Questions, always questions. Give me some coffee. Another cigarette. Now what?

Why did I call Henry Bissell?

Maybe I had a slight fit of mercy. Maybe I thought Bissell would talk to her, excite her sympathy, and she'd go back to his house, try to think things out. If she was alone with the kid, I could get to the rabbit and nobody'd ever know. With her and Malone together, I had trouble.

Maybe I was showing no mercy at all; maybe I knew I was going to have to kill them all before it was over. Maybe I just wanted Bissell to know. The old one-two punch. One, she's cheating on you. Two, she's dead.

Maybe I even wanted Dale and Malone to know I was watching. It would be dangerous, but I told you, I like the edge.

Maybe I didn't call him at all—ever think of that? There are malicious people around here. My mother, for instance. My dear, sweet mother who always acted so dignified and holier-than-thou. Dear old Mom, the Queen of the Dead. My father was a hypocrite, but at least he was honest enough to admit he was one. Dear old Dad. He bowed to the queen at last, and they both bowed to me.

Chapter Thirteen

Rachel disengaged herself from him. She touched her forehead wearily. "Do you still have that sherry? I can't think. Too much has happened."

He went to the bar, poured a glass and handed it to her.

She took it, glancing uneasily toward the draperies that hid the glass doors to the deck. "Do you think somebody's still watching us? Now?"

He shrugged, his usual frown in place. She knew he believed it.

She sipped the sherry, glad of its distracting burn. It did not seem real that someone could be watching them from the woods. Yet Thornton had watched *her* place. . . .

"Castor?" she asked. "Do you think he's the one?"

He shook his head, unsure. "He's known what we've known from the start. This is his territory. He's given us information. But he's held it back, too. About the feds digging at your house. I can't believe he didn't know that. It's almost as if he's playing with us."

She nodded. Castor had looked at them this morning as if he'd known how they'd spent the night.

"I don't know," he said from between his teeth. He frowned harder this time. "Maybe."

She glanced nervously at the draperies again. "I don't care how it feels. I don't trust him. If you can't trust the police, what do you do?"

"Trust yourself." Jay's face went grimmer than before. Except for the beat of rain on the roof there was silence.

"Do you think," Rachel asked hesitantly, "that the call to Henry had anything to do with the break-in at my place?"

Jay went to the cupboard, took out a glass, filled it with water. "Maybe. Otherwise it's another one of those damned coincidences." He drank the water in two long pulls.

She wondered if it was hard for him not to drink. She took a sip of sherry, wishing she hadn't asked for it.

He set his glass down and stared at the closed curtains as if, by concentrating, he could see beyond them to what lay concealed by the night.

She stared into the last of her sherry, disturbed. Why would someone call Henry? To hurt him? To hurt her? How did the person even know what the situation was between herself and Henry—or did the whole town know? And did she and Jay only imagine people suspected their relationship?

"Was Henry friendly with people down here?" Jay asked.

She raised one brow as if sadly amused. "Henry? Friendly? No. Not outside his own circle. He did know Nessa Berryman. And a few men he fished with—I can't even remember their names."

She finished the sherry, went to the sink, set the glass down and frowned. "But why would anyone break into my—into his house? Why did they take such strange things? What were they looking for? Or were they just trying to scare me?"

He watched her. Her long body was graceful, even in tension. Her profile was lovely, even in worry. He wished at that moment he could give her the world. He couldn't even give her a good answer.

He pushed his hand through his hair. "I don't know what they wanted. I don't know why they'd want to scare you."

Rachel frowned, still staring at the counter. She twisted one long leg nervously. "Except it wasn't frightening, was it?" She looked up and met his eyes.

"I mean," she went on, her brow creasing, "if somebody wanted to scare us, he could have done a better job. Ransacked us, written things on the walls. No, if they wanted to scare us, they'd have done a better job."

She turned from him, biting her lip. It was a lovely lip, he thought, too lovely to be set so sadly or bitten in worry. Pushing aside the curtain covering the window over the sink, she stared into the rainy darkness.

She shook her head. "No," she said. "They wanted something. But what? It makes no sense. An old VCR. A cheap camera. Toys, for God's sake. Cheap jewelry...."

She shook her head again so that her thick hair swung. He clenched his fists to keep from reaching out and touching her.

"Rachel?"

She turned to him. Worry stared out of her eyes, had settled into the troubled line of her mouth. "You know what?" she asked. "If they were looking for something, they must not have found it."

He wanted to reach out to her, but he had no business doing that right now. She needed protection, and so did Mercer and Kip. It was up to him to try to find a way out of this crazy mess. He couldn't see one.

"If they'd found what they wanted," she mused, "why would they keep on watching? But they did. They saw the suitcases. They know we're here. So if it's something they're after, and it's back at the house..."

He raised his eyes to meet her questioning ones. "If it's back at your house," he said, "they've got a clear shot at it now. Nobody's there to stop them."

"Exactly," she said, seeming a bit relieved. "So maybe they're there—not here, watching us." She brightened still more. "Maybe *that's* why they called Henry. Look, let's think this out. Should I make us coffee or something?"

He scowled slightly, too restless to watch somebody else work. "I'll make it." He reached for the coffeepot. "What do you mean, maybe that's why they called Henry?"

She colored, recalling the humiliation of Henry's words. "Easy," she said, her chin high. "He told me not to go back to the house. I'll have to, of course, to get the rest of our things. But he doesn't want me there. So anybody who wants in can get in."

He stared at her in disbelief. "Henry doesn't want you in the house? He'd just kick you and your child out?"

Rachel's face was stiff with control. "It's his right. I...disappointed him. Why would he want me back?"

He tossed the coffee scoop down and faced her. "My God," he said. "What man *wouldn't* want you back? He should crawl here on his hands and knees. If you were mine—"

"I wasn't *his,*" Rachel interrupted, an edge to her voice. "I'm my own person. I just thought, for a time, he and I would be good as companions. I was wrong."

He ignored her objection. "If you were mine, I wouldn't give you up without a fight."

She winced, as if surprised or disturbed by the passion in his words. He wanted to move toward her but did not. She'd needed time, she'd said. He had to try to give it to her.

"What I mean," he said more gently, "is if I left you all alone and somebody came along when you needed somebody, I'd be hurt. All right, angry, too. But, if I loved you..."

He stopped and swallowed. "If I loved you, I'd forgive you anything before I'd lose you. Understand?"

She looked away, disconcerted. She seemed to listen to the beat of the rain. "No," she said. "I guess I don't."

"Rachel," he said in frustration, "you're a psychologist. What would you tell some guy if he said his wife had been with somebody else? Would you tell him to divorce her? To kick her out? Never to see her again?"

She shook her head. "Of course not, if he loved her. He should find out what went wrong. He should work to keep what they had...."

"Right," he answered with his familiar intensity. "And if *I* know it, then a big honcho shrink like Henry should know it." His voice grew lower, raspier, yet more tender. "You should, too, kid."

She managed half a smile. He didn't smile back. Instead, he put on the coffee, then pushed back the curtain over the sink. The sky was just as black and the rain drummed just as hard as before. "I think she died here. Missy Proteus," he said quietly.

"I know," she answered. "I think *somebody* died here."

"I think Thornton was murdered," he said, still staring into the darkness.

"I know," she said.

"It's too damned convenient that his mother died so soon afterward. Cutting her throat. People don't usually commit suicide that way, do they?"

"No," she answered. "They don't."

"So it's possible somebody killed her, too," Jay mused. "Nobody'd suspect. Why should they? Her only kid's dead. She's distraught. Who'd question suicide?"

"Nobody," Rachel said, feeling hollow and frightened again. "Except you and me. And maybe we've lost touch with reality."

He gave her the hint of a bitter smile. "We even think we're being watched. Isn't that what crazy people always think?"

"Sometimes. But we don't say 'crazy' anymore."

Jay's smile died. "Yeah. I forgot. It isn't politically correct."

"Jay? If they've been watching us, is it because they think we suspect?"

He shook his head, unsure. "I don't know."

"Or is it because of something I have? Or we have? And if that's so, what is it?"

"I don't know that, either."

Unwanted tears stung her eyes again. "But if we *are* being watched, and there *have* been killings, we're in trouble, aren't we? You and me and the children. Aren't we?"

"Yeah," he said, letting the curtain drop. "I felt it from the first. You feel it now, too, don't you?"

She was silent for the space of a heartbeat, then two, then three. "Yes," she said, going to his arms. "I feel it, too."

She had come to him, he hadn't gone after her, so it was all right. He buried his face against her hair and held her tightly. He would take care of her if he could. He would watch over all of them if he could. He held her more tightly still, kissing her as if kissing alone could keep her from vanishing.

THEY MADE LOVE with the desperation and tenderness of people whose time is running out. When it was over he held her in his arms, knowing that neither of them would sleep.

"Jay?" she whispered, her fingers toying with the thick hair on his chest. Her breath was warm, tickling his throat.

"Yeah?"

"I should never have been involved with Henry."

"I know." He kissed the top of her head, drawing her closer. His fingertips caressed her cheek. His lips pressed her forehead, then her temple. "I knew that from the first."

Her hand moved up to grip the warm solidity of his shoulder. "I'm going to have to start all over. Scrap my dissertation. Go in another direction."

"That's fine, kid." His finger traced the line of her eyebrow, then her jaw. "People start over all the time. I'm starting over myself. We'll do it together."

"Jay?"

"Yes?"

"What *will* you do? Do you know?"

He sighed heavily. "I don't know. Maybe buy a farm. A farm should be good for a kid. Maybe a sporting-goods store. I don't know yet."

"Jay...I'm frightened."

He ran his hands up and down her body. "Try not to be."

"All this reminds me of what happened when I was little—that canoe trip. At first everything is nice and peaceful and calm. And then suddenly everything changes—it's dangerous. It pulls you down, and you feel you're going to drown in it."

"Don't talk that way," he said, his arms locking around her possessively.

"Jay..."

"Shh," he whispered. "I want to make love to you again. Kiss me."

"Jay..."

"Kiss me. Love me."

She lost herself in the deep wells of desire. She felt as if, after years of wandering aimlessly, she had come home at last.

THEY SAT IN THE KITCHEN at the counter, drinking coffee, listening to the beat of rain on the roof, its tap against the windows. They talked quietly, as always, so as not to wake the children.

Rachel's body still tingled from their lovemaking, and she felt as if they were married, had been together forever.

From time to time she reached out to touch him or he did so to her. It was as if they were assuring themselves that the other was truly there. But their conversation, there in the golden light cast by the kitchen's lamp, was hardly domestic.

As they talked, Jay alternately paged through his stack of old newspapers and Tarquin Menander's booklet on Stokes. Rachel made notes, trying to extract some pattern, some sense from everything that had happened.

"All right," said Jay. "Who knew what Thornton said? Let's get that down."

Rachel wrote out a list:

1. Mercer
2. Kip
3. Evan
4. Me
5. Jay
6. Minnie Crabtree
7. Ruby Fuller
8. Castor Bevins
9. Powell Crabtree
10. Cleve Rinehart
11. The Menanders
12. Henry

"Oh, it's no good," Rachel said in frustration, looking at the length of the list. "Powell said Castor was laughing about it in the coffee shop, so who knows who all heard it? Besides, I have the feeling that if Katherine Menander knew, she would have told everybody. Half the town might know."

"Maybe," Jay said, scanning another newspaper. "But let's keep it narrowed down. How did each person react— besides you and I, Minnie and Ruby?"

Rachel made notations beside each name as she spoke. "Well, you saw Castor—he just seemed amused. Powell acted insulted—as if I were casting a slur on his properties. Cleve Rinehart was the one who acted strange. As for the the Menanders, I don't know. And all Henry said was, 'Poppycock.'"

Jay gazed at the list and frowned. "A few of those people have some sort of relation to Stokes, though."

Rachel nodded and made another set of marks. "Castor? None we know of—we don't even know for sure if he was *with* the sheriff's department when Stokes was here." She put a question mark beside his name.

"But Powell Crabtree knew him, at least. Cleve Rinehart was his aide—and from what Katherine Menander said, he and Stokes were close. As for Tarquin Menander, well, a dissertation takes a long time to research and write. He's an expert on Stokes and he might have known him. Katherine said he'd been down here other summers.''

''And Henry?''

Rachel gave a rueful laugh. ''Henry's been coming here forever, but he's the last one we need to suspect.''

''Isn't that always who did it—the last one you suspect? Was he ever friendly with Stokes? Did he ever say anything about him?''

''Nothing. Not a thing.'' Henry had never mentioned Stokes at all. Wouldn't he have said it if he had known him?

''And if a murder happened in this house,'' Jay said with a frown, ''how would Thornton know? How could he have seen the body?''

Rachel shook her head wearily. ''I don't know. That's always where I run into a blank wall. Oh, Jay, it comes back to me—how I didn't believe it at first. There's no proof. There's no evidence. There's no motive. And yet I *feel* something's happened. And that it's still happening.''

''I know.''

''And if somebody broke into my house looking for something, what did they want? Why did they take such a strange assortment of things?''

''To make it look like a burglary. After all, they broke the door.''

''But why those particular things?'' she asked, wrinkling her brow. ''Or is everything really only in our imaginations? Are we just fooling ourselves, being paranoid?''

Jay shook his head and opened another newspaper. ''Maybe we should stop this. Maybe we should just go to bed and get some rest. That's what I should do—get you into bed and just hang on to you all night, the way Kip does to that rabbit.''

She smiled wanly. ''You mean clown.''

''It used to be the rabbit. Now it's the clown. I don't even know where it came from.'' He rattled the newspaper. ''There are about seven more of these to get through, then let's quit. We're driving ourselves crazy.''

A very small and silent explosion took place in Rachel's mind. She went cold, so cold she felt prickly with it. "Jay?"

"Yeah?"

"You don't know where the clown came from?"

He shook his head and turned a page.

She tried to take a deep breath, but her chest felt constricted. "Jay, that rabbit Mercer's been carrying around? The one she said came from Pluto? I don't know where it came from, either. It just seemed to appear. All of a sudden she had it. And a toy rabbit was one of the things taken from the house."

He looked up at her, one dark brow cocked in an unspoken question.

Her heart beat so hard she could feel it pound against her ribs. "And you noticed the clown just lately?" she asked.

His eyes didn't leave hers. He set down the paper. "Right. It just appeared." He frowned harder. "And that's almost exactly when Kip started acting scared again. He hasn't let go of the thing."

They rose from the table almost simultaneously, their eyes still locked. Then Rachel licked her lips and quickly stepped down the hall to the children's room. Jay followed, standing tensely by the door as she opened it, slipped inside and reemerged with Mercer's beanbag rabbit.

He stared down at it. She held it upside down so he could see the silvery duct tape bandaging its stomach. Neither of them spoke as they moved back to the kitchen. Rachel set the rabbit, belly up, on the table. Jay reached down and stripped the tape away. He turned the rabbit over so that the beans spilled onto the opened newspaper in a cascading rattle.

Rachel held her breath. Then a small object, wrapped in white, hit the table with an unexpectedly heavy clunk. Jay picked it up. It was crudely covered by several layers of facial tissue. Jay unwrapped them.

"My God," he said, and Rachel gasped. There, in his palm, lay a small, heavy sculpture of a peanut, perhaps an inch long. It shimmered with the brilliance of pure gold.

"A peanut?" he said in disbelief, testing its weight in his hand. "This thing feels like solid gold."

She reached to touch it, as if to prove to herself it was real. "I've read about these," she breathed, her fingertips tracing the curves of the shell. "They were buried in the tombs of great kings in South America. Food for the journey to the next world. Grave goods."

She looked up at him. "The pre-Columbian gold. What the authorities were looking for."

"The sort of thing Stokes collected," Jay said, holding the peanut so the rich metal caught the light. "My God, look at this thing. I can see why somebody'd break the law for it. It's like magic. But how in hell did it get into the rabbit? And where'd the rabbit come from?"

"Thornton," Rachel said, feeling colder than before. "He said he had gold charms to protect him. This must be one. It has to be. He must have put them into the toys. I saw him watching the house that night after he told the children about the body. He must have been trying to get it to Mercer."

She shuddered and Jay put his arm around her. Both of them stared at the gleaming gold. "So he was right about the gold," Jay said in a low voice. "That means he may have been right about the body. Even down to the green hair."

They looked at each other.

Rachel felt a frisson of sheer terror. *What we've found is worth killing for. Somebody died in this house because of it; Thornton and Ruby died because of it, and we could die, too.*

"We'd better call the police," Rachel said, swallowing hard. Now she knew all too well why they had been watched. She feared, with sick certainty, that they were being watched still.

She stepped to the phone, picked up the receiver and started to dial. But no comforting hum buzzed from the earpiece, only an ominous silence. She stared hopelessly at Jay. "The line's dead." She stood as if paralyzed.

Jay took the phone from her hand, listened a moment, then set the receiver back into the cradle. He could have told her something comforting, that the rain had taken a line down, or that his phone had been acting strange for weeks, but neither of them would have believed it.

He was thinking the same thing she was: the line had been cut.

He pressed the peanut into her hand, closing her fingers around it. He kissed her briefly, almost brusquely. "Keep this. Get the kids. Grab that damned clown. I'm going to make sure the car starts. Then we're getting the hell out of here."

She clutched his arm. "Jay...don't go out there. There may be somebody. Maybe more than one. Please. Don't go."

"I'm not waiting for them to come in *here*," he said relentlessly. "Our kids are in here. You're in here. And I'm not taking you out into the open until I'm sure the coast is clear and they haven't done anything to the car."

"No," she pleaded, "don't go—please." But he ignored her.

He took the poker from the fireplace and held it out to her. "Take this." Reluctantly she clasped it. It was cold and unwieldy in her hand.

He went to a kitchen drawer and pulled out a carving knife. "I'm going out the back way. Lock the door behind me."

"Don't..." she repeated, but with a soundless movement he had slid the deck door open.

"Don't...please," she said. He stepped past the draperies, out of her sight and into the darkness. The door slid shut behind him.

She stood, frozen in disbelief, then rushed to lock the door with shaking hands. For a long moment, she simply stood, her eyes shut, trying to pray, but too frightened to do so.

It was like the time she nearly drowned, she thought again, dazed. Everything seemed placid, then, without warning, life veered out of control and into overwhelming danger.

A muted rattling noise came from outside, near the front of the house, a clattering like the spill of tossed gravel. She whirled, turning toward the noise, edging away from the glass doors, keeping her back to the wall. She drew a breath and held it, listening.

Only the faintest whisper of the rain filled the silence. She listened more intently.

A scuttling sound, louder than before, rustled again near the front door. She tensed and gripped the poker more tightly.

The children, she thought. *Protect the children*. She moved to the near end of the hallway and positioned herself like a guard. She stood, listening to the silence.

She flinched when she heard a smothered clash outside, a sound that could have been body striking body. Faint irregular thuds came to her ears, and rustling, and the breaking of small branches. *They're struggling*, she thought.

Then she heard a soft zinging sound that she didn't recognize. She stiffened. It sounded again. *Zingggg*. Soft but clear, like a string being plucked.

Then more silence. She drew another deep breath. The rain beat harder. For a moment it rattled against roof and window, dripped from the eaves. Then it slowed again, became a soft, steady, almost imperceptible rhythm.

Someone moved slowly around the side of the house. She listened. The movement was clumsy, as if the person was dragging something, or was tired or wounded.

She closed her eyes and prayed. *Dear God, keep the children safe. Keep Jay safe. Please.*

Someone trod heavily on the bottom step of the stairs that led up to the deck. She heard more footfalls lumbering upward. The gait was slow, uneven.

She opened her eyes and stared at the curtains. She listened, her heart beating so hard she could barely breathe. Footsteps, halting and heavy, neared the doors.

It was Jay, she thought desperately. He was hurt, but he was all right. He was alive and coming back for them.

The steps halted. "Jay?" she called, moving nearer to the curtains. "Jay?"

All she had to do, she told herself, was to hear his voice and unlock the door. Then everything would be fine.

Everything would be fine. She would hear his voice and unlock the door.

"Jay?" she said again. She waited for his answer.

Instead, the door exploded. The glass around the lock shattered and filled the air with icelike shards, and the lock itself blew away.

A black-gloved hand pushed back what was left of the door. A man stepped inside. It was not Jay.

Chapter Fourteen

He was a big man, and a ski mask covered his face. He wore dark clothing, wet with rain. In his hand was a gun with an odd attachment at the end of the barrel. The gun pointed at Rachel.

A silencer, she thought, dazed and clenching the poker. *He's got a gun with a silencer. That was the zing sound. He's shot Jay.*

Blood reddened the man's thigh. He, too, had been shot or stabbed, she thought desperately—but his wound seemed only to slow him, not stop him.

Something in his height, his build, the shape of his jaw looked familiar. But her numbed mind recognized him in only the most elemental way: *enemy.*

She backed toward the hallway to block his way to the children. "Get out," she ordered, brandishing the poker. "Get out—or you'll have to fight me."

He aimed the gun at her face. "Lady, I'll *kill* you. Drop that thing."

She gripped the poker more tightly. "Get out. What did you do to Jay? Get the hell out of here."

The man's thin lips twisted in a sneer. "He's dead. Drop the poker."

No, she thought. *He isn't dead. I won't let him be dead. No.*

Her feet were apart, her knees slightly bent, and she was coiled instinctively in a fighter's position. "No," she said

"Thornton said the corpse had green hair," Jay said. "We've talked to Missy Proteus's father. He said her hair was green—a bad dye job."

"Oh, hell," Castor muttered, "that old souse'd tell you elephants are pink and porcupines are purple. He called up the sheriff's department once screaming that big spotted spiders were coming out of the cracks of his house."

Now Jay's going to tell him him about the earring he found and the green hair, Rachel thought. *And then he'll believe we're crazy for sure.*

But instead, Jay's anger seemed to evaporate as suddenly as it had gathered. He clapped Castor on the shoulder companionably enough, although he didn't smile. "All right. It gets to me, that's all. We've got an odd sequence of events here."

Castor shrugged, but didn't appear mollified. "Life is mostly an odd sequence of events," he said pompously. "Your job isn't to invent mysteries. It's to raise those wonderful kiddies of yours out there." He nodded toward the lake, where the children played, holding their toys.

RACHEL AND JAY agreed to tell the children nothing yet. They feared that learning of the deaths of Thornton and his mother so close after the break-in would be too much for them to deal with, particularly for Kip.

Jay repaired the lock as best he could, wedged the door into place with a block of wood and convinced Rachel that she should return to his place. He didn't want her and Mercer staying alone in a house so isolated and vulnerable. To his surprise, she agreed almost without argument.

She had become quiet after discovering the break-in, almost as subdued and troubled looking as Kip. He instinctively knew better than to press her about what she was thinking; she was somewhere deep inside herself, mulling things over. He had things to think over himself.

Rachel packed suitcases for herself and Mercer, and Jay loaded her computer and files into her car. She drove behind him to his place. They passed Castor Bevins, back at work, parked beside the road apparently waiting for speeders but looking suspiciously as if he was napping.

Mercer and Kip rode with Rachel. "Will Henry get mad if you stay at Mr. Malone's house again?" Mercer asked, hanging over the back of the seat.

"Our door's broken," Rachel said with artificial calm. "We can't stay in a house with a broken door. I'll call Henry and explain."

But deep within she thought, *I can't explain anything anymore, even to myself.*

THAT AFTERNOON, on the surface Rachel and Jay acted casual, confident and not deeply concerned about the break-in. Beneath the surface, he seethed with his feelings and she with a new set of fears and doubts.

Kip seemed especially nervous and anxious to stay near the adults. The day turned rainy, and the children stayed underfoot, leaving Rachel and Jay little privacy.

They learned to speak without speaking aloud, to communicate by a glance, the movement of an eyebrow, a slight shake of the head, a quirk of the mouth.

They knew the only sure way to keep the children from hearing about Thornton and Ruby was to keep them isolated from the outside world for the time being. When Jay realized food was running low, Rachel drove alone into Sangria to get supplies.

With an involuntary shudder, she passed the large Victorian house that was the town's funeral home, Berryman's. She swallowed hard as she drove past.

Ruby Fuller would be lying there now, pale and powdered. Soon, her only son would be at her side, the two of them dead within forty-eight hours of each other.

Over Main Street, the red, white and blue bunting flapped placidly in the breeze. Stokes Day balloons of bright yellow had appeared everywhere, bobbing and cheerful. The banners and posters seemed inappropriately jolly in light of the double tragedy the town had just suffered.

But when Rachel went to the little mall with the super-market and discount store, no face registered tragedy. Shoppers looked caught up in their own worlds, apathetic, happy or irritable. No sense of loss seemed to touch them.

As Rachel left the supermarket she paused by the news-paper racks on the sidewalk and bought a copy of the *Sangria Herald*. The lead story on the front page recounted the robbery of the Chamber of Commerce. Another story listed the events of the upcoming Stokes Day celebration.

In the bottom corner she finally found mention of Thornton: "Local Youth Victim of Hit and Run." Only a short paragraph followed. The story was continued on page eight. At the story's end, Ruby Fuller was named as Thorn-ton's survivor. The paper, too, caught up in the local festiv-ities, hadn't had time to register news of Ruby's death.

She stuffed the paper into the nearest trash receptacle, feeling angry and impotent. To Sangria, Thornton's death was not big news. And Ruby's death was not news at all.

She put the groceries into the back of her car and walked to the big discount store on the corner to get Kip a nose clip for swimming. The store windows were plastered with Stokes Day posters, and outside stood a vendor selling Stokes Day buttons, T-shirts and booklets.

In the aisle of the sporting-goods section, Rachel found Katherine Menander talking to a plump, middle-aged clerk with a name tag that said Adelle. Sean Alan stood next to his mother, his finger exploring the interior of his nostril.

"Why, Rachel Dale," chirped Katherine. "How *are* you? I've been trying to phone you—and where's Mercer?"

"With a friend," Rachel said vaguely.

"Isn't it a shame about Thornton?" Katherine said, her eyes widening. "And I heard you found him. Ick! I'd have tossed my cookies. I phoned Tark right away, and he said I should *insist* you and Mercer come over to spend the night. But I couldn't get you. When Tark got home this morning, he was *so* disappointed you weren't there. He's such a com-passionate man, my Tark. Won't you come stay with us?

Sean and I'd love to have you. And Tark has to go away again tonight.''

"We're fine," Rachel said. "We're staying with... friends.''

"Well, our door is always open, Tark's and mine. But I can't imagine—finding a body. Ugh!" She shuddered daintily, then lowered her voice. "Did you hear about... his mother?''

Rachel nodded numbly. Katherine seemed unpleasantly excited by the events.

"Well, I don't wonder that Ruby did it," Katherine said with a *tsk*. "Letting him ride all over on that bicycle! Irresponsible is what she was. How could she live with herself? She *should* have cut her throat, I say.''

She nodded in righteous satisfaction, and the clerk named Adelle nodded, too. Rachel blinked, shocked at the two women's harshness.

"It was a blow for poor Sean Alan not to have play group today," Katherine said. "He got so restless I had to bring him into town. I wonder how long Minnie Crabtree thinks she'll have to mourn? All week, I suppose, with it being both her sister and her nephew like that. Oh, I do wish you and Mercer would come stay with us. It'd be so good for Sean Alan.''

"It's all too bad," Adelle remarked. "But to tell the truth, Thornton used to frighten the tourists—if they didn't know him. It's been a problem. It has. Well, looks like he and Ruby are going to make up with Nessa at last. It all comes round. Me, I always said I'd never fight with Nessa—she gets us all in the end." She shook her head.

Rachel felt her nerve ends prickle. She stared at the clerk's round, bland face. "What did you say?" she asked.

"Vanessa Berryman," Adelle said, stifling a yawn. "My, rainy days make me sleepy. You know, she runs the funeral home. She was Ruby's sister, Thornton's aunt. Wonder how it feels, laying out your own family like that. Brr.''

Rachel frowned. Ruby Fuller had said—more than once—that Minnie Crabtree was the only living relative that defiantly. She didn't think she could stop him, but she had no other choice than to try. She couldn't let him near the children. And she had to get to Jay.

"What the heck?" said a drowsy, irritable young voice behind her. "How's a person supposed to sleep?"

Rachel whirled and saw Mercer standing behind her, rubbing her eyes and looking cranky. She carried her Raggedy Andy doll. "Mercer!" Rachel cried.

"Drop the poker," the man said quietly. "Now."

Mercer squinted at him. "Who broke the door? Hey, your voice sounds familiar. I know—you're the real-estate man."

Rachel stiffened, shocked by what Mercer had said. She had seen the man only twice before, once when he'd come to the condo and once in his office, when she'd gone with Jay. It was Minnie's son, Powell Crabtree.

"Drop the poker, or I'll blow her smart-mouth head off," the man said, aiming at Mercer.

Rachel stared at him. Powell Crabtree, local realtor, always so hail-fellow-well-met. Powell, the amiable golfer and lecher, son of a grade-school teacher and a minister. Powell Crabtree stood amidst the shattered glass, wearing a ski mask, pointing a gun at her child.

Rational thought fled. The most primitive part of her took over. It told her, *Fight or die.*

She did not drop the poker. Instead she flung it at him with all her might. "Mercer, run!" she screamed and, ducking, grabbed the child by the hand and sprang down the hall, dragging her.

The dull end of the poker struck Powell in the shoulder and bounced off harmlessly. He squeezed the trigger, and Rachel was conscious of the zinging sound as the plaster of the wall shattered behind her.

There was a second zing, and a second patch of plaster exploded, only inches in front of Rachel's face. Dust and fragments of wall spattered her, temporarily blinding her, but she kept running. She threw herself into Kip's room, yanking Mercer behind her. She slammed the door shut.

Using strength she didn't know she possessed, she grabbed Kip's dresser and shoved it against the closed door. She held it in place and ducked when the top of the door splintered and a bullet knocked into the wall behind her, spraying paint and plaster.

"Hey!" Mercer yelled, affronted.

"Get down!" Rachel ordered. She ducked but held the dresser in place. Kip crouched on his bed, his face white, clutching his clown doll.

Another shot shivered the door, hurled into the plaster, and rained dust and rubble down on Kip. Wildly Rachel lurched for the mattress on Mercer's bed, grabbed it and hauled it upright, slamming it against the dresser and door. She half stood, half crouched, her arms braced against it. She prayed that if the mattress would not stop Powell's bullets, at least it would slow them.

"The window!" Rachel flung at Mercer. "Open the window and get out. Both of you. Run. Don't let the man near you."

"Mom?" Mercer said, fear suddenly in her voice.

"Get out!" Rachel ordered desperately. "Run. Stay away from the man. Now."

But Mercer stood as one paralyzed, and Kip, still clutching his doll, darted into his closet, like a small, frightened animal in search of shelter.

Tears of frustration sprang to Rachel's eyes. "Mercer!" she cried. "Get Kip and run!"

Just then the top of the door split farther apart, and Rachel gasped as the bullet hit the mattress, then grazed her shoulder, throwing her backward against Kip's bed.

He's going to kill us all, she thought wildly, grabbing Mercer. Her shoulder hurt, but no blood spilled from it. Dimly she realized the bullet must have struck but not pierced her. Partly crawling, partly stumbling, she made her way to the window to wrench it open, still clutching Mercer in one arm.

Powell crashed through the ruined door, shoving the dresser out of his way and knocking the mattress aside. "Get away from that window!" he ordered. Rachel froze, hugging Mercer to her, keeping her body between Powell and her child.

Her mind whirled. How many shots could an automatic fire? Up to fifteen, she knew. He might have plenty of bullets left. Or he might have none. He might not even know himself. Her heart beat madly. Mercer twisted in her arms, whimpering.

"Put the kid down," Powell said. He breathed hard, and the bloody place on his leg had darkened, become a larger, wetter spot. "Where's the other one? Where's the boy?"

Rachel set Mercer down carefully, still blocking her child from Powell's view.

"Where's the boy?" he asked again, almost hissing.

"I don't know," Rachel lied.

Powell leaned against the wall to ease the strain on his leg. Once again he leveled the gun at Rachel's head, smiling tightly against his pain. "Where's the boy?"

She took a deep breath, determined to stall. "You might as well take off the mask. We know who you are."

To her surprise, he pushed the mask up and wiped his face, which was sweating and pallid. He glanced down at his leg. "God," he said in disgust. "God."

"Look," Rachel said, "you'd better tie that up. You're going to bleed to death."

"Shut up," he said.

"Take the pillow case," she said, nodding toward a pillow that had fallen to the floor. "It's the right size. You're bleeding a lot. It's going to be hard to explain."

"Shut up," he repeated, and wiped his face again. He took a deep, rasping breath. "Where's the rabbit?" he demanded. "Give it to me. Where's the clown?"

She stiffened, realizing it was the gold he was after and he would kill for it. Where was Jay? He couldn't be dead. He couldn't be. Yet here she was herself, at gunpoint. Behind her, Mercer squirmed in fright and confusion.

"I've seen them," Powell said, a twist to his mouth. "He said there were three. He put one in Rinehart's mailbox—I found it. Two he left for the kids. He told me what they were and where they were. And she described them. I've seen them. Where are they?''

"He? She?" Rachel asked, shifting her weight, moving imperceptibly closer to him.

Think, she commanded herself frantically. It was possible to take a man's gun. Every year police officers were killed with their own guns, wrested away from them. She knew; she'd read statistics. A gun could be taken. It could be done.

"Who took three toys? Thornton? Who described them? His mother?"

He grimaced with pain. "Where are they?"

"Look," she said, stepping toward him, "you're going to pass out. You will. You'd better tie it up. I'll tie it up for you. You can keep the gun on me."

"Stay there," he ordered, waving the gun slightly, so that it aimed first at her stomach, then at her face.

"Did you kill them both?" She made no further move toward him. She held her arms out slightly, stretching open her hands to show she was harmless.

"He shouldn't have talked."

"Why Ruby? Why did she have to die? Did she know, too?"

"Of course she knew. Now, where the hell are they? Don't make me beat it out of you."

"What'll you do?" she challenged. "Hold a knife to my throat, the way you did to Ruby?"

"It did wonders for her powers of observation."

Don't think about that, she warned herself. *Just keep him talking.*

"Why were you looking in the Rineharts' mailbox? What did you find there?"

Powell smiled cynically. "Katherine Menander *asked* me to look. She was afraid of snakes. What I found was that I had to go on a little scavenger hunt. The toys—where are they?"

"Why do you want them?" she asked, her heart pounding thunderously. "The toys?"

"Just hand them over. Where's the rabbit?" The bean-bag rabbit was still on the kitchen table, gutted. In her pocket she could feel the weight of the gold peanut. Lying half-hidden beneath one bed was Kip's favorite stuffed rabbit with its worn, satin-lined ears.

"There are two rabbits," she said, nodding toward the floor. "I only see one."

"Put it on the bed." He gestured with the gun at the rumpled bed. "Nothing funny. I'll have my gun on your kid."

Rachel nodded. She knelt, slowly, carefully, and picked up the rabbit. Then she stood up, just as slowly and carefully. When she set it on the bed she was closer still to Powell and his gun. She did not move back; she kept the ground she'd gained, but made sure she was still positioned between Powell and Mercer.

"This doesn't look promising," Powell said, picking up the satin-eared rabbit. Like the beanbag rabbit, it was worn and white. The two toys might look the same from a distance. Rachel, desperate for time, prayed that they did.

Keeping the gun trained on Rachel, Powell ripped the rabbit open. He reached inside, but all he withdrew were ropes of wadded cotton. He flung the torn rabbit to the bed in disgust.

"Where's the other one?"

She took a deep breath. She carefully measured the distance between herself and Powell. She had to keep playing for time. "We already opened it. We know. About the gold."

He swore, clutched his injured leg and kept the gun aimed at her face. "Hand it over."

"Why did Thornton put it there?" she asked, inching a bit closer to him. "Why?"

"Who knows what went on in his crazy head?" Powell leaned against the wall again, resting his leg. "Hand it over. Where's the clown? Where's the other kid?"

"I don't know," Rachel repeated. "Does the clown have one, too? Where did he get them?"

"He took them," Powell said shortly. "Nobody knew it. If he hadn't taken them, you wouldn't be in this mess. But he did. Where's the gold? Give it to me."

"It's hidden," Rachel said. "Jay hid it. I'm not sure where. I'll have to look. It's somewhere in the living room, I think."

Powell swore and lowered the gun so that it was aimed at her knees. "Do better than that. I want the gold—*now*."

Rachel paled and dug into the pocket of her jeans. She twisted her body as she did so, inching imperceptibly closer to Powell. "Here," she said, holding it out to him. When he didn't reach for it, she took a small step nearer to him. "Here," she repeated, wondering if she dared another step.

"Drop it on the bed," he ordered.

She did so. It bounced once, then lay among the rumpled sheets.

"Where's the boy?" Powell demanded. "He's been hanging on to that clown—I've watched. Where is he?"

"He must be hiding somewhere in the house," Rachel said and licked her dry lips. "Listen, you'd better not shoot us. He'll never come to you. You'll need us." She wondered if anything she could say would take him by surprise and decided to give it a try.

"This is about Missy Proteus, isn't it?" she asked. "The girl with the green hair. She died here in this house, didn't she?"

His face went blank for a moment. Rachel took advantage of the moment to edge nearer. If she could get only six inches closer, she could grab for the gun.

Get his wrist, she thought. *Get his wrist, knee him in the bad leg, knee him in the groin, bite, scratch, kick, do whatever you have to do. And yell like crazy for Mercer to get out of the way.*

"Why did Missy die? Who killed her? You? Or Stokes?"

"It was an accident," Powell said bitterly, his face distorting with pain.

"Who did it? You? Stokes?" she probed.

"She was nobody," he said between clenched teeth. "Nobody. Who was she to bring such a great man down?"

He put a peculiar twist, a sarcastic one, on the words "great man." Rachel noted the tone, and the sudden hardness in his eyes. If Powell had a weak spot, was it somehow connected to Stokes?

"You did it to protect Stokes," she guessed. "You had an interest in him, right?" Once again she licked her lips in nervousness. "But how did my house get mixed up in it? And Thornton? How did he see her? And why did he say you took her to my house?"

"You're smart," Powell said with an unpleasant nod, "but too curious. Call the kid. Now. Tell him to come out, that I won't hurt him."

Rachel shook her head. "No. Tell me first. If the boy hears me screaming or suspects I'm hurt, he won't come. Tell me. Then I'll call. How did my house get mixed up in it?"

He swallowed. His bad leg trembled. "You want to play games? Fine. I like games. We were going to bury her at your place, in the basement. Your side was empty. The old woman next door was in the hospital. But it was risky, and then I thought of my mother. Who could hide a body better?" He made the barrel of the gun describe an S up her body so that it ended at her face again. "Call the kid. Or I'll just set fire to the house and wait for him to run like a rat."

Rachel thought he was bluffing. He didn't dare set fire to the house with Kip still hidden, and he knew it. He couldn't chance the third gold piece being lost in the flames. Then, in the ruins, anyone might find it.

Keep calm, she told herself. *Act like a psychologist. Everything he says is interesting and none of it shocks or scares you.*

"Your mother?" she said, sounding truly surprised. She leaned toward him slightly. She shifted her weight, moved her feet a fraction of an inch. "Minnie is mixed up in this, too?"

"Not Minnie," Powell said with contempt. "No. Nessa Berryman. Dear old Mom."

He looked feverish, and suddenly he looked a bit fanatical.

"Nessa Berryman's your mother?" she asked carefully. "I thought Minnie was."

Powell's mouth twitched in contempt. "Minnie wasn't even good at *pretending* to be my mother. And Nessa never wanted to admit it. But she paid for that. Oh, yes. She paid for that."

Sweat glistened on his upper lip, and the bitterness on his face now mixed with an expression of gloating. He had hissed the name "Nessa Berryman" with such venom that Rachel knew he hated the woman, despised her.

She chose her words carefully. "You never seemed to be like Minnie to me. I could see why the two of you wouldn't get along. You must have resented your real mother for giving you away."

Powell wiped the back of his hand across his sweating lip. "Resent her?" he said with a laugh. "I don't resent her. I've *destroyed* her. Her and my stingy aunt who brought me up. Nothing I ever did was good enough for her. I was *marked*. I was *unclean*."

"Why did you take Missy's body to Nessa Berryman's?"

"Bodies are her business," Powell sneered. "The Queen of the Dead. The business made her rich. So I forced her to get rid of Missy. She had to, if she didn't want everybody to know I was her own true son—and she was my mommy dearest."

His eyes glittered with rabid hate. Rachel knew she must try to use that hate to her advantage. "You forced her to get rid of Missy? How? Did she put her into a casket with someone else? How?"

Powell's leg had started to tremble. "Do you think I'm stupid? Someone could find her. No. I made her cremate her. There is no girl. There is no body. Nothing but a handful of ashes on the wind."

Rachel's stomach gave a sickening lurch. "Very ingenious," she forced herself to say. "But what about—"

"Shut up!" he ordered vehemently. "Yes. I'm ingenious. I always have been. *You* thought I was a buffoon, didn't you? Too bad. Never underestimate the enemy. Never."

He sucked in a long breath between his teeth. "Now get the boy," he said. "Get him *and* the clown, and I'll kill you fast. You want to play games? Here's the setup: I can kill you fast, I can kill you slow. As for the kids—"

"No—I'll do it," Rachel said hastily. His mind had veered sharply from one mode to another, and she knew her best course was to follow, not to try to lead. "I . . . I'll have to call from the door. He could be anywhere. I don't know if he can hear me from here."

Powell stared at her, gnawing his lips. He seemed to weigh her words. *Please, God,* thought Rachel, *let him believe me. If he believes me, I can get close enough to try for the gun. Please, God. Please.*

Powell started to nod, to let her go to the door. But at that same moment, a small muffled sound came from the closet. It was a child's sneeze. Rachel's heart constricted so sharply it felt as if it had collapsed in upon itself, ruined. Her frightened eyes met Powell's suddenly satisfied ones.

"Well, well," he said. He smiled a small, extremely crooked smile.

He took a limping step toward the closet. He opened the door wide with his free hand. Rachel's heart grew tighter, more hopeless. He had moved well out of easy range now. And he had Kip cornered. He had him.

"Come out, little boy," Powell said with false heartiness. "I know you're in there. Come out and bring the clown."

There was the noise of stirring in the closet, as if Kip was backing into its farthest depths.

"Come out, little boy," Powell repeated, his voice growing harsh. "I've got a gun. I'll shoot you if you don't."

Kip, Kip, she thought. *Don't come out. Don't. If he has to look inside for you, I'll go for him. Don't come out. Don't. Don't.*

Powell turned, his eyes icy, and spoke to Mercer. "Little girl, tell him to come out. Or I'll shoot your mother."

Mercer stood against the wall beneath the bedroom window. She had been watching Powell with wide dark eyes. Her face was white and she swallowed hard. "Kipper," she said in a shaky voice, "I . . . I think you better come out."

"Kip, don't—" Rachel cried, but it was already too late.

Kip, a wildness in his face, sprang from the closet, holding a broken plastic coat hanger like a knife. He hurled himself at Powell's legs like a desperate tiger cub, stabbing at his injured leg.

Powell gasped first in surprise, then in pain. His knee buckled and he screamed. Kip screamed, too, in primal terror and rage, but hung on to Powell's leg.

Rachel hurled herself across the room, crashing against Powell, seizing his wrist. "Mercer! Kip! Hide!"

But Kip was at Powell, screaming about his mother. "My mama," he cried, hammering at Powell's leg with his fist. "You hurt my mama!"

Rachel knocked the man against the floor and struggled for the gun. Powell backhanded her face. Ignoring the pain, she hung on to his wrist, trying to twist it. She kneed him as hard as she could in the ribs, the only spot she could reach, then kneed him again.

He flung Kip off him. Then Powell struck at Rachel. She ducked, so that he only drove his fist into her shoulder. He knocked her backward, but he didn't knock her loose.

"Mercer!" Rachel screamed. "Get Kip. Run! Save him!" She heard Mercer dragging Kip's desk chair to the window. She heard the twisting of the window latch.

She shifted and tried to knee Powell in the groin, but couldn't connect. He wrenched away from her, but she hung on to the gun with all her strength, trying to keep it twisted away from her.

She heard the window being pushed up. *Get out, get out, get out,* she wanted to scream, but Powell had knocked the breath from her.

"I'll kill you," Powell gasped.

Straining, he torturously bent his wrist against her grasp until the gun was pressed next to her arm. Another few inches and it would be against her heart.

"Mercer, Kip," she breathed raggedly, "run!"

"I'll kill you all," Powell repeated, his face contorted.

Suddenly there was a sickening sound. Powell's eyes rolled backward. He sagged away from Rachel, his wrist going limp in her hand. The gun slid easily from his grasp.

Rachel seized it and looked up, stunned.

Jay stood above them, holding the poker she had hurled at Powell. He held it like a club, and he glared down at Powell, upper teeth bared in a snarl.

"Jay!"

"Don't ever touch my kid," Jay said to Powell's motionless form. He spoke from between his teeth. "Or my woman. I'll kill you. I swear to God I'll kill you."

He drew back the poker to strike Powell again, fury in his eyes.

"Jay, don't!" she cried, half shielding Powell with her body. "You'll kill him. Don't!"

"He deserves killing," Jay said, his face savage. But then, without warning, his knees buckled and he fell to the floor beside her and Powell.

"You're hurt," she said, dimly aware of Kip's sobbing.

"This?" Jay said contemptuously. He touched his side and his hand came away bloody. "This is nothing. You all right?"

He reached and awkwardly touched her face. He looked as if he was in shock. His eyes, slightly glazed, studied her face, then shifted to Kip.

Kip sat on the floor, leaning helplessly against the bed, convulsed with tears. He reached trembling arms toward Jay. Mercer, white faced, had crept to Kip's side. Looking dazed, she ran to Rachel, who snatched her and held her convulsively.

Kip cried harder, his arms still stretched out.

"Kip," Jay said, a faint, crooked smile tilting his mouth a bit drunkenly. "Kip, my man."

He tried to rise, staggered a bit and came down on his knees next to the boy.

"Jay," Rachel begged, "don't move. You're hurt."

Jay shook his head, rose and staggered again. He sank next to Kip and pulled the weeping boy into his arms. Kip threw his arms around his father's neck and buried his face against Jay's shoulder.

Jay held him as tightly as he could. "It's all right, son, it's all right," he soothed, squeezing his eyes shut as he pressed his cheek against the boy's fair hair. "Daddy's here. Daddy's here."

CONFESSION

To tell the truth, I don't remember trying to kill them. I don't. Dale and Malone may be lying about the whole thing.

I remember waiting in the rain. Waiting out there in the blackness. Hell, weren't they ever going to sleep? And any minute they might stumble onto the gold.

I knew I was going to have to make my move. They'd given me no choice. So I cut the phone line. I was going to give them another half hour to turn out the lights. If they didn't, then I'd move in on them.

I can't remember much else. Malone hit me so hard, I still get headaches all the time. If I ever get out of here, I will kill him—you can count on it.

But don't worry. I don't really want out. I like it here. I love the intelligent company.

Besides, I did exactly what I wanted most. I destroyed every one of them that I originally wanted to. I couldn't have done it nearly as well if I'd succeeded that night.

See, my failure is actually my success. If I'd gotten away with it, people wouldn't have been hurt nearly as badly.

*That I'm sitting here is the final twist of the knife to them;
it means the truth is out. Out at last. All of it. Nothing could
hurt them more.*

I've done a brilliant job. If I do say so.

*Sometimes I just sit here, and I have to smile. Yes, I con-
sider myself a happy man, to tell the truth. A very happy
man.*

*Tell my mother that, will you? Tell her I'm a very happy
man.*

Chapter Fifteen

"Everybody got to beat up the bad guy but me," Mercer complained when Rachel took the children to pick up Jay.

"Hush," Rachel said. "You helped tie him up."

"I should have given him a good punch," Mercer said combatively.

"Hush," Rachel repeated. She hated remembering that night, and Kip still had great trouble talking about it.

They were driving to the hospital to check Jay out. He had a grazed head, four broken ribs and a nicked lung.

He had also, in four short days, garnered the title of worst patient in the history of Sangria's St. Mary's Hospital. The kindest thing Rachel had heard said of him was that he was tough. The usual thing she heard was that he was impossible.

He kept grumbling, "To hell with the whole damn hospital." He didn't hurt that much—he just wanted to get home to her and Kip and Mercer.

Powell Crabtree lay in the intensive care unit of the same hospital, a police guard at his door. He still hadn't recovered consciousness, but a nurse had said it might happen any time now. Although there was a warrant out for Nessa Berryman, she had disappeared from Sangria and was nowhere to be found.

The police were closemouthed. They told neither Jay nor Rachel anything. Their silence made Rachel nervous and put Jay in a foul mood.

The police refused to discuss the idea that the great Albert Pike Stokes might have been involved in anything unsavory. They told both Rachel and Jay they declined to speculate about Stokes's involvement with anything at this point. The Stokes Day celebration was to go on as scheduled.

Minnie Crabtree was questioned, but all she would say was that, yes, when she was a young married woman in Florida, she had adopted her younger sister's illegitimate child.

Their father, she said bitterly, had insisted on it. In doing so, she maintained, he had ruined all their lives. She refused to speak further of it. She had cut off all relations with Nessa for decades. She had disowned Powell years ago. She said she would speak no more of them, not even when threatened with a court order.

All Jay and Rachel learned was that Castor Bevins was no relation in any way to Nessa Berryman. Nessa's legitimate son, Samuel Berryman, Jr., was a police officer in St. Joseph. He had no knowledge of his vanished mother's whereabouts.

In a final irony, Stokes Day fell on the day Jay got out of the hospital, and the drive home was held up by the Stokes Day parade. Jay glowered at the floats and marching bands and police cars. He swore, more than once, even though the children were in the car.

"I can't believe this," he muttered. Kip sat on his lap, and he hugged the child closer to him. "A parade for the old hypocrite—Powell practically admitted to you that Stokes killed the girl. They can't find Nessa Berryman, and they haven't even *arrested* Powell yet."

Rachel shrugged in resignation. "They can't arrest an unconscious man. He's in protective custody. When he's conscious and rational again, then we'll know what happened."

"Ha," Jay said cynically. "He'll hide behind an army of lawyers, and nobody'll ever know what happened. There's no justice. Nobody gives a damn."

"Jay," she said, casting him a frustrated look, "let's just see what happens, all right? Let's be grateful we're all safe."

"I don't want to wait. Why should I be grateful? If the police had been awake, nobody would ever have been in danger. Least of all you and the kids."

Rachel gripped the wheel more firmly. "Your son is extremely glad you're home. So why don't you save your energy for that?"

"Yeah," Jay said darkly. He knew Rachel was worried about the boy, and he was, too. He glanced at her uneasily. He wanted to ask her if she would stay with them. They needed her, both he and Kip. He hoped she needed them, too. But they couldn't talk yet. Not in front of the kids.

It maddened him, this lack of privacy. It made him want to bang his head against the car door. But he didn't. He just settled back against the car seat and watched the last of the parade pass by. He pulled Kip closer to him and kissed the boy's ear. Kip hugged him and Jay tried to keep from wincing. He still hurt all over.

At last the parade passed, and the final police car disappeared up Main Street. Rachel put the car into gear and drove homeward, to Jay's place.

For the rest of the trip, Jay said little. He kept one hand laced firmly through Rachel's, leaving her to drive left-handed. She found it awkward, but rather lovely.

His other arm he kept tightly around Kip, who sat stroking the satin ear of his mended rabbit. The police had taken the clown doll. What they had found in it, they kept to themselves, but Kip had finally told Rachel and Jay about Thornton giving him the doll. Rachel had told the police, who took the information and, as usual, kept silent about it.

Now Mercer, feeling in exile in the back seat, was anything but silent. "Then Kip bopped him, then Mom bopped him, then Jay bopped him," she intoned. "Next the police bopped him. Bop, bop, bop. Jay, did Mom tell you she called the university? She said she wants to change her dissertation and have a different adviser. She said she and

Henry have personal differences. She's not gonna study murder anymore."

"I like you, Mercer," Jay said out of the corner of his mouth. "You get things out into the open. Maybe we'll follow you both to Nebraska. Buy a farm. Have they got farms in Nebraska?"

"Of course they've got farms," Mercer said. "Would you buy Kip a pony?"

"I could," he said and kissed his son's ear. "Do you need a pony, man?"

Kip said nothing, only snuggled closer to his father. Rachel turned off the highway and down the lane that led to Jay's house. Mercer babbled on, Jay held his son tightly and kept his fingers laced with Rachel's.

When they came in sight of the house, Rachel blinked in surprise. Beside Jay's black Corvette was parked a large, late-model car, a dove gray Lincoln sedan. Inside sat a woman dressed in black. When she saw them approaching, she got out and stood as if awaiting them. She was slender and, although not tall, she held herself as if she were. She was about fifty and strikingly attractive, with curly dark hair and high cheekbones.

Rachel drove up and parked beside the spot where the woman stood. She rolled down the window and cast her a questioning look. "Yes?"

"I'd like to talk to you," she said, clasping her black-gloved hands before her. Her green eyes met Rachel's without wavering. "I'm Vanessa Berryman."

Rachel's heart leapt with fright. Speechless, she squeezed Jay's hand, her own grown cold.

Jay leaned so he could see the woman more clearly through Rachel's window. "Mrs. Berryman," he said evenly, "the police are looking for you."

"I know," she replied, her tone calm. "I'd like you to call them. But I also want to talk to you. Alone, if you please." She glanced meaningfully at the children.

Rachel shook her head, dubious, but Jay nodded. He turned and spoke over the back seat to Mercer. "Go play," he ordered. Mercer stared at him in challenge, found herself stared down and opened the door. When Kip climbed out, she grabbed his hand and ran toward the lake.

Jay, too, got out more slowly. He walked around and opened Rachel's door. When she stood, he put his arm around her protectively. He looked Nessa Berryman up and down. "Come in," he said. Rachel gazed at him anxiously.

Keeping his arm around Rachel, he let Vanessa Berryman precede them up the stairs. Rachel looked at the woman's trim legs, her straight back. There was no question: of the three sisters, Minnie, Nessa and Ruby, Nessa was the family beauty. Her car, her clothing, her bearing gave silent witness that she was the best off financially, as well.

"I do intend to call the police, Mrs. Berryman," Jay said when the three of them entered the living room. "Would you care to have a seat? A drink?"

"I *wish* you to call the police," the woman said, her chin high. "Thank you, I'll sit. No, I don't want a drink. I want only to explain."

Jay walked to the kitchen counter, picked up the phone and started dialing. Nessa watched him without apparent emotion, and Rachel watched Nessa. A tiny muscle jumped in the woman's cheek as Jay spoke to the sheriff's department, and once she took a deep breath. She seemed to have herself under the strictest emotional control.

She took another deep breath when Jay set down the receiver. He returned to the living room and sat next to Rachel on the couch. He reached for her hand and held it. The three of them sat staring at each other. "They'll be here directly, Mrs. Berryman. Now, what do you want to explain?"

Nessa Berryman seemed suddenly ill at ease. The almost military straightness of her shoulders sagged slightly. Rachel felt an unexpected twinge of sympathy for the woman, who sat looking as if she wanted to speak but could not.

"Mrs. Berryman," Rachel said, "what did you want to say?"

Nessa shook her head hopelessly. She folded her hands tightly in her lap and stared down at them. "That I'm sorry," she said in a choked voice. She squeezed her eyes shut, and Rachel feared the woman was going to cry.

But Nessa seemed to reach within and find the strength to go on. She opened her eyes, laced her gloved fingers more tightly together and met first Rachel's gaze, then Jay's.

She took two more deep breaths. Then she spoke. "I ran away the morning I heard that Ruby'd died. I knew why she'd died. And Thornton. I thought I'd be next. That he'd kill me, too. I didn't know you were in danger—either of you. Or your children. If I'd known that, I'd have stayed, talked. I would have talked long ago if I'd known it would save Thornton and Ruby. But I didn't. None of us did. You see, Powell made us all feel . . . trapped."

Tears glistened in the woman's green eyes, but she blinked them away. She shook her head sternly. "No," she said as if to herself. "I don't intend to break now. He'd like that. To think he broke me. Do you mind if I smoke?"

"Of course not," Rachel said. She nudged a crystal ashtray across the coffee table.

Nessa stripped off her gloves, opened her purse and took out cigarettes and a lighter. As she lit the cigarette, she looked about the large living room with its vaulted ceiling.

"So this is the fine home," she said vaguely. "I was never invited here. But Powell was."

She exhaled a blue stream of smoke. "Did Powell tell you I'm his mother?" she asked.

As Jay nodded, watching her, Rachel said, "Yes, he told."

"I supposed he might. He'd want to tell. And it's the truth. He was my child."

Her voice choked oddly on the word "child," and she hurried to go on. "I had him when I was sixteen. My father was an upstanding man in this town, a religious man. He didn't want my life ruined. But he also thought it immoral not to care for the baby. He trumped up some story that I was supposed to go to Florida—for my health. Minnie and her husband lived there." She gave a small bitter laugh.

Rachel could see the strain in Nessa's face. Each moment that she talked seemed to age her more. "Mrs. Berryman, you don't have to—" Rachel began.

Nessa held up a hand to silence her. Her diamonds flashed. "I do have to," she said. "He nearly killed you. And it's time I told the truth. Who is there that more deserves to hear the truth than you? I read about you in the papers. I didn't go very far away. I've just been waiting. Getting myself ready for it."

She inhaled smoke deeply, released it with a sigh. "My father talked Minnie and her husband into adopting the baby. Father could be very persuasive. They did. And I came home as if nothing had happened."

She paused again and Rachel felt another surge of sympathy. Jay squeezed her hand.

Nessa smiled and stared up through her smoke at the ceiling. "Minnie and Raymond were very—how can I put this?—straitlaced. Judgmental. It didn't take much for Raymond to resent Powell, especially when he learned that he and Minnie would never have children of their own.

"Then Raymond decided Florida was sinful—he insisted on moving back to Sangria. I was married by that time to Sam Berryman. I was almost happy."

She crossed her feet at the ankles, demurely, like a lady. "We had a child of our own by then. Samuel, Jr."

Rachel drew in her breath, not knowing what to expect next. "Yes. We'd heard you'd had a son."

"He probably wouldn't claim me," Nessa said tightly, tapping the ash from her cigarette. "The older he got, the less we got along. But I tried. Truly I tried."

She shook her head sadly. "But my life was hell with Minnie and Raymond...and Powell back. Every time Minnie spoke to me I saw the contempt in her eyes. And every time I saw Powell, my stomach churned. That's not the way a mother should feel, but there was something repellent about him. Even back then. My husband had money.

I don't deny it. And every time Powell looked at me, I saw the sheer *jealousy* in his eyes.

"At last I couldn't stand it any longer. I cut off relations with them. Out of some warped sense of guilt, I tried to spoil my son, and the more I did, the worse he became."

She leveled her gaze again on Rachel. "My husband and I gave our son every advantage. He seemed to delight in throwing it in our faces. We sent him to the finest colleges—he flunked out of every one. He got a young girl in trouble and wouldn't marry her. It nearly killed my husband. He was a proud man, a dignified man. Reputation was everything to him."

She ground out the cigarette. A cold poise had seemed to descend over her, but she lit another cigarette immediately.

"Then there was Powell. He quarreled as much with Minnie and Raymond as my son did with me. He was nothing like them, nothing like any of us. He was vulgar and pushing and cunning. And jealous. He was still jealous of us. I could tell by the way he looked at me on the street."

She fell silent and stared up through the smoke.

"Mrs. Berryman," Rachel said gently, "did Powell know you were his mother? Did he know who his real father was? Why did he do what he did?"

Nessa examined her hand, adjusted a diamond ring. "He didn't know. It came as a shock. He quarreled terribly with Minnie one day, I heard, and the truth came out."

She swallowed and played a bit with the diamond. "He came to me. I told him I wanted nothing to do with him. He threatened to tell the whole town the truth. I . . . I paid him not to. I don't think my husband could have borne it. He wasn't well himself, then. I did all the accounts. It was easy to give Powell what he wanted.

"And what he wanted—" she paused again "—was to make something of himself, to show us all. He seemed to do well for himself—though he used *my* money to do it. Then Ambassador Stokes came back to Sangria. To build a summer house. His fine summer house. *This* house."

Once again she glanced about the living room. "If only he hadn't come back—but that's a foolish wish. He did. And it started all over again. So here we are. Here we are."

Jay leaned forward, his elbows on his knees. "What do you mean, Mrs. Berryman, 'It started all over again'?"

"The womanizing, Mr. Malone," Nessa said calmly. "The womanizing. Powell was like his father. Like me, his father never formally acknowledged him. But unlike me, he did accept him—unofficially. If there was a favor to turn Powell's way, he turned it. If there was influence to be wielded on his behalf, he wielded it. Discreetly, of course. In return for Powell's discretion—about their relationship."

Rachel blinked, wondering if she understood correctly. "Mrs. Berryman, are you saying that *Ambassador Stokes* was Powell's father?"

Nessa nodded and drew on her cigarette. "Yes. Only he wasn't Ambassador Stokes then. Just a representative. A very handsome, irresistible representative—at least to a gullible sixteen-year-old like me."

Nessa straightened her shoulders and stubbed out the second cigarette, half-smoked. "He and Powell shared several passions. One was young women. Powell became—how shall I put it?—his father's summer procurer. Yes, that will do—procurer."

"Wait," Jay said, tensing beside Rachel. "You mean it was Powell who brought Missy Proteus here? For Stokes?"

Nessa stared at him coolly. "It was. And it was Powell Stokes called when he'd nearly killed the girl."

"Hold on," Jay said with a frown. "What do you mean *nearly* killed?"

"That's what Stokes told me that night. The night they brought her to me. Both of you know the rumors about the gold?"

Rachel nodded, encouraging her to go on.

"We know the rumors," Jay said tonelessly.

A siren whined in the distance. Another joined it.

"They were *true*." Nessa inspected her gloves, flicked away a speck of lint. "I saw it myself. The girl had a cheap suitcase holding dozens of pieces of it—they didn't even know. Stokes had awakened and found her filling her purse. He'd just gotten the stuff. He bought contraband art all the time—another of his endless passions."

The sirens grew closer. Nessa drew on her gloves, adjusting them with minute care. "They both loved *show*, father and son. They both loved flash and finery. Somehow the girl found his new treasure. Maybe he was careless. Maybe he'd shown it to her. But he woke up and found her filling her purse. They struggled and she struck her head. He thought he'd killed her."

She opened her purse, took out a gleaming black-and-gold compact, snapped it open. "Excuse me," she said. "Stokes thought he'd killed her, and he called Powell. He told me this at the mortuary after they brought her in. He was shaking like a leaf. Suddenly he looked like an old man."

She patted a stray hair into place. "Stokes had carried the girl back to the bedroom. Powell arrived, went in and looked at her. Then he came out of the bedroom, took up the poker—" she nodded at the fireplace "—went back into the bedroom and locked the door. He killed her, I'm sure. Then he came back out and said to Stokes—oh, how Stokes shook when he told me this—'She's dead, Daddy. I figure we better find an alibi for you now.' Then he took a gun and took Stokes's little dog and shot it, so there'd be an excuse for all the blood."

She snapped the compact shut and put it back neatly in her purse. She sat with the purse on her lap, as if she were ready to leave for an appointment. Her manner seemed resigned. "Ruby and I were still close when it happened. Her husband was in the hospital. She and Thornton had come to stay with me—I'd just been widowed myself. That's the one thing Powell hadn't counted on—Ruby and Thornton being there."

She paused and shook her head as if slightly dazed. "I think *I* woke Thornton. They said I screamed. Powell slapped me, and he *said* I'd been screaming. He said he'd taken the body to another place to bury it, then decided to bring it to me instead. He called me the Queen of the Dead. He said he might as well get both parents involved. He said he would ruin me if I didn't help. It was at that moment I looked up and saw Thornton there, standing in the doorway, and Ruby, looking terrified, only a few steps behind him. And Powell laughed when he saw them and said something like, 'Hell, let's make it almost the whole damned family.'"

The sirens sounded quite close now, as if they had turned off the highway and were coming down the lane. Nessa smoothed her skirt, held her purse more tightly. "From that night, he owned us all. He'd turned the tables. He had his father in his power. He had me. He even had Thornton and Ruby."

The keening of the sirens stopped. The police were in the yard now, and Nessa rose, nervously smoothing her skirt. "I'd rather go out alone if you don't mind," she said, not looking at either Rachel or Jay. "I'd rather go to them than be taken."

Rachel and Jay stood, too. Jay took a step toward Nessa. "Mrs. Berryman," he said, his voice low, "let me walk you out there. It'll be easier."

She gave him a haunted, skeptical look. "No, Mr. Malone. This is easier. I won't lean on anyone. Powell grew up so full of hate he wanted to ruin all of us. Now he's done it. But there is one thing he can't do. He will not make me bend or lean. Whatever waits for me, I'll walk toward it alone. I thank you for your time. And I apologize profoundly for the trouble I brought into your lives."

She straightened her back and walked to the front door. Rachel started to move after her, but Jay stopped her. "Let her do it her way," he said softly.

Nessa opened the door, stepped through it with dignity, then closed it firmly behind her. Rachel and Jay moved to the window to watch, his arm around her tensed shoulders.

The deputies had gotten out of their cars. They stood on the lawn and looked up at Nessa on the deck. She nodded once, said something, then descended the stairs. She walked to the nearest deputy and, her back straighter than before, thrust her gloved wrists toward him so that he could handcuff her.

He gave her a searching look, snapped the cuffs into place and helped her into the back seat of the patrol car. She sat as stiffly and formally as a queen. The car pulled away. The other two deputies looked after it a moment, then ascended the stairs.

"What will they want with us?" Rachel asked, tears brimming n her eyes.

Jay held her tighter. "Answers. This time we have them."

The children had run up from the shore and stood apprehensively watching the deputies knocking at the door.

"Yes," Rachel breathed. "We finally have them. Don't we?"

AFTER THE DEPUTIES LEFT and the children had calmed down enough to go back to play, Rachel was still pensive. "What about Nessa Berryman? What'll happen to her?"

"I don't know," Jay answered. "It'll be up to the courts. But they'll try Powell for what he did to Missy Proteus—and Thornton and Ruby—and what he tried to do to us. And I don't imagine after this year, there'll be any more Stokes Day celebrations."

"No," she agreed. "This is the first. And the last."

"Too bad. They seem short on heroes in this neck of the woods."

I don't think so, Rachel thought, looking at him.

Jay's face was taut. "Stokes is dead," he said, his voice harsh. "But he'll still pay. In reputation. It's the highest price he could pay. And he will."

"I can't believe it," Rachel said numbly. "Justice. It finally happened. For poor Missy Proteus. And I hope for Thornton. And Ruby."

"Hey," he said, leaning and kissing her cheek. "Don't take everything so hard."

She squared her shoulders. "You said nobody saw the sparrow that fell. That nobody cared. But you cared. When something like this happens, all anyone can hope for is justice. But nobody cared about that, either. Until you came along."

"Ah, come on," he said, seeming almost embarrassed. He took her into his arms. "It wouldn't have happened without you. Both of us needed to be there."

She rested against his shoulder, careful not to move in a way that would hurt him. His arm around her shoulder felt wonderful, right. She kissed his throat. He kissed her temple.

"Should I follow you to Nebraska?" he said. "I can raise cattle or sell hockey pucks there as well as anywhere. Probably better."

"If you don't follow us back to Nebraska, I can't go," she said, snuggling more closely into the comfort of his warmth. "I'd have to start from square one somewhere else."

The back door slammed open. "Hey!" yelled Mercer, when she saw them embracing. "Is that what mothers and fathers do the minute a kid's back is turned?"

Startled, Rachel tried to pull away, but Jay held her fast. "Yeah," he said, glancing coolly at Mercer over his shoulder. "This is what mothers and fathers do. Get used to it, all right?"

Mercer stood watching them with interest. She scratched a mosquito bite on her stomach. "All right," she said agreeably. "I just came in to tell you Kip and I are playing psychologist."

"Fine," Jay said. "Go play. We'll be out in a bit. I just want to talk to your mother in private for a minute—*if* it's possible."

Mercer smiled her most guileless smile and backed out the door. She closed it quietly one of the few times in her life.

"Hello, Mom," Jay whispered, pulling Rachel to him. "I think I love you. How about it?"

"I love you back," she said, tears in her eyes. He bent and kissed her. It was a long hungry kiss, because both knew that there would be little time for kissing until that night, when the children were asleep, and night seemed an eternity away. Rachel's lips tasted all the sweeter for that to Jay, and his to her. They clung to each other as if nothing could draw them apart again.

Outside, Mercer made Kip lie down on the bottom step of the back deck stairs. She squatted beside him, sitting on a cement block. "I get to ask you all these personal questions," she instructed him. "And you gotta answer the truth. You *gotta*. Understand?"

Kip nodded and held on to his rabbit with the satin ears. He stared up at the clear blue sky.

"Okay," Mercer said, putting her elbow on her knee and her chin in her hand. "How did you feel when the man came for you in the closet?"

"Scared!" Kip said emphatically, and began to suck his thumb.

"And then what did you feel?" Mercer persisted, studying him with interest.

"Mad!" Kip said just as emphatically, and quit sucking his thumb.

"So how do you feel *now?*" she asked.

"Better," he said with conviction.

Ah, Mercer thought. This job was a snap. She liked it. She closed in for a big question. "How will you feel if I'm your sister? If they get married?"

Kip stared up at the sky for a moment in silence. Then he burst out, "Glad!" He threw out his arms and said it so loudly that it startled Mercer, and she fell off her cement block, her legs waving in the air.

She began to giggle madly and so did Kip. He giggled so hard he rolled off the step and into the grass beside her.

Above them, in the maple trees, the sparrows sang their undistinguished song. In the sky, at the edge of town, a sky rocket went up from the city park, celebrating the first and last Stokes Day in history.

Inside, Rachel sighed against Jay's lips. "The kids are laughing awfully hard. Should we see why?"

He sighed, too. "I suppose. I forgot it was this nutty."

"What's nutty?" she asked.

"Family," he said, and kissed her again.

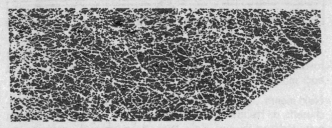

HARLEQUIN

AMERICAN ◆ ROMANCE®

American Romance's yearlong celebration continues.... Join your favorite authors as they celebrate love set against the special times each month throughout 1992.

Next month ... Spooky things were expected in Salem, Massachusetts, on Halloween. But when a tall, dark and gorgeous man emerged from the mist, Holly Bennett thought that was going too far. Was he a real man ... or a warlock? Find out in:

OCTOBER

S	M	T	W	T	F	S
				1	2	3
4				8	9	10
11	12		15	16	17
18	19			23	24
25	26	27	28	29	30	31

**#457
UNDER HIS SPELL
by Linda Randall Wisdom**

Read all the *Calendar of Romance* titles, coming to you one per month, all year, only in American Romance.

WELCOME TO

The quintessential small town, where everyone
knows everybody else!

Finally, books that capture the pleasure
of tuning in to your favorite TV show!

Join your friends at Tyler in the eighth book, BACHELOR'S PUZZLE by Ginger
Chambers, available in October.

*What do Tyler's librarian and a cosmopolitan architect have in common? What
does the coroner's office have to reveal?*

GREAT READING...GREAT SAVINGS...
AND A FABULOUS FREE GIFT!

Each book set in Tyler is a self-contained love story; together, the twelve novels
stitch the fabric of the community. You can't miss the Tyler books on the shelves
because the covers honor the old American tradition of quilting; each cover
depicts a patch of the large Tyler quilt!

And you can receive a FABULOUS GIFT, ABSOLUTELY FREE, by collecting
proofs-of-purchase found in each Tyler book, *and* use our Tyler coupons to save
on your next TYLER book purchase.

HARLEQUIN®

Temptation®

the Fortune Boys

A funny, sexy miniseries from bestselling
author Elise Title!

**LOSING THEIR HEARTS MEANT
LOSING THEIR FORTUNES...**
If any of the four Fortune brothers were unfortunate
enough to wed, they'd be permanently divorced from
the Fortune millions—thanks to their father's last will
and testament.

**BUT CUPID HAD OTHER PLANS FOR
DENVER'S MOST ELIGIBLE BACHELORS!**
Meet Adam in #412 **ADAM & EVE** (Sept. 1992)
Meet Peter in #416 **FOR THE LOVE OF PETE**
  (Oct. 1992)
Meet Truman in #420 **TRUE LOVE** (Nov. 1992)
Meet Taylor in #424 **TAYLOR MADE** (Dec. 1992)

**WATCH THESE FOUR MEN TRY TO WIN AT
LOVE AND NOT FORFEIT $$$**

HARLEQUIN®

INTRIGUE®

A SPAULDING AND DARIEN MYSTERY

Amateur sleuths Jenny Spaulding and Peter Darien have set
the date for their wedding. But before they walk down the
aisle, love must pass a final test. This time, they won't have to
solve a murder, they'll have to prevent one—Jenny's.
Don't miss the chilling conclusion to the SPAULDING AND
DARIEN MYSTERY series in October. Watch for:

#197 WHEN SHE WAS BAD by Robin Francis

Look for the identifying series flash—A SPAULDING AND
DARIEN MYSTERY—and join Jenny and Peter for danger and
romance. . . .

HARLEQUIN
I N T R I G U E®

ABOUT THE AUTHOR
Bethany Campbell, a former English teacher and textbook consultant,
writes full-time for Harlequin. Her imagination knows no bounds—
which, according to Bethany, sometimes gets her into trouble. When
she's not writing, she enjoys traveling and collecting cartoon art. She is
married, has one son and lives in Alabama.

Books by Bethany Campbell
HARLEQUIN INTRIGUE
  65—PROS AND CONS
116—ROSES OF CONSTANT
151—DEAD OPPOSITES

HARLEQUIN ROMANCE
2726—AFTER THE STARS FALL
2779—ONLY A WOMAN
2803—A THOUSAND ROSES
2815—SEA PROMISES
2852—THE LONG WAY HOME
2877—HEARTLAND
2911—FLIRTATION RIVER
2949—THE DIAMOND TRAP
3000—THE LOST MOON FLOWER

Don't miss any of our special offers. Write to us at the following address
for information on our newest releases.

Harlequin Reader Service
P.O. Box 1397, Buffalo, NY 14240
Canadian address: P.O. Box 603,
Fort Erie, Ont. L2A 5X3

BCB10